MW01199341

BEAST

BIANCA COLE

BEAST PLAYLIST

"Cravin'"—Stiletto feat Kendyle Paige

"On Your Knees"—Ex Habit

"Eyes don't lie sped up"—Isabel LaRosa

"The Devil is a Gentleman"—Merci Raines

"Bite Marks"—Ari Abdul

"Flames"—R3hab, ZAYN, Jungleboi

"Cold Blooded"—Chris Grey

"Morally Grey- Nation Haven Editon"–April Jai

"Drive you insane"—Daniel Di Angelo

"Here's My Heart"—SayWeCanFly

Listen on Spotify

AUTHOR'S NOTE

Hello reader,

This is a warning to let you know that this book is a **dark** mafia romance much like many of my other books, which means there are some sensitive subject matters addressed. If you've got any triggers, it would be a good idea to proceed with caution.

As well as a dark and controlling anti-hero, this book addresses some sensitive subjects. A full list of these can be found here. As always, this book has a HEA and there's no cheating.

If you have any triggers, then it's best to read the warnings and not proceed if any could be triggering for you. However, if none of these are an issue for you, read on and enjoy!

BLAKE

*T*he clang of a door slamming echoes through the stark, empty cell. I jump to my feet. Being cooped up in this cell is driving me insane. I need to get out. Never before have I been in such a small space with nothing to do for so long, and I don't have my meds either.

Kali tenses, glancing at me. "What is it?"

"I don't know." Tapping my foot on the floor, I turn away from her. "I'm about ready to chew my way through those fucking bars at this point."

Kali bites her lip. "It must be hell for you even more than us here."

I narrow my eyes. "What's that supposed to mean?"

She gives me a look that already irritates me. "With your condition."

I grind my teeth together because everyone sees my ADHD as a disability, but I beg to differ. I like to see it as a strength. I'm never too tired to do something and always ready to put my all into things, even if I get sidetracked sometimes. "You know I hate people calling it that."

She sighs. "Sorry, I know." She runs a hand through her dark locks. "I'm so stressed."

Luna paces up and down the cell, muttering something under her breath. For the first God knows how many days we were separated. Alice and Luna were in one cell, and Kali and I were in another.

They started our "training" yesterday, and we were all placed in one cell together afterward. I'll never know why they waited to train us, but we're all struggling to hold it together after yesterday's first session.

To say it was perverse is an understatement, but I know it could have been ten times worse. It will get ten times worse.

"They'll no doubt start our training soon," Alice says, sitting on a hay bale in the corner and staring blankly at the bars of our cell. "We've got to remain strong."

I take a deep breath, trying to calm the restless energy coursing through my veins. Being cooped up in this cage is absolute torture. I need to move, to do something, anything. The minutes drag by at an agonizing pace.

Kali gives me a sympathetic look, no doubt noticing my agitation. "We've got to hold it together," she says softly. "For each other."

Luna nods, her usual bubbly demeanor subdued. "Kali's right. We can get through this if we lean on each other."

I appreciate their words, but it's not that simple for me.

The itch beneath my skin is maddening. I can't keep still and decide to join Luna, pacing back and forth across the tiny cell.

Suddenly, there's a loud clang and echo of footsteps approaching. Luna and I stop pacing and move toward Alice on the hay bale, as does Kali. And then they appear. The three men in charge of our "training."

Taren, Matias, and Thiago. My heart sinks. It's time for day two of their fucked up training. It appears Taren is in control, but there seemed to be a lot of tension between the three men yesterday.

He unlocks the cell doors and steps inside, looking at us emotionlessly. Although, I notice a slight flash in his eyes when he looks at Alice. "Strip," he orders. "Everything off."

Kali and I exchange uneasy glances, but we comply and remove our clothes. I grit my teeth together and toss my shirt, shorts, and underwear on the floor.

"Now on your knees," Taren orders.

We witnessed what kind of violence we'll be subjected to if we don't comply yesterday. Luna still has a bruise across her face from where Taren struck her. Immediately, all four of us drop to our knees, painfully aware that they hold our lives in their hands.

What fresh hell will they put us through today?

The coarse surface of the floor scrapes against my skin while I adjust myself. Vulnerability is like a second skin wrapping around me under their hungry, watchful gazes. Kali is to my left, her breath coming out in quiet pants.

Luna is to my right, her head bowed and eyes fixed on the ground.

They may force us to our knees, but I won't bow my head. Instead, I watch the three. Taren stands in the middle, scanning us with an unreadable expression. Matias and Thiago flank him on either side, smirking like they're watching their favorite show unfold.

"Keep your eyes down," Taren instructs, his voice a steel thread weaving through the tense air.

Motherfucker.

A part of me longs to defy him, but I comply, lowering my gaze despite every muscle in my body screaming to fight, lash out, and claw my way out of this nightmare.

Matias steps forward, the smirk growing wider. "Why don't we make them—"

"No." Taren's voice slices through Matias's suggestion like a knife through silk before he can even say it. "That's not what they're here for."

Matias bristles at the interruption, his jaw clenching. "But—"

Taren turns to him, a silent threat emanating from him. "They're here to learn obedience and submission," he says firmly. "Not to be playthings for your amusement."

The tension ratchets up another notch. And I find myself holding my breath. What is with these three? Clearly, some issues need to be solved about who is in charge. I sense that we're merely pawns on their chessboard. Nothing more than a game.

Glancing up briefly, I notice Thiago scowl, but he remains silent, his arms crossed over his chest.

"Now," Taren continues, returning his gaze to us with that unreadable expression and forcing me to bow my head again. "You will obey my commands without question or hesitation."

The statement hangs heavy in the air. My friends' fear is so acute that I can practically feel its weight.

We nod mutely. Compliance is our only option to survive this hell. My heart pounds against my ribcage like a caged bird desperate for freedom.

Taren walks around us, assessing our submission with a predator's keen gaze. His presence feels oppressive—a weight I can't shake off no matter how hard I try.

"Stand up," he barks.

All of us scramble to our feet quickly. He barks more orders at us; turn around, hands behind your back, stand on one foot and we all follow them mechanically like animals forced to perform at a circus. It's dehumanizing. We're nothing more than objects to shape into submissive creatures with no minds of our own.

Deep down, beneath my fear, a spark of defiance burns within me. Sure that nothing they could do to me will ever snub it out and I'll cling to it as long as I'm breathing.

Thiago steps forward, a predatory glint in his eyes. "Now, on your backs," he commands, his tone laced with amusement. "Spread those thighs for us, as that's the position you'll be in most of the time once someone buys you."

Thiago's words send a spike of dread shooting through me. Just like yesterday, they want to humiliate us.

How on earth did we end up here?

Nothing more than cattle to be sold at market. The thought of some tyrant purchasing me or my friends fills me with a primal fear—fear that surpasses being here because at least here I am with my friends.

"Fucking bastards," I mutter under my breath, my hands balling into fists at my sides while rage floods me. "This is so humiliating." Hesitation rules me, that stubborn flame kicking into life. Spreading my legs for these men—no monsters– is degrading and disgusting. All I want to do is lash out and hurt them in some way, but I know they'll make our lives a living hell if I do.

Matias, the unhinged one, approaches with a violent delight flashing in his dark brown eyes. He loves this. I noticed it yesterday. This man feeds off our pain and humiliation.

"Do you want me to force you into that position?" he taunts, his voice dripping with malice. "Because if I do, I can't promise I won't fuck your tight little cunt in the process."

My stomach churns at his words. This is the kind of man he is—a predator, a monster who takes pleasure in the suffering of others. I can feel the heat rise to my cheeks, a mix of anger and fear coursing through me and something else I can't quite name.

Before I can respond, Taren steps forward, his expression grim. "Stop it, Matias," he commands, his voice authoritative. "You're not going to do that to her, and she's going to do as she's told." His gaze moves to me and sends shivers down my spine. "Aren't you, Blake?"

I nod and sigh in relief despite knowing it'll be short-lived. Taren is here right now to be a buffer between me and Matias, but the look in Matias's eyes suggests he isn't finished with me. The thought sends a shiver down my spine.

"Lie down and spread your thighs," Taren repeats.

My mind races with strategies to survive this place while I lower myself to the ground. I need to be smart, not just strong. Humiliation spreads through me when I spread my legs, noticing the dark flash in Matias' eyes as he watches me.

Fuck.

I close my eyes while I lie there, exposed and vulnerable. The rough and cold concrete floor scraping against my back is a stark reminder of my place here and my powerlessness.

Taren circles us slowly, inspecting our submission. My stomach churns as his eyes rake over me, forcing me to fight the urge to cross my arms over my chest. That would only anger him, so I remain still, my thighs spread wide.

"Good," he says finally, his voice betraying no emotion. "You're learning quickly. A compliant slave will be highly valued."

His words make my skin crawl. I'm not a slave. I'm a human fucking being. But I bite my tongue and say nothing. There's no point arguing with these monsters.

"Now, on your hands and knees," Taren orders.

I comply, getting onto all fours. The others do the same, Kali's face burning red with shame. She meets my gaze briefly, and I try to give her a smile, but it feels more like a grimace.

"Arch your backs," comes the next command. "Stick those asses out."

This entire fucking situation goes against everything I stand for. Grinding my teeth together, I do as I say and arch my back. This position makes me feel like an animal, and I hate it.

"Good. You're learning how to display your assets properly." He smacks my ass lightly, and I flinch. "With training, you'll fetch top dollar at auction."

Auction.

The word sends ice through my veins. Who knows what our buyers will do to us? Men who buy women aren't the kind of men you ever want to meet.

I shudder at the thought but remain silent. Taren continues walking around us, occasionally delivering a smack to our backsides. The blows are light, meant to humiliate rather than hurt.

Suddenly, Taren drops a huge dildo in front of me and one in front of each of my friends. "Time for us to see how well you take a cock. Now lie on your backs and fuck yourselves with the dildo until you climax. There'll be no stopping until you come."

Matias groans and paws at his bulging crotch. "Fuck,

we should be deep in their tight little cunts. A cock is better than a piece of fucking rubber."

Taren glares at him. "Control yourself, Matias. You're a fucking embarrassment." There's an odd edge to his tone as he glares at Matias.

Matias growls and marches toward Taren with his fists clenched, but Thiago quickly stops him. "Back down, brother."

It's the same as yesterday. They're having a pissing contest over who's in charge.

Fuck ourselves with a dildo in front of them? The thought makes my skin crawl. However, I guess it's a natural progression. Yesterday, it was fingering ourselves to climax.

"I can't," I say, my voice barely above a whisper. The fact is, I never come from penetration alone. I'll be doing it all fucking day. Kali and Luna look equally horrified. Only Alice seems resigned, her eyes dull and defeated.

Taren's expression hardens. "You'll do as I say, or there'll be consequences."

His threat hangs heavy in the air. I know he has the power to make our lives a living hell. But this feels like too much.

"Please," I beg, hating the desperation in my voice. "Don't make us do this."

For a moment, Taren's eyes soften almost imperceptibly. But then the mask slams back down, and his face becomes an emotionless slate.

"Enough stalling," he barks. "Do it now."

My hands shake as I reach for the dildo and lie down on my back. My friends do the same, resigned misery etched on their faces. Only Matias seems excited, his eyes bright with sick delight.

I hesitate, my fingers curling around the rubber shaft. This feels so wrong, being forced to fuck myself in front of these monsters. But I know I've got no choice.

With a shaking hand, I bring the tip to my entrance, bracing myself for the invasion. Slowly, I slide it inside, clenching my jaw at the feeling. Once it's fully seated, I begin moving it in and out mechanically.

I keep my eyes squeezed shut, pretending I'm somewhere else, somewhere safe. But I can feel their eyes burning into me, hear their lewd comments and groans of arousal. Bile rises in my throat, and I have to fight back the urge to vomit.

Despite my revulsion, my traitorous body starts responding. As I move the dildo, friction builds, and a warmth blooms low in my belly. It's unlike anything I've experienced before from penetration.

No, I can't get off, not like this, not for their entertainment.

But my body has other ideas, as my inner muscles start to clench around the dildo. My breathing comes faster, and I can't hold back a quiet moan. Shame floods through me even as my hips move of their own volition, seeking more stimulation.

Unable to stop myself, I crack my eyes open. Matias is stroking himself with his big cock poking through his pants. His eyes bore into us, in turn like lasers. When our gazes meet, his lips curl into a cruel smirk.

"That's right, slut," he rasps. "You love performing for us, don't you?"

I shut my eyes again, refusing to let him see the tears building. It's too much, all of it. The humiliation, the degradation, the loss of control over my own body.

I focus on my friends instead, drawing strength from their solidarity. We'll get through this nightmare together, I tell myself. We'll be free one day.

I move the dildo faster now, my inner muscles starting to flutter. I bite my lip, holding back the cries, trying to break free. I won't give them the satisfaction of hearing me come.

Finally, it hits me—a wave of unwanted pleasure that I can't stop. My back arches, and my toes curl as I ride it out silently. It's over.

When I open my eyes again, the men are grinning triumphantly. Bile rises in my throat, but I force it down. I got through it. I survived.

And someday, I'll make them pay for what they've done. I vow, despite knowing I'll probably never get the chance.

2

BLAKE

*S*oft snores echo through the cell as I toss and turn on my hay bale, trying to quieten my mind. All three of my friends are fast asleep, but my mind is racing at one hundred miles a minute. It feels like there's no end in sight. Even if we survive their training, we'll be split up and sold off into possibly worse fates.

Without my meds, my ADHD makes it impossible to focus, and sleep is challenging. Everything is amplified—the sounds, the smells, the sensations. I can't find peace or quiet in the chaos of my mind.

Soft footsteps approaching draw my attention to the bars of our cell, and then Matias appears from the shadows.

His eyes flash with delight when they meet mine. "Good, one of you is awake. Get up," he growls. "It's time for your special one-on-one training."

Ice-cold fear freezes me in place as a tremor travels

from my head to my toes. I can't move or speak, staring blankly as he approaches.

He grabs my arm and yanks me to my feet, dragging me out of the cell while my friends remain asleep. A part of me wants to scream to wake them, but I know they can't stop this. They can't save me.

"What do you want?" I ask as he leads me down a dark corridor to an empty cell.

Instead of answering, he shoves me inside and slams the door shut, locking it behind him.

I'm trapped with a beast.

Adrenaline kicks in as I lift my arms, preparing for a fight. "I'll fight you."

Matias smirks at me, his eyes glinting with amusement. "You're feisty, aren't you?" he says. "I like that."

He steps closer and grabs my wrists, forcing them down easily. A shiver races through me when his hot breath ghosts my face. His gaze burns into me with a predatory intensity, making my skin crawl. It's so intense I try to pull away but he grabs my chin, forcing me to meet his gaze.

"I like you and the dark-haired girl you were trapped in a cell with at first. Kali, isn't it?" he muses, the glint in his eyes betraying the psychopath within. "I have this dream of you both servicing my cock at the same time. Both of you bound and helpless," he murmurs.

I shake my head, trying to break free from his grip. "You're sick," I hiss.

He laughs a cruel, heartless sound. "Oh, I know," he

says. "But that's what makes it so much fun." He leans in close, his breath hot on my face. "You're going to enjoy this," he whispers. "I'm going to make you enjoy it."

Using all my strength, I attempt to yank myself out of his grasp, but he's stronger than I expected. He pins my arms behind my back and forces me to meet his gaze. His eyes are dark and predatory like a wolf sizing up its prey.

"You're mine now," he growls. "And you're going to do everything I say. Do you understand?"

"Yes," I whisper.

He smiles heartlessly. "Good girl," he says. "Strip."

I shiver but don't hesitate, pulling off my clothes and folding my arms over my chest.

"Now, let's begin." He unbuckles his belt, the leather scraping against the metal buckle. I watch in horror as he pulls the belt out and whips it through the air ominously.

"This is going to hurt," he says, his voice devoid of emotion. "But it's going to be worth it. Turn your back on me."

He raises the belt and brings it down on my back, the leather biting into my flesh. The stinging pain is intense, making me cry out, but he doesn't stop. An odd sensation builds between my thighs, making me shudder. He continues, using the belt to sting me with welts.

Frozen by fear and disgust, I fix my eyes on the stone wall before me. After he's wound me up tighter than a coil with the pain, he finally stops. Why the hell am I aroused right now?

"That was just a taste of what I'm capable of if you disobey," he says. "Now, on your knees and turn around."

Like a robot, I do as I'm told, turning to face him in time to see him pull out his huge, hard cock. Dread seizes hold of me while I stare at it, the tip dripping with cum. I clench my eyes and drop to my knees, trying to block out what's happening. But Matias grabs a fistful of my hair and yanks my head backward.

"Open your eyes and look at me," he commands. Slowly, I force my eyes open. His gaze bores into me, twisted and cruel.

"Now be a good little bitch and open up." He taps the head of his cock against my tightly closed lips. I try to turn my head away, but his grip on my hair is too strong.

The pain intensifies as he twists harder. Tears spring to my eyes. If I refuse, there's no telling what he'll do. So, I part my lips.

Matias chuckles darkly as he shoves himself into my mouth. I gag, overwhelmed by his size, as he hits the back of my throat. But he doesn't stop, roughly fucking my face while holding my head in place. Saliva spills everywhere, and hot tears flood my cheeks.

"That's it, just like that," he groans. I feel nauseous, struggling not to literally throw up as he fucks the back of my throat over and over. All the while, I can feel my body responding, dampening between my thighs at his rough treatment.

What the hell?

Perhaps it's because of my ADHD. Maybe this is giving

me an outlet. Or maybe I've got a seriously fucked up case of Stockholm Syndrome.

After what feels like an eternity, Matias finally pulls out, leaving me gasping for air. He smirks down at me while idly stroking himself.

"That was good, Blake," he says. "But we're just getting started." He gestures to the corner of the cell where a small, dingy, stained mattress lies. "Get on the bed. On your hands and knees."

My heart sinks. I know what's coming next. Moving mechanically, I crawl onto the mattress. The scratchy fabric irritates my skin. I position myself as he ordered, staring at the stained, threadbare surface.

Behind me, I hear Matias' boots thudding against the concrete as he approaches. His hands grasp my hips tight enough to bruise. I flinch as he flips up the back of my shirt and tears down my shorts and underwear.

Expecting him to slam into me, I brace myself. Instead, I feel his tongue against my pussy. My heart skips a beat.

His tongue flicks over my clit, sending a jolt of unwanted pleasure through me. I clench my fists into the mattress, fighting back tears.

"God, you're already soaked. You like that, don't you?" Matias taunts. His stubble scrapes against my inner thighs as his tongue explores my most intimate areas.

Despite how fucked this is, my body responds. And he's right. I am wet. It makes me hate myself.

"Please, stop," I beg weakly, my voice breaking. But Matias ignores me. His hands grip my hips harder as he eats me out aggressively, like an animal devouring its prey.

I bury my face in the mattress, willing myself to disconnect, to pretend I'm somewhere far away. But the sensations won't let me escape. My breaths come faster, and I can't hold back a small moan.

Matias lifts his head and chuckles. "I knew you'd enjoy this." I hear him spit, then feel his fingers roughly enter me, stretching me open. I whimper at the intrusion, but he shows no mercy, curling his fingers inside me until I cry out.

"That's it, let it out," Matias says. He withdraws his fingers and runs the head of his hard cock through my lips. "Don't worry, I won't fuck your pussy. At least not yet. God, I have some hot fucking fantasies about you, me and Kali together, though."

I freeze at the thought. Matias has had his eyes on Kali from the moment he saw her. He looks at her like a ravenous beast, and for some fucked up reason, he's also taken a liking to me.

Has he done this to Kali, too, or is she next?

"Now, I want you to come for me," he demands, thrusting his fingers deeper and hitting a spot inside that lights me up.

Just like with the dildo, I find myself so turned on it's sick.

I bite my lip, trying to resist the pleasure building inside me. But Matias' skilled fingers find all the right spots, playing my body like an instrument.

"That's it, just let go," he urges as I tremble on the brink, my legs quaking. With a few more strokes, he pushes me over the edge, and I come hard, crying out for release.

Matias doesn't stop, dragging out my orgasm until I'm overstimulated and writhing. Only then does he pull his fingers free, leaving me panting and spent on the mattress.

"You're even more responsive than I thought," he says, pleased. I feel disgusted, hating my body for betraying me like this.

Matias moves up behind me on the bed. I tense, expecting him to force himself inside. But instead, I feel the head of his cock nudging at my ass. My eyes go wide.

He strokes himself, rubbing the head of his dick right from my clit and back up to my ass. "I'm going to cum on your ass. Hold still."

I clench my eyes shut and brace myself as Matias continues stroking himself. The head of his cock drags along my wet pussy, and I feel utterly violated.

"Please stop," I beg weakly, even though I know it's futile. Matias just chuckles darkly.

"Keep begging. It makes this even hotter," he says. I hear him start to breathe heavier and know he must be close.

Sure enough, moments later, I feel the hot spurts of his cum landing across my lower back and ass. Matias groans loudly as he finishes, pumping himself through his orgasm. The sticky fluid drips over my skin, marking me.

"That's a good look for you," Matias says when he's

done. I stay frozen in place, feeling defeated. He smacks my ass hard, making me yelp after the whipping he gave me.

"Get up and clean yourself off," he orders. On shaky legs, I rise. There's a small grimy sink in the corner of the cell. I wet a rag and wipe away the evidence of what he did.

Matias watches me with a smug smile, casually doing his pants back up. "That was round one," he says. "I'll be back for more soon."

Dread washes over me. This is the beginning of a nightmare I can't wake up from. As long as I'm trapped here, Matias can use me however he wants. And when he comes in the night, there's no one around to stop him.

3

GASTON

I stroll through the lavish entrance of Ileana Navarro's mansion, an air of familiarity settling around me. The scent of expensive perfume and old money hangs heavily in the air, a testament to the business conducted here. I can't deny the anticipation that stirs within me, a thrill I always feel when I step into Ileana's world.

But I keep my expression impassive, being careful to hide my eagerness. No point in showing one's cards too early in the game, after all. I've played this game before and know the rules too well. The product I'm after isn't exactly a common commodity.

Ileana greets me with a knowing smile, her eyes gleaming with practiced coyness. She's a shrewd business-woman, knowing exactly how to appeal to her clients' specific tastes. "Gaston, always a pleasure," she purrs, extending a hand adorned in expensive jewelry. "I've got some new stock I think you'll find enticing."

I smirk at her. "No doubt they'll be up to the usual standard. I was glad you called. The last purchase didn't last as long as usual."

Her eyes flash with sadistic glee. She no doubt believes I murder my girls once I've had enough of fucking them, but that's not my style. Ileana's language is always violence, whereas mine is business first and foremost. They work for me once I'm fed up with fucking them.

"Shall we have a drink?" She gestures toward the ornate dining room.

The table is set for three, meaning her right-hand man, Taren, will be joining us. A lavish feast awaits us; she always knows how to put on a show. I incline my head, following her into the room. The air is thick with the aroma of well-aged wine and roasted meats, a sensory experience designed to set one at ease and open the purse strings.

She pours a deep crimson liquid into two crystal glasses. The wine is undoubtedly one of her finest, another subtle aspect of her sales tactics. Accepting the glass, I swirl the wine around before lifting it toward her, "Salud."

She clinks her glass against mine. "Salud."

Then I bring the glass to my face and inhale, savoring the rich, full-bodied aroma before taking a sip.

"Have a seat," Ileana says, gesturing at the table.

Complying, I sit down and wonder what this "stock" is like that Illeana is so excited to show me. Hopefully, it is nothing like the last ones; otherwise, this will be a wasted and disappointing trip. The last girl had no fire or spark, and that's what I want—a girl who puts up a fight.

While my thoughts wander, the doors open, and Taren strides in. He cuts an imposing figure at six foot three tall, wearing a suit that doesn't match as always. Although on this occasion the contrast is more subtle than others. He wears a pair of black suit pants and a gray suit jacket. The moment his eyes meet mine, they flicker with recognition. "Gaston, what a surprise," he greets, genuinely surprised by my presence. Illeana didn't tell him I was coming.

Taren and Ileana's relationship is weird, to say the least. She's raised him since he was a kid after murdering his entire family in cold blood in Mexico City. But I learned not so long ago that she also makes him sleep with her, something that I don't condone. I may be dark, but she's acted like his mother. She even makes him call her mother, but there's one thing I've never been in denial of. Ileana Navarro is sick in the head.

Ileana flashes him a warning glance as he sits. "I told you we were having a guest," she says.

Taren's glare could cut through ice. "You didn't say who, though, did you?" He tilts his head, staring at his boss, mother, and God knows what else. "You realize they've hardly started their training."

That's what I like to hear. I clap my hands together. "Perfect. You know I prefer a hands-on approach with my girls." Often, their training breaks their spirit, and that's not what I'm after.

Taren grits his teeth and nods. "Of course, Gaston. Whatever you say. Are we eating first, or do you wish to see the girls?" he asks, keeping his voice steady.

I smile. "I'd love to see the girls first." Why wait through dinner merely wondering if any will take my fancy.

Taren nods and stands, leading me out of the room toward the basement. He's off. Tense. Normally, he's not like this, but there's tension between him and Illeana. We walk in silence down the hallway toward the basement. Again, unlike Taren. He'd normally engage in some kind of bullshit conversation.

We reach the cell, and Taren clears his throat.

"On your feet, girls. You have a visitor."

The four girls scramble to their feet and put their arms behind their backs, staring at the floor.

"Not completely untrained, are they, Taren?"

Taren avoids my gaze. "They've been training for a few days."

He unlocks the cell door, leading me inside. I keep my eyes on him, wondering why he's acting off.

I inspect the four girls, circling them. While I do, I keep an eye on Taren's reaction, noticing that he tenses up every time I get near the beautiful, curvy girl with red hair.

That's his problem.

Taren has a thing for one of the prisoners. A part of me likes the idea of taking her away from him, watching his reaction as I select the girl he craves.

"Why don't you tell me about this one?" I ask, signaling to the girl.

The rage on his face is amusing. "That's Alice," he says, keeping his gaze off her. "She's spirited." He tries to sound detached, but I can read him like a fucking book.

I chuckle. "Spirited, eh? I do enjoy a good challenge." I move closer to Alice and lift her chin, looking into her blue eyes.

Out of the corner of my eye, I see Taren's fists clenching.

"But the spirit can be broken, can't it, Taren?" I meet his gaze, smirking to make it clear that he's obsessed with her. Releasing her chin, I turn to a dark-haired girl beside Alice.

All the girls are beautiful in their own right, but one caught my eye the moment we stepped in. Tall, blonde, and just downright fucking gorgeous. Even so, I give time to each of the girls. But when I get to the blonde at the end, I spend the most time admiring her. "And who's this?"

"Blake," Taren answers, his voice flat.

"Blake," I say, testing her name on my lips. I grip her chin and lift it, making her meet my gaze. The defiance in her azure eyes strikes me like a bolt of lightning, igniting something within me. Her spirit doesn't just challenge me. It captivates me. My pants tighten around my crotch as I gaze into her eyes.

They blaze with a wild defiance, unyielding and fierce. She stands there, her posture rigid with resistance, and I find myself momentarily at a loss for words. "She's the one. I'll take her."

The dark-haired girl beside her gasps. "No! You can't take her! You sick son of a bitch."

I smirk at the insolence, watching as Taren approaches the girl and slams his hand into her face, forcing her to the floor. "Apologies for that, Gaston. We'll sort out the paperwork over dinner. I'll have someone prepare her for you."

I laugh at the utter dread in my girl's eyes. And the way her jaw clenches in barely contained anger. What she doesn't know is any girl I buy lives in luxury. In a sense, I'm saving her. She'll want for nothing. Her time at my home will be a far cry from this shit hole.

"Perfect," I reply, holding Blake's gaze. "I look forward to playing with you, beautiful."

She glares back at me. "Fuck you!" she spits.

My smile widens at the feisty response. "I'm going to have a lot of fun with this one, Taren. Aren't I?"

Taren nods. "It would seem so." He turns, leading me away from the cell and my purchase back toward the dining room.

Ileana is a snake waiting for us with a false smile. "Gaston, Taren," she greets, rising to her feet. "How did you find our girls?" she asks, looking at me.

I run a hand through my hair. "Beautiful. I selected one of them." I tilt my head. "Usual price?" I ask, despite knowing Ileana believes these girls are worth more than the usual price.

Ileana clears her throat. "These are more expensive, as I

explained on the phone." She pulls out a seat at the table. "Come, sit and eat, and we'll discuss the details."

I nod, sliding into the chair. "We can negotiate."

Ileana takes her seat at the head of the table, a cocky smirk on her lips. I've never been fond of her, but she's always got the best girls. I don't need the entanglement of romantic relationships, so purchasing a beautiful woman has always been my go-to. They're treated well, considering, and they keep my bed warm at night until I get bored of them and upgrade.

"I want fifteen million and not a penny less," Ileana says, sipping her wine. "Agreed?"

I chuckle at her audacity. "That's five million more than your standard fee."

"I've seen the girls. All four of them are worth five million more because none of them are 'standard.' They're more beautiful than any girls you've bought from me before. Fifteen million, or I'll sell them to the highest bidder." Her eyes narrow. "I'll get over fifteen, I'd expect, for the one you want. Blonde, right?"

I lean back. Ileana drives a hard bargain. She's right, though. I've never come across such a beautiful girl in any auction before. Blake is supermodel standard with golden hair that cascades down her shoulders like a silken waterfall. Her features are delicate and perfectly proportioned, with high cheekbones, a straight nose, and full, kissable lips. She stands tall and proud, almost six feet tall, with a graceful and voluptuous body. Her breasts are full and perfectly round, and her hips flare out in a tantalizing curve.

I've never been hard for a girl from one meeting like that. My dick is still semi-hard now, thinking about her.

"Yes, and tall."

Ileana nods. "She could be a supermodel. Perhaps if you don't want to pay—"

"Fifteen it is," I agree, knowing I won't quibble over five million dollars. She's worth all the money in the world. "Get your man to write up the contract." I nod toward Taren, knowing it'll wind him up. He's fun to tease.

Taren glares at me. "I'm not a fucking lawyer."

Ileana clears her throat. "My lawyer will be here shortly to sort it out."

I nod and lean forward, grabbing some lobster and putting it on my plate. "Perfect." I take a sip of my wine. "Now that business is out of the way, how have you been, Ileana?"

"Not the best." Her eyes narrow. "Have you heard about the Estrada cartel trying to secure Mexico City?"

Oh shit. I should have known Ileana would have caught wind of the plot to fuck her over. A plot I fully support. While Ileana might supply me with great girls, she's paranoid and psychotic. Ileana Navarro is a liability to the entirety of Mexico. "No," I lie.

"Don't lie to me, Gaston," Ileana responds.

She's not stupid. My influence in Mexico City means I know everything that goes on. "I may have heard some rumors, but nothing more."

"Tell me everything you've heard," Ileana demands.

I sip my drink. "Just that he's making waves and buying up real estate in the city."

"So he's trying to gain control of the city?" Ileana murmurs, pulling out her phone and typing something furiously.

I watch her, wondering who the fuck she's contacting. No one wants Ileana to have power in this territory anymore. It's a universal fact that she's a nightmare. "I wouldn't worry too much, Ileana. No one has controlled Mexico City for centuries." I shake my head. "I doubt Pablo Estrada is going to change that."

I don't believe that, as he's making waves, but I can't let her paranoia spiral.

Ileana scowls at me, her eyes gleaming with suspicion. "I've been in this game a long time. I know when someone's lying to me."

I take another sip of my wine, trying to hide my amusement. Ileana is a shrewd leader, but she's also paranoid and impulsive. She's been in power for too long, making her reckless.

"I don't know what you're talking about," I say, keeping my voice steady. "I've told you everything I know."

Ileana leans forward, her eyes narrowed. "You're hiding something, Gaston. I can see it in your eyes."

I chuckle. "You're imagining things, Ileana. I've got no reason to lie to you."

She glares at me, but I can see the doubt in her eyes.

She knows I'm lying, but she can't prove it. And that's the way I like it.

"Well, if you hear anything else, let me know," Ileana says, her voice hard. "And don't think you can play me, Gaston. I'm not as stupid as you think I am."

I raise an eyebrow. "I wouldn't dream of it, Ileana."

She growls softly before turning her attention back to her food. We finish our meal in relative silence with a bit of small talk here and there, but the tension between us remains. I know Ileana is suspicious of me, but I don't care. I'm not afraid of her. In fact, I'm looking forward to watching the other cartel leaders take her down.

She's been a thorn in the side of Mexico's elite for too long, and it's time for her to go.

4

BLAKE

*G*ray, cold eyes haunt my mind as I pace the floor frantically. Eyes belonging to a man so handsome it's hard to believe he's real.

"What are we going to do? That fucking bastard is going to buy me!"

Kali and Alice exchange a look. They don't think I notice, but I do. There's nothing that can be done. We're about to be torn apart far earlier than I expected.

"Let's try the vent again," Luna suggests, staring up at the air vent, which Alice tried climbing out of.

Alice shakes her head. "We've got no chance of getting out of there. It was too tight once I actually stuck my head up. We'd probably all end up stuck."

Kali joins me, pacing. "We can't just let him take her. We have to fight this!"

"If we fight, all four of us will end up dead or worse. Fighting these people will only make our situation unbearable," Alice points out, always the voice of reason. Out of all of us, she has a level head no matter the situation.

Kali shakes her head. "So, what's the option? Let that guy take her?"

Luna grabs Kali's hand, squeezing. "This is about survival now." She glances at me. "And Blake is strong."

I nod because Luna is right about that. There's no way I'm going down without a fight. "I'll try my best to escape and rescue you guys."

"We make a pact right now. Whoever gets out first comes to rescue the others, okay?" Luna suggests.

We all nod and place our hands in a circle together. While it's a show of solidarity, I can't deny I'm skeptical of our pact ever working out. Who are we kidding? The likelihood is I'll never see my friends again. A pain claws at my throat, but I ignore it. This isn't the time to break down.

"We're in this together, to the bitter end," Kali announces. "We survive, we escape, we come back for each other. Remember, we're stronger than they think we are."

A stark silence falls over us after that. We all break apart to either pace the floor or sit on the hay bales. I can't sit. The energy inside me is too restless.

Time seems to crawl by as I wait. Expecting my new owner to return and claim me. After a while, I hear footsteps approaching. My stomach sinks when Matias appears on the other side of the bars.

"Looks like Gaston has a liking for blondes. Blake has been purchased, which means I need to get her ready."

My stomach churns as flashbacks of him shoving his

cock down my throat resurface the moment his dark eyes meet mine.

The tension in the air is so thick you could slice through it with a knife. Out of nowhere, Alice lunges at Matias. "Not so fast, creep!" It's completely unlike her, but Matias barely even flinches as he brings a heavy hand down across her face, slamming her into the floor. "Don't try anything else," he warns, gazing at the rest of us.

Kali ignores his warnings and punches him in the stomach while focusing on me. Luna joins in a kicks him in the shin. All I can do is stare both moved and shocked that my friends are risking their lives for me.

Matias growls at Luna before turning his attention to Kali. He lifts her and pushes her against the wall, yanking her dress up. Kali's body stiffens when he whispers something into her ear, and I can only imagine what kind of disgusting, lewd things he's saying since I've been in a similar position.

We've been "trained" for six days now in total. Yesterday, they decided to make us suck their cocks all at the same time. Although Matias used me and Kali simultaneously. But what no one realizes is that he's been using me and Kali personally, too, at night or early morning. I've pretended to be asleep when he's taken Kali from the cell. The guy is a psychopath, and he needs to be locked up.

Matias's hand moves to cup her pussy, and she whimpers, utterly powerless and held against the wall by the beast of a man. Alice jumps to her feet again, a look of pure rage twisting her features. "Get off her, you sick bastard!" she screams, running at him again.

Matias doesn't hit her this time; he laughs and keeps Kali pinned to the wall. I've never seen Alice so angry.

The sound of someone clearing their throat draws our attention to the cell door. Taren. There's a look of pure rage in his eyes. "What the fuck do you think you're doing, Matias?"

Matias's eyes widen, and he glances at Taren. Suddenly, that callous smirk is gone, and he releases Kali. She gasps for breath, sliding down the wall to the floor.

"I was asked to retrieve the girl," Matias growls, his eyes glinting dangerously. "Which means I'll do it however I see fit. It's none of your business."

Taren steps forward, his face a mask of controlled rage. "It became my business when you laid your hands on them," he retorts in an icy cold voice.

Someone follows him inside. Those eyes cut to mine and it feels like my world crumbles. It's the man who bought me. His gray gaze is fixated on me for a few beats, stealing all the air from my lungs.

Why the fuck would a man like him need to buy women?

He turns his attention to Matias, giving me a welcome reprieve. "And I don't like how you treat the assets I'm paying for."

Matias growls. "You're only buying one, and I didn't touch her."

He strides toward Matias, a confidence in his step.

"Maybe not on this occasion, but if you treat the girls this way once. You'll do it all the time." He runs a hand through his thick, dark brown hair. "Perhaps I shall cancel my sale and tell Ileana I don't like how her men treat the assets I'm paying top dollar for."

It's amusing to see the fear in Matias' eyes. He backs off and bows his head. "I apologize. It won't happen again."

The man walks toward Matias, his gray-blue eyes assessing him. Despite his completely put-together look, I sense it's a disguise. There's a monster lurking beneath his pristine exterior, too.

Suddenly, he grabs Matias by the throat, squeezing so hard his eyes bug out of his skull. "Perhaps I should just murder you right here and now. As I'm not a fool. You've put your hands on my asset more than once since she arrived here, haven't you?"

Matias struggles to draw in the air, grabbing the man's wrists. An odd gratitude coils through me seeing this man harm the man who has put me through so much shit. Although, I sense it will be just as bad with him.

Taren clears his throat. "Gaston, please release my man."

Gaston.

That's the name of my new owner. A shiver races down my spine.

He doesn't comply immediately, but after a few moments, he releases Matias. There's a sinister smile on his lips. "Your man needs to learn his place, Taren." He adjusts his cufflinks, which appear to be solid gold with diamonds. As for the asset..." His cold gaze moves to me, and I can hardly think, let alone move, under his intense gaze.

Asset.

That's what he keeps calling us. That's what he views me as.

"I trust she'll be worth every penny." His gaze lingers momentarily before he turns and walks out of the cell.

Weakness wins out the moment he's gone, and a stray tear escapes my eyes. I see Alice notice and quickly brush it away, not wanting my friends to see how upset I am.

Blake is strong.

That's what Luna said, and I always believed I was, but this situation tests me to my limits.

"That son of a bitch almost killed me," Matias growls.

"About time someone taught you a lesson," Taren replies, but he's not looking at Matias. He's looking at Alice. "Did you strike Alice?"

Matias growls at him. "What the fuck is with your obsession with Alice?"

"Did you strike her?" he repeats the question.

Matias folds his arms over his chest. "She fucking came at me. So, I stopped her."

That is true, but he was brutal with her. That's why she's got a bruise on her face already.

Suddenly, Taren's cool and calm demeanor morphs, and he knocks Matias to the ground with a swift punch.

His fists are a blur as they repeatedly connect with Matias's face. "You don't touch her," he hisses through gritted teeth, pommeling him.

Matias tries to fight, but Taren overpowers him. It's as if he's not human, as with each punch Matias lands, Taren shows no sign of pain or slowing down. Once the ground is painted in blood, Taren pulls back with raw and bleeding knuckles.

Taren looks at me. "Come with me, now."

"Can I at least give my friends a hug goodbye?"

A softness I don't expect to see resonates from Taren's eyes as he nods.

Quickly, I move toward my friends, and we come into a big group hug in the middle. The tears spill, then. I can't keep them back. God knows when or if I'll ever see them again.

"I love you all," I murmur, wiping the tears from my face. "We will see each other again," I vow, despite knowing it's probably not true.

Matias glares at me through his busted eyes, hobbling out of the cell. Taren grabs my wrist and drags me away. "It's time." He leads me down the corridor and then turns to me. "Discard your clothes there." He points at a bin and then nods at a shower. "And go wash."

I do as I'm told, thankful to be able to wash the grime and dirt away. The shower is not very warm, but it suffices. After I've been in for about five minutes, I hear Taren's voice.

"No lingering. Gaston is waiting, and he doesn't like being kept long!"

I swallow hard and shut off the faucet, toweling myself off and drying my hair. My stomach churns as I've got no clothes.

"Taren, what do I—"

"There's a dress on the back of the door and panties on the side. Put them on."

That's when I spot it. A dark black short dress which will hardly cover my ass. And a tiny pair of lace panties. I shudder at the thought of wearing both but do as I'm told, slipping into the soft satin fabric.

When I return to his side, Taren gives a nod. "Perfect. Come on."

Taren leads me out of the Navarro mansion, and I feel torn. I'm leaving my best friends behind, Luna, Kali & Alice, but I hope this might be my first chance to escape. Maybe once I'm with Gaston, I'll find a way back home. A way to save my friends, too.

The limo waits before the mansion, and Taren opens the door for me. I hesitate before sliding inside to find Gaston. Those gray eyes pierce through me as if they can see right to my soul. He's so unnaturally beautiful it's unnerving.

I glare back at him, which seems to ignite something in his eyes.

He moves closer to me. "So, Blake, isn't it?" he asks, touching my thigh. "You're so gorgeous. I can't wait to play with you."

"Keep your hands off me," I retort, shifting my leg away from him.

Gaston grabs a fistful of my hair and angles my head back, looming over me. I may be tall, but he still towers me by at least five or six inches.

"Listen here," he growls. "I paid millions of dollars for you. Do you really think you have any say in what happens to you now? I'll touch you whenever and however I please. Understand?"

Defiance flares to life within me as I glare back at him.

He tightens his grasp on my hair, pulling my face so close to his that our lips are almost touching. "That's not an answer, Blake," he says softly but threateningly. "Do you understand?"

I toy with the idea of ignoring him again, but the glint in his eyes serves as a warning. This man is dangerous, and pushing him might be a bad fucking idea. "Yes," I say quietly, hating that I crumbled so easily.

"Good girl," he says approvingly, releasing his hold on my hair.

Gaston's praise sends a strange rush of pleasure through me, and I realize that I'm getting turned on. I quickly squeeze my thighs together, trying to hide my arousal.

He notices my reaction and grins wickedly. "You're enjoying this, aren't you, Blake?"

I shake my head, trying to deny it, but my body betrays me. My nipples harden, and I can feel the heat rising between my legs.

Gaston leans in closer, his breath hot against my ear. "Maybe you're the perfect little submissive after all. The kind who loves getting praised, who craves the attention of a dominant man."

His words send a thrill through me, and I can't help but feel a strange sense of excitement. I've always been fiercely independent and strong-willed. Still, there's something about men being dominant with me sexually that I've never experienced before. Something that makes me want to submit and relinquish control.

Ignoring his musings about my desire to submit to him, I look into his cold, gray eyes. "What are you going to do with me?"

"Well," he begins, running a finger along my jawline. "Your job now is to serve me in every way I want. You'll address me as 'sir' at all times, and you'll obey every command I give you without question. And since my cock is currently hard," he grabs himself through his pants, "it's your job to satisfy me."

"Fuck you!" I spit.

His laugh is dark and yet has an unwanted effect on me. "I love it when my toys talk back." Roughly, he grabs my arm and yanks me onto his lap. "Let's see if you still feel the same after some 'training.'"

My instinct to fight slams into me. I bring my hand up to slap him, but he anticipates my move and captures both my wrists with his large hands, stopping me. He pins my arms behind my back with one hand. "No fighting." He leans in close enough that his breath tickles my earlobe. "If you continue to disobey, there'll be consequences. Severe ones."

My stomach flip flops as I notice the hard press of his cock through the fabric of his pants. The only thing between us is the fabric of his pants and the little lacy panties I'm wearing.

"Now that we've got that clear, I want you to grind your pussy against my cock."

I'm ashamed that I'm getting wet at the feel of his hard cock pressing into me. Even though I know it's foolish, I resist and focus on his chest and the intricate tattoos visible through the white fabric of his shirt.

"Grind on it, Blake," he orders, his voice menacing. "Show me what a good fucktoy you can be."

Steel coats my nerves as I meet his gaze and glare at him instead.

He chuckles. "Fuck, this is going to be so much fun," he muses, hiking my dress to my hips and cupping my ass cheeks roughly. "You'll obey in the end." He spanks my ass hard, making me gasp. The sting only serves to heighten my arousal.

Fear wraps around me as I recall how good it felt when Matias inflicted pain. Clearly, I'm broken. And I don't want Gaston to know that about me, so I do as I'm told, gyrating my hips and grinding my pussy on his hard cock through his pants.

The wetness between my thighs has soaked my panties and must be making a mess of his pants.

He groans and grabs the back of my neck, forcing me to

meet his gaze. "That's more like it," he praises, giving me another harsh spank. "Grind on that dick and make my pants wet with your perfect little cunt," he orders.

This should be humiliating. It is. And yet my nipples are hard, and I'm gushing for him. More turned on than I've ever been. An ache builds inside me while I stare into those beautiful gray eyes. An ache for more than friction against my clit.

"Such a good girl," he murmurs, grabbing my hips. My breathing is erratic, and I can feel myself teetering on the edge of climax. "I want you to do something else for me now." He maneuvers me off his lap, and I almost cry in protest, my clit throbbing desperately for the friction he just tore from me.

And then, he forces me to my knees on the ground of the limo between his thick muscular thighs. I watch him unzip his pants which are straining from the bulge of his cock, and slowly pull it out. A flash of need sweeps through me at the size. It's longer and thicker than any man's cock I've ever seen. The girth looks almost impossible to fit in any hole.

"Suck it, Blake," he demands, grabbing a fistful of my hair and forcing my head toward the tip. "Show me that you can be a good girl."

Despite the shame, I do as I'm told, opening my mouth and taking his huge girth into my mouth.

He groans. "Fuck yes, baby girl, suck on it just like that."

I can't believe I'm doing this. Forced to my knees and

sucking a complete stranger's cock. Heat spreads through my body, rising to my cheeks. It's not merely from embarrassment but from the arousal spiking through my body. I'm so turned on. Gaston is a beautiful, powerful man who can do whatever he wants with me. And for some sick reason, I like that.

He watches me, his eyes gleaming with lust. His fist tightens in my hair and forces his cock deep into my throat. I gag, but he doesn't stop. He keeps shoving it deeper and deeper into my throat.

"That's it, Blake. Show me what a good girl you can be," he growls. "Take that cock right into the back of your throat."

I struggle against him, but he's too strong. All I can do is take every inch down my throat. His cock is so big it's like he's trying to strangle me with it. A whimper escapes my lips as I push at him.

"You're not done just yet, breath through your nose," he murmurs, pushing deeper. "Show me what a good little cock sucker you can be."

Tears spring to my eyes as I choke on his cock. He's holding me so tight now it hurts, and the pain intensifies my desire. My pussy is so wet I can feel my arousal wetting my thighs. Focusing on breathing through my nose, I begin to accept him deeper. My jaw aches, but I ignore it. In that short moment, all I want is to please him.

Gaston chuckles, his hands tightening in my hair again. "Good girl," he praises. "Your throat feels so fucking good."

Gaston thrusts his hips, driving himself deeper into my throat. My eyes water, and I gag everywhere, soaking his pants with saliva and tears. And he's relentless, watching me with those ice-cold eyes as he uses me for his pleasure.

My orgasm is so close. The orgasm he denied me when he stopped me from grinding against him. Clearly, my mind has short-circuited. This shouldn't get me off. It's like I'm being split in two, one part of me hating every moment while the other loves it. I'm so confused and ashamed by my reaction, but there's no denying it's happening. My pussy clenches with each thrust of his cock down my throat.

I can hardly believe it as a moan tears from my throat, and a flood of white-hot pleasure slams into me so hard it makes my body shake. A gush of liquid squirts from my cunt onto the limousine floor, making a mess. Without a doubt, it's the most explosive orgasm I've ever experienced.

Lifting my gaze to meet Gaston's, my heartbeat stutters. The rage in his eyes, mixed with desire, scares me. "Did I give you permission to come, baby girl?"

Fuck.

When he calls me baby girl, it threatens to ruin me. The way he says it with his slight Spanish accent is beyond sexy. And then he slams into my throat harder than before, growling as his release washes over him.

I feel his hot, salty cum hit the back of my throat, and I try to swallow it all, but there's so much. A flood of cum spills from my lips as he continues to thrust through his orgasm, draining every drop.

When he pulls out of my mouth, I gasp for air.

But then he grabs my throat hard with one huge hand and squeezes. "You need to learn discipline, baby girl. Coming without permission is strictly against the rules." His eyes darken. "Even if it was hot that you couldn't control yourself while I fucked that perfect little throat." He releases me after several agonizing seconds, leaving me breathless and coughing. "Next time, you'll wait until I tell you to come. Understand?"

"Yes."

His eyes narrow, and he grabs my throat again, squeezing so hard. "Yes, what?"

I grind my teeth together. "Yes, sir," I respond.

He smirks at me. "Good girl." Then he spins me around so I'm facing away from him and lands another hard smack on my ass.

I cry out in surprise.

"You have the sweetest ass, baby girl." My face grows red with shame as he laughs. "So tight and round, perfect for keeping my cock warm on the long journey home. Now sit on my lap with my dick between your thighs and be quiet."

I sit on Gaston's lap with his semi-hard cock between my thighs. And despite how degrading it is and the shame I feel at coming from such rough treatment, the desire and need still pulse between my thighs.

The limo drives us further away from my friends

toward my new home with my new owner. His warm breath tickles my neck as he holds me against his hard, muscular chest while he glances out the window. Gaston moves one large hand onto my thigh and squeezes gently. Whether it's meant to comfort or serve as a move of possession, it only reminds me how trapped I am.

5

GASTON

*M*y beauty's rhythmic breathing as she sleeps on my lap is like my personal symphony. After two hours of attempting to remain awake, she gave in and slumped against my chest. I've held her ever since, loving how she feels on my lap with my now solid cock gripped between her thighs.

Never before in my thirty-four years have I been so turned on.

Blake might act like a feisty vixen, but her submissive nature shines through the moment she's being used. It's exactly how I like my women. Fighter when out of the bedroom, but the moment you have them on their knees servicing your cock, their putty in your hands. It's a rare trait to find indeed.

A strange stirring ignites in my gut while I watch her sleep. Blake is different. She's a challenge—one I can't wait to conquer.

Reaching out, I trace my finger along her jawline, savoring the softness of her skin. My hands move down her neck and over her collarbone before dipping to the slope of her breasts. She doesn't wake, but I feel her heartbeat quicken.

God, she's so fucking tempting. She smells divine like the ocean tinged with a sweet scent of strawberries.

I push her dress down so her tits are free, softly caressing them. Her breath catches in her throat, but she remains asleep, making me smile. The desire to continue my exploration is unavoidable. So, I let my hand dip lower over her stomach and beneath the hem of her short dress.

Blake moans softly in her sleep.

"Are you dreaming of me, baby girl?" I whisper into her ear.

She arches into my touch as I trace my fingers along her inner thigh, getting closer to her perfect little cunt. Pressing my lips against the pulse point at the base of her throat, I can feel her heart racing beneath my lips. Slowly, I rip apart the lace covering her pussy and touch her clit.

"You've got such a wet cunt for me," I murmur quietly, not wanting to wake her yet. In fact, I don't want to wake her at all. This is my secret exploration of her body, all for me. "Keep sleeping, baby girl," I breathe into her ear. "Can you do that for me?" I ask, despite knowing she can't answer. Slowly, I slip a finger into her tight cunt.

"Fuck," I breathe, my cock jumping between her thighs in response.

She groans in her sleep as I finger her softly. I've never

felt this hooked on one of the girls I've bought. Scratch that. I've never felt this hooked on any girl at all.

My cock leaks over her inner thighs, and the sight is fucking hot. She's splayed out over me as I finger her pussy, my cock mere inches from it. Gently removing my fingers, I rub my cock against her cunt, coating myself in her arousal.

"I'm going to have so much fun playing with you, beautiful," I murmur. "So much fun."

Blake groans and moves a little, warning me she's starting to wake. Quickly, I suck her arousal from my fingers, groaning at how goddamn good she tastes, and pull my cell phone from my pocket, flicking through my emails casually.

Suddenly, she bolts upright in my lap and almost falls forward.

I steady her with my hand. "Calm down. You're right where you're supposed to be."

She tenses at the sound of my voice. "Shit, did I fall asleep." I notice her gaze dip down to my cock between her thighs and the sticky precum that's leaked onto her skin.

"Yeah, and I got fucking hard watching you," I breathe against the back of her neck, holding her close. "Turn around and straddle me so I can look into your pretty blue eyes."

She doesn't move at first, testing my patience. "Do I need to remind you of the rules?" I tease my hand over her throat, threatening to block her airway.

Quickly, she moves and straddles my thighs, pressing

my dick against her pussy as she does. Her brow furrows as she glances down. "What the—"

"I played with you a little while you slept and tore your panties."

Her eyes widen. "What the fuck?"

My hand circles her throat. "No dirty language. Good girls don't swear."

Her reply is a nod. I consider demanding she reply with words, but instead, I turn my attention to polite conversation. "Tell me something about yourself. What did you do in America before you were kidnapped?"

She clenches her jaw, clearly irritated that I'm changing the subject considering I played with her while she slept. My cock is throbbing against her pussy, and since she woke, she's got even wetter. "I was a student," she says simply.

"What were you studying?" I trace a finger along her cheekbone, a feather-light touch that makes her visibly shiver.

"Psychology."

My smirk grows. "Convenient. I'm sure you'd have a lot of psychoanalysis when it comes to me, beautiful, wouldn't you?"

Her eyes narrow. "Yes, I already know you're a sociopath or perhaps borderline psychopath."

"And what about you, baby girl? Shouldn't you psycho-analyze yourself? After all, you orgasmed with my cock choking your throat. Clearly, that says something about your psychology, does it not?"

Her expression turns furious. "No, it's common when women are put in those situations to have a physiological response to the assault. It doesn't mean I wanted it."

I laugh. "The thing is, Blake, I know you wanted it. I saw the way your eyes lit up when my cock hit the back of your throat. Hell, I saw it the moment you set eyes on it." I wrap a hand around the back of her neck, gripping tightly. "Let's not play games here. You love every second of this." I lean in closer, allowing my breath to tease against her ear. "You're so wet for me right now, my cock is covered in your cum."

"Sir, we're here," Jorge, my driver, speaks through the intercom.

I clench my jaw at the interruption and force Blake into the seat beside me. "Time for you to see your new home," I say, switching my tone to casual. I stuff my cock back into my pants and zip them up, ignoring the fact I've got a wet patch when her pussy was leaking all over me.

Jorge pulls up in front of Elysium, my apartment building where I own the penthouse. And then he gets out and opens the door for Blake, who slides out onto the sidewalk, yanking her dress down self-consciously. It's just like Ileana to dress my purchase in such a trashy outfit when she knows I value class. Not that it matters. Blake has a whole new wardrobe waiting for her inside.

I slip a hand onto the small of her back and guide her toward the entrance of the apartment building. "Welcome to Elysium, baby girl."

She scoffs, glaring at me. "Something tells me Elysium will contradict what it's like living here."

I tilt my head. "I wouldn't be so sure." Pressing harder against her back, I lead her into the opulent lobby adorned with marble and crystal chandeliers.

The security guard nods at me. "Welcome home, Mr. Marques."

I give him a nod. "Thanks." And then, I press the button for the top floor and wait for the elevator to arrive. While waiting, I study Blake. She's standing in front of me, her posture rigid, her hands clasped.

It shouldn't be possible for a girl to look so strikingly beautiful in a dress so fucking trashy.

The elevator arrives with a soft ding, and we step inside. I press the button for the top floor and look into the eye scanner on the wall above. It IDs me and then moves upward while I tap my foot impatiently. Blake hasn't said a word since we left the limo, and the silence feels more palpable in such a tight, confined space.

"What are you thinking?" I demand, wondering why I ever care what she's thinking. It's not often I concern myself with the thoughts and feelings of women I buy.

She doesn't respond, staring at the elevator walls as we ascend to my apartment.

"I asked you a question, beautiful." I move my hand from the small of her back to the back of her neck and squeeze. "Answer me."

"I'm thinking I'm in hell," she mutters.

She might be right. Many people have referred to me as

a devil disguised in a suit. She just doesn't realize yet how good it can be to live on the dark side.

The doors slide open when we reach my floor to reveal my penthouse. It's spacious and modern, with floor-to-ceiling windows that offer a panoramic view of the city. There's a large yet comfortable living room that leads into the open-plan kitchen and dining area. The floor-to-ceiling doors in the living room lead out to a balcony with a swimming pool and jacuzzi.

"Welcome home, Blake," I say as we exit the elevator.

She looks around, her eyes wide with surprise and awe. "It's beautiful," she whispers, her voice barely audible.

"It is, isn't it?" I reply, taking her hand and leading her into the apartment. "And it's your home now. Let me give you a tour."

"This is the kitchen," I say, showing her the spacious modern kitchen with state-of-the-art appliances and a large center island. "You'll find everything you need here to cook for us."

Her jaw clenches. "I'm not a good cook, so I hope you like mac and cheese. It's about the extent of my culinary skills."

My eyes narrow. "We'll see about that." She'll learn to cook for me, it's part of the requirement for all the girls I buy. Her job is not just to warm my bed but to become my domestic slave. I walk into the adjoining dining area. "And this is the dining area," I say. "We can eat here or on the balcony when the weather is nice."

Blake's eyes widen. "Balcony?"

"Yes," I say, leading her through the floor-to-ceiling doors from the kitchen to the balcony. "It's out here."

We step out onto the balcony, and Blake gasps. The view is breathtaking. We're on the top floor of the building, and we can see the entire city spread out before us.

"Wow," Blake whispers.

I smirk, glad that she's impressed by my home.

Her expression sours when she notices the look on my face. "Amazing what being a douchebag with millions of dollars can buy you."

I narrow my eyes. "Try billions, baby girl. And if you call me a douchebag one more time, you won't like what happens." Tightening my grasp on her hand, I pull her back into the kitchen and onto the pool terrace.

Her jaw falls open then. "Nice pool."

"Do you like to swim?"

She meets my gaze. "Yes, although I prefer the sea."

"Perhaps if you're a good girl for me, we'll visit the seaside sometime." Next, I take her into the library lined with books from floor to ceiling.

"This is the library." Blake walks toward the bookshelf and runs her fingers over the spines of some of my first editions.

"Do you like to read?" I ask.

There's an odd look in her eyes as she glances at me. "Not really." I wonder what that look is about. I've never wanted to understand someone the way I want to understand her.

We continue through the apartment, and I show Blake

the home cinema equipped with a state-of-the-art sound system and a huge screen.

"This is amazing," Blake says. "I've never seen anything like it."

"You don't like to read, but movies are more your thing?" I ask.

She shrugs. "I like movies if they're good."

"Come on, we've got the best room to see yet."

Her eyes narrow when I grab her hand again, leading her to my bedroom—our bedroom for as long as I keep her here. It's the largest bedroom in the apartment, decorated in luxurious creams and gold. There's a king-size bed in the center of the room, and the walls are adorned with expensive paintings. "This is our room."

Blake's face pales.

"The closet is behind that door on the left, and the bathroom is behind the door on the right. Get freshened up and dressed into something more suitable." I let my eyes drop down her stunning figure. "And once you're ready, come and meet me in the kitchen. Understood?"

She nods.

I click my tongue. "Use your words for me, beautiful."

"Yes, sir," she replies, averting her gaze.

It takes all my strength to walk away from her. All I want is to bend her over that bed and feast on her for the rest of the night. Turning away, I walk back to the kitchen and pour myself a glass of whiskey. Grinding my teeth, I don't understand why I hate being away from her when she's only down the corridor. Maybe it's because my cock is so fucking hard.

It's been hard ever since I set eyes on her. The need to fuck her is so damn excruciating, but she's not ready yet. When I finally fuck my girl, she'll be begging for my cock like a dirty little slut. My dirty little slut. And she will beg. That's something I guarantee.

6

BLAKE

*T*he mirror in the opulent adjoining bathroom reflects my vacant stare.

How the hell did I get here?

Gaston is a misogynistic pig who believes women are supposed to submit to men. He's the kind of man that makes my blood boil, and now he owns me.

Sighing heavily, I turn to the shower and turn on the faucet. Despite the situation I find myself in, there's no denying that this place is a million times better than the filth I've been kept in by the Navarro cartel.

The question is, is this hell disguised as heaven?

Dropping the horrible, trashy dress to the floor, I step out of it and then remove my torn panties. I still can't believe that bastard played with me while I was sleeping. Stretching my arms above my head, I step under the spray of hot warm and sigh. It's heaven. While I may have had a quick shower in lukewarm water earlier, it wasn't like this.

The water cascades over me, washing away the grime and the horrors of the past couple of weeks. It's cathartic, almost—a rare moment of solitude and sanctuary in a world that has become unrecognizable. I close my eyes and allow the steam to envelop me, trying to cleanse not just my body, but my soul from the taint of the past God knows how long. Since being kidnapped, I've lost track of time.

The warmth soothes my skin, but it does little to calm the storm raging inside me. I'm torn between the relief of immediate safety and the gnawing fear of what comes next. How do I retain my sense of self when every decision is made for me? The thought of facing him again sends a shiver down my spine that not even the hot water can chase away.

And then there's that traitorous ache that pulses deep whenever I think about him. The way he made me sit on his lap with his cock between my thighs was weird and yet oddly arousing. He's so powerful, so handsome, so manly...

"No, Blake. He bought you, for fuck's sake," I mutter to myself.

The stark contrast between my hatred for the situation and the peculiar allure I feel toward him baffles me. And I felt it, although not so intensely, when I was with Matias too. It feels akin to Stockholm Syndrome, developing an empathy or connection with one's captor. Even though I know it's not possible. I've only just met him, and the syndrome takes some time to manifest.

Gaston is my captor. My owner. My master. That thought alone should be enough to extinguish any misguided affection or attraction I might harbor. Yet, as I stand under the soothing water, trying to rinse away the complexities of my emotions, I find myself grappling with an unsettling truth.

Despite the circumstances, despite the logic screaming at me, there's an undeniable spark—a dangerous desire for the man who now claims ownership over me.

After a long time in the shower, I hear a banging on the door. "Blake! You've been in there an hour. I expected you out by now."

Shit.

"Sorry," I call back. "I'll get out and be dressed in ten minutes!"

"You better be and not a minute longer."

I swallow hard and shut off the water, wrapping myself in the softest and thickest towel I've ever felt in my life. Quickly, I towel dry my hair and then walk out with it wrapped around myself. There's no sign of Gaston, but on the bed, he's placed a stunning red Valentino dress, a garter belt, and matching black lace underwear.

Taking the hint that he wants me to wear that, I quickly dress and then glance in the mirror. I've got no makeup on, but then he's never seen me with it on anyway. Swallowing hard, I open the door and walk swiftly toward the kitchen to find him sitting at the kitchen island on his cell phone.

For a moment, I have a chance to really study him before he notices me. He's gorgeous with sharp, angular features that are softened slightly by the warm glow of the kitchen lights. His jawline is chiseled, framing a pair of thin lips often set in a firm line, giving him a look of perpetual determination.

His hair, a rich shade of midnight black styled meticulously. What truly captivates me, however, are his eyes. They're a striking shade of gray, reminiscent of the sky on a stormy day, holding depths that seem to hint at both torment and passion.

Suddenly, he notices me and looks up from his phone. Those gray eyes flash with fire as he drags them slowly down the length of my body. "Perfect," he mutters but then shakes his head. "If only you'd be on time."

I arch a brow. "I don't remember you giving me a time limit." It's the truth. He merely told me to get ready.

Gaston nods at the bags on the counter. "I ordered some food while you were getting ready. I figured we could get to know each other and save you cooking. But since you took your sweet time, it's all cold now."

A wave of annoyance washes over me. "That's not my fault. You didn't tell me how quick to be."

"You should've known better than to take so long."

I clench my hands into fists. "I hadn't had a hot shower in God knows how long, so I was enjoying myself."

He arches a brow. "Enjoying yourself how? I hope you weren't touching your pussy, as that belongs to me now." He stands from the stool he is sitting on and steps closer, his eyes gleaming with a dangerous intensity. "No one, not even you, gets to touch it. Not now I own it—own you."

I take a step back, my heart pounding in my chest. "I'm a human being, not your property."

He chuckles. "That's exactly what you are. I bought you, and now you belong to me." He reaches out and grabs my arm, pulling me toward him. "Do you understand?"

I glare at him. "Let me go."

"I asked you a question."

I nod in reply. "I understand; now, please release me."

He laughs. "I don't think so." He yanks me closer and then crashes his lips to mine. My resistance lasts a few moments, but the feel of his solid, hard body against mine and his tongue thrusting into my mouth turns me into jelly.

His tongue tangles with mine, claiming me, possessing me. His large hands roam over my body, gripping my hips and pulling me flush against him so that I can feel the hard length of his cock against my stomach.

A shiver runs down my spine. I hate him. I hate what he's doing to me. But I can't deny the way my body responds to his touch. It's like he knows exactly how to play me, how to make me weak with desire.

He breaks the kiss, his lips trailing down my neck. "You're mine," he growls against my skin. "Every inch of you belongs to me."

There's an argument on the tip of my tongue, but when he grazes his teeth over my pulse, it dies out. Instead, I whimper.

His lips curve into a smile against my skin. "That's it, beautiful," he murmurs. "Give in to me. You know you want to." His hands slide down to my ass, squeezing roughly.

I gasp, my hips bucking involuntarily against him.

"You can't fight it," he says, his voice low and seductive. "You're mine and always will be."

He kisses me again, and I find myself melting into him. My hands fist in his shirt, pulling him closer. I hate myself for it, but I can't help the way my body responds.

He cups my breasts through the fabric of my dress, his thumbs brushing over my painfully hard nipples. I moan into his mouth, my back arching as pleasure courses through me.

He breaks the kiss, his eyes dark with desire. "I'm going to make you scream my name," he promises. "I'm going to ruin you for anyone else." And then his gray eyes flash with sadistic glee. "But not yet. Now it's time to eat."

Bastard.

He's got me all worked up on purpose. I clench my thighs together and don't react to his torment.

He moves around the kitchen, grabbing plates out of the oven and the food he ordered. My mouth dries as he rolls the sleeves of his shirt up, revealing ink over both of his corded arms.

Fuck.

This man is a literal God, even if he is a fucking asshole.

He grabs a corkscrew and opens a bottle of red wine. When he turns around, I don't realize until he speaks that I'm staring.

"Like what you see, beautiful?"

I narrow my eyes. "If you're talking about the wine, yes."

He laughs. "You, Blake, are a terrible liar. You should work on that."

Moving to the other side of the kitchen, he grabs two wine glasses and pours us each one. And then he passes me a glass. I take it, knowing I'll need it to get through this evening. The red liquid sloshes around as I bring it to my lips, taking a long sip. It's rich and smooth, probably some expensive vintage that costs more than my entire wardrobe at home.

Gaston smirks at me as he takes his own glass, his eyes never leaving mine. "I hope you like it. It's a rare Cabernet Sauvignon from a small vineyard in Napa Valley."

I shrug, feigning indifference. "It's fine, I guess." I don't want to give him any satisfaction.

He chuckles a low, dark sound that sends a shiver down my spine. "I can see right through you, Blake."

Rage coils through me as I place the glass down on the counter. "You don't know anything about me."

He steps toward me, closing the distance in two short strides. "I know enough. You're stubborn and defiant but fiercely loyal to your friends. You're intelligent and quick-witted but can be impulsive and reckless too."

Bile rises up my throat as it's all true, but how could he know that? Perhaps Taren gave him information on me.

Gaston reaches out to tuck a strand of hair behind my ear, his fingers lingering on my skin. "And I know that deep down, you crave submission. You want someone to take control and dominate you in every way possible."

I jerk away from his touch, my cheeks burning with a mixture of anger and embarrassment. "You're wrong," I snap, but even I can hear the lack of conviction in my voice.

There's a predatory gleam in his eyes. "Am I? We'll soon find out, won't we?"

He turns back to the food, opening the containers and placing them on the counter. The aroma of spices and grilled meat fills the air, making my stomach growl despite my best efforts to ignore it.

"I hope you're hungry," Gaston says, handing me a plate. "I ordered a little bit of everything, so you can try whatever you like."

I take the plate from him, my fingers brushing against his. The contact sends a jolt of electricity through me, and I quickly pull away, busying myself with loading my plate.

Gaston's eyes remain on me like a hawk while we sit to eat. It's unnerving and, at the same time, thrilling how interested he is in me. I take another sip of wine, hoping it will calm my nerves.

Instead, the alcohol only makes me more acutely aware of his proximity and how fucking beautiful he is.

God, what is wrong with me?

I should be disgusted by him, repulsed by everything he stands for. Gaston is a man richer than God with all the power in the world, and he abuses it by buying women. But instead, I find myself drawn to him, like a moth to a flame. And the problem is, flames always burn you.

7

GASTON

*S*itting at the boardroom table of my company, QuantumTech Solutions, I find myself distracted. A rarity in my life. Distractions are the makings of failure, and yet here I am, thinking of nothing but the beauty I've got locked away in my penthouse apartment.

It's been a week since Blake came home with me. A week of teasing and tormenting each other. I haven't even touched her since we got back to Mexico City because she's hellbent on proving she's not affected by me when we both know it's a lie. And when I fuck her, she's going to be begging me for it.

"Gaston, what's your input on this?"

I glance at Javier, the head of operations. "Sorry, what was the question?"

His brow furrows. "Is there something wrong, sir?"

"No, I just didn't sleep well last night."

Javier runs through some bullshit issues with staffing again, and I tell him to do whatever he wants. If he needs more staff, hire. This kind of shit is below my station.

"Okay, sir. I'll get on it."

I shake my head. "Great, if that's everything. I need to—"

"No, sir," Damien interrupts. "There's an issue with Pablo Estrada attempting to buy our land. He's very persistent."

I straighten at the mention of Pablo, as he's one of the men working against Ileana. "Did he mention why he wants the land?"

Damien shakes his head. "No, but he keeps asking for a meeting with you personally, sir. And I know—"

"Arrange it. I want to hear what he has to say."

Damien looks shocked that I want to meet with him, as usually I refuse all in person meetings, but he bows his head. "Of course, sir. I'll send you the details as soon as I have them."

I glance around the table, seeing no other concerns from my team.

"Alright, if there's nothing else, this meeting is adjourned," I say, gathering my notes and standing. The others murmur their goodbyes while I stride out of the boardroom, eager to get back to the privacy of my office.

Sitting down at my desk, I wake my computer from sleep mode, intending to go through some emails and proposals. But I'm distracted again, thinking of the fiery beauty I've got waiting for me back home. Unable to resist, I bring up the security feeds from my penthouse.

There's Blake, making a mess of my kitchen as she attempts to cook something. Flour is dusted across the countertops, spices litter the floor, and smoke rises from a pan on the stove. She coughs, waving her hand in front of her face. I can't help but chuckle. She wasn't lying about being a terrible cook.

Just watching her move around my kitchen so domestically makes my cock stir. I palm my dick through my pants while she struggles to save whatever concoction she's whipped up. Her brows are furrowed in concentration, lips pursed, and sweat glistening on her forehead.

Fuck, she's sexy even like this.

Unable to take it anymore, I unzip my pants and pull out my rapidly hardening cock. Gripping it firmly, I stroke myself while I watch Blake on the monitor. I groan, imagining her on her knees before me, lips wrapped around my thick cock.

Soon. Soon I'll have her begging for me like a good little slut.

I can't stop thinking about her all day, every day. Blake. The little firecracker. She's gotten off lightly this first week, but that's all going to change. I may be playing the long game for once, resisting the urge to just take what I want from her, but I can have some fun.

It's not usual that I care whether or not a girl wants me before I fuck her. But Blake is special. I want her to crave my touch so badly that she'll do anything I ask.

I know she's getting antsy. Bored. She thinks I don't notice the way her body reacts when I get close to her. The quickening of her breath, the slight flush on her cheeks. She hates how much she wants me already.

It won't be long. A woman like Blake needs excitement, thrills, and pleasure. And I'm the only one who can give her what she truly needs. I'll push her right to the edge, teasing and tempting, until she shatters and submits to me wholly.

I recall how incredible it felt to have her on her knees before me with her pretty pink lips wrapped around my throbbing cock. The way she'd looked at me with those gorgeous baby blue eyes.

My dick twitches in my hand, precum dripping down my shaft.

The image of her spread out on my bed, bound and moaning as I explore every inch of her body, flashes into my mind. She's going to love every second when the time comes.

Blake can deny that she wants me all she wants, but I see the truth when she looks at me. In those stunning blue eyes, I see a mix of desire and intrigue, and all it would take is one push to unravel her.

My cock swells as I imagine her tight little cunt bouncing up and down my cock, her tits in my face as I suck her nipples into my mouth. What I'd give to have her here right now, sitting on my dick in my office, moaning while she rides me.

The thought brings me to climax as I shoot my cum

across the polished wood of my desk. God. I've not mastur-bated for years. It's pathetic. I'm thirty-four years old, not fourteen.

I sit back in my chair, trying to catch my breath. A sudden knock at my office door forces me to tuck myself back into my pants and quickly wipe up my cum from the desk. "Come in," I call.

Damien steps inside, looking flustered. "Sir, I apologize for the interruption, but there's an urgent matter that requires your attention."

I raise a brow. "What is it?"

"It's about the Estrada situation. He's here, sir. Demanding to speak with you immediately."

My jaw tightens at the audacity. Showing up without an appointment and demanding he be seen immediately is typical of Estrada. "Very well. Show him in."

Damien nods and steps aside, allowing a tall, imposing man to stride into my office. Pablo Estrada.

"Marques," he greets, his tone clipped.

I lean back in my chair, eyeing him coolly. "Estrada. To what do I owe the pleasure?" Pablo takes a seat across from my desk without invitation. The insolence of this man never ceases to amaze me.

"I believe you know why I'm here," he says, dark eyes boring into mine. "You've got something I want."

I lean back in my chair, clasping my hands together. "And what might that be? I've got many things that people want."

A muscle in his jaw ticks. "The land. The property you recently acquired in the heart of Mexico City. I want it."

I chuckle humorlessly. "Ah yes, that little piece of real estate. Well, I hate to disappoint you, but it's not for sale."

Estrada leans forward, his gaze intense. "Everything has a price, Marques. Name yours."

I study him for a long moment, weighing my options. The truth is, I've got no intention of selling that land to Estrada or anyone else. It's a strategic acquisition, one that'll give me even more power and influence in this city.

"I appreciate your offer," I say smoothly, "but as I said, the property is not on the market. My plans for it are extensive."

Estrada's eyes narrow. "Plans? What kind of plans?"

I wave a dismissive hand. "Nothing that concerns you, I assure you. Now, if there's nothing else..."

Standing, I signal the meeting is over. But Estrada remains seated, his posture tense. "I urge you to reconsider," he says. "It would be in your best interest to cooperate with me on this."

"Are you threatening me, Estrada? Because I promise you, that's not a wise course of action."

We stare at one another, the tension kicking up a notch. After a few moments, Estrada finally relents. He stands and adjusts his suit jacket before glaring at me. "This isn't over," he warns. "I'll have that land, one way or another."

With that, he turns and strides out of my office, slamming the door behind him. I sink back into my chair, rubbing a hand over my face.

While I support his attempt to get ride of Illeana Navarro, I won't stand by if he proves to be a thorn in my side. Perhaps I underestimated the crime boss, but I've got no intention of backing down or bowing to his demands. That land is mine, and I'll do whatever it takes to keep it that way.

8

BLAKE

*P*acing Gaston's apartment, I'm going to lose my mind if I don't get out of here soon. He refuses to allow me out of the penthouse, stating I'm not trustworthy enough yet.

But how the fuck do I earn his trust when he hasn't even touched me since we got here?

I thought he was going to fuck me, but every night I've slept in his bed, and not once has he tried anything. The ding of the elevator arriving warns me he's home, and I quickly stop pacing and dive onto the sofa.

He marches into the living room looking frustrated as he yanks his tie off and chucks it down on the back of the sofa. It takes him a moment to notice me, but when he does some of that tension eases.

"Hey, beautiful," he murmurs, moving toward me and kissing my cheek softly. "What's for dinner?"

I can't deny that this entire setup is weird. He treats me

like I'm his girlfriend or wife. "I had a stab at tacos. Hopefully, they'll be more edible than the lasagna."

I wasn't lying when I told him I'm a terrible cook. I am. But I'm trying to learn. The fact is, without my meds, I find it very hard to focus on anything, but telling him about my condition would give him power I don't want him to have.

His chuckle is low and sexy. "If it's not, we'll order pizza."

Pizza sounds good. Really fucking good, actually. I cross my fingers and hope my attempt at tacos tastes as bad as I think it will.

"You look tense," I comment, following him into the kitchen. He's rolling up his shirt sleeves, exposing his tattooed, muscular forearms.

He glances at me, lips twitching. "Work was...trying."

"Oh?" I raise my brows. "Anything I can help with?"

He laughs then, a deep rumble that echoes around the kitchen. "Not unless you're suddenly an expert in land development."

I hop onto the counter, watching as he opens the oven and pulls out the tray of tacos. The smell that wafts free isn't promising. "Sorry, I think I'll stick to terrible cooking and being a pain in your ass."

He sets the tray on the counter and turns to me, a dangerous glint in his eyes. "Beautiful, you've got no idea what a pain in my ass you are."

I tilt my head. "Why don't you enlighten me then?"

His hands settle on the counter either side of my hips and he leans in close, his warm breath caressing my face.

"Having you in my home and not touching you, claiming you, is a special kind of torture."

I tilt my head, unsure what he's getting at. "Then why don't you? You bought me, right?"

His gray eyes bore into mine, a mixture of lust and frustration swirling in their depths. "Because, baby girl, I want you to beg for it. I want you to crave my touch and my cock so badly that you can't think straight."

I swallow hard, my body responding to his words even while my mind rebels. He can't win. He can't break me. But fuck, the way he's looking at me makes me want to surrender and drop to my knees before him.

"And what if I don't?" I challenge, my voice coming out breathier than I intended. "What if I never beg?"

His lips curve into a smirk, and he grabs my hips, digging his fingers in. "You will. It's only a matter of time."

I lean forward, my lips an inch from his. "Don't be so sure, Gaston. I'm not like the other girls you've had."

"No, you're not," he agrees, his gaze dropping to my mouth. "You're a fucking wildcat, and I can't wait to tame you."

My heart pounds in my chest, and my skin feels too tight over my flesh. There's this deep and dark part of me that wants to give in and beg him, but that would be admitting defeat.

I slide off the counter, pressing my body against his for a fleeting moment before stepping away. "Keep dreaming. Let's find out if these tacos are edible, shall we?"

Grabbing the tray, I carry it to the dining table. My

hands are shaking slightly, and I don't want him to see, but I can feel his eyes on me, burning into my back.

Gaston follows and takes his usual seat across from me. Silence falls over the table as we serve ourselves, and surprisingly, the tacos aren't awful. I take a sip of wine, watching Gaston as he leans back in his chair, studying me with those intense eyes.

"Tell me how your day was," he demands.

"As boring as all the other days I've been trapped in this apartment."

He sighs, pinching the bridge of his nose. "There's plenty to do here. Swim, use the home gym, home cinema, read, surely you can't already be bored?"

I shrug and eat more of my taco.

Gaston leans forward. "Tell me something about yourself. About your friends and family before you got captured."

I stiffen memories of my loved ones flashing through my mind. Memories of my three best friends are still stuck in hell. They might have been bought already, or maybe they're still 'training.' "I don't want to talk about them."

Gaston frowns, his brow furrowing. "Why not?"

I meet his gaze with steely resolve. "Because it's none of your fucking business."

A slow smile spreads across his face, his eyes glinting with something that makes my stomach flip. "Fair enough," he says, leaning back in his chair once more. "But just know, everything about you is my business now. You belong to me."

"I don't belong to anyone."

Gaston smirks, his gaze raking over me possessively.

I clear the dinner plates from the table, feeling him watch me. My skin prickles with awareness of his presence. I set the dishes in the sink and turn on the faucet, letting the sound of running water fill the tense silence.

I sense him before I hear him, the heat of his body alerting me to how close he is. Gaston moves behind me, caging me against the counter with his arms on either side of me. My breath catches as I feel his erection press into my backside through our clothes.

The frustration I feel at being cooped up in the apartment without my meds is making me act crazy. And the thrill of Gaston's nearness is the most tempting thing to happen all fucking week. The desire to resist is strong, but the desire to take out my frustration on this man by fucking him senseless is stronger.

Gaston's breath is hot against my neck. "You drive me crazy, baby girl," he rasps. "I'm trying to be a gentleman, but it's so hard with you tempting me."

My lips part, and I focus on steadying my breathing. I shouldn't want this, shouldn't want him, yet I do. Gaston's hand trails down my arm, and I shiver at his touch.

"You're anything but a gentleman," I manage weakly, even as my back arches.

He chuckles, nuzzling my hair. "Your body is yearning for me, belleza. But you're so stubborn, aren't you?"

He steps back, and I sag forward against the counter,

pulse racing. I don't know how much more of this tension I can take. I spin to look at him.

Gaston regards me with hooded eyes before turning away. "I've got some work to finish. I'll see you later."

He leaves me standing there, frustrated and confused. Turning back to the washing up, I force myself to breathe and gain control of myself. Gaston leaves the kitchen, but his words and touch still linger on my skin.

Deciding I need a moment to myself, I head to our shared bedroom and slip inside, locking the door.

Why am I letting him get to me?

Sighing, I walk into the bathroom and lean on the sink counter, staring at myself in the mirror. I hate how crazy I'm feeling right now. Without my meds, I feel like I want to climb the walls. So, I turn on the shower, hoping it will help clear my mind.

The warm spray feels heavenly against my heated skin when I step under it. I let my eyes close, the water cascading over me while I try to clear my mind.

But it's no use. Gaston's presence is seared into my every thought. I can still feel the ghost of his hands on my body, the intensity of his gaze burning me from the inside out.

Lathering the soap over my skin, I can't help but imagine what it would be like to give in to the desire that coils low in my belly whenever he's near—let him take control and have his way with me.

My fingers trail down my neck, over my breasts, lower

still until I'm cupping myself. I bite my lip, a soft moan escaping as I gently caress the sensitive bundle of nerves.

I know I shouldn't be doing this and thinking of him. But in this moment of privacy, with the water cascading over my body and my own touch igniting sparks of pleasure, I can't bring myself to care. The thought of being his, of belonging to him in every way, sends a shiver down my spine.

I press my forehead against the cool tiles, my breath coming in ragged gasps as I chase my release. The idea of Gaston taking me, claiming me, pushes me closer and closer to the edge.

Just as I feel that familiar tightening in my core, I know I'm close to the edge. "Gaston," I groan his name into the shower, knowing he won't hear me. Here in the privacy of the bathroom, I keep my dirty secret while I picture him fucking me. But then, just as I'm about to climax, I stop.

"No." I let out a frustrated growl.

This isn't happening.

If I come while imagining him, then he's already won. As he says, it's only a matter of time. I must refrain. So, frustrated and heated, I finish washing and step out of the shower, wrapping myself in a towel.

There's one thing that's clear. I need to get a handle on my desires before they consume me entirely and I do something I regret.

9

GASTON

I sit at my desk, fingers dancing across the keyboard as I bring up the security feeds throughout the penthouse. My eyes linger on the bathroom camera, where Blake stands under the steady stream of the shower.

Her face is tilted into the water, eyes closed. I zoom in, drinking in every inch of her naked form. The sight of her makes my cock stir every damn time, but I ignore it. I've not jerked off this much ever.

Her hands wander across her own body, pinching her nipples until they stand to attention. A soft moan escapes her lips, and her other hand moves over the flat plane of her stomach until her fingers find her clit.

"Oh, God," she breathes, and the camera catches her perfect, breathy voice. Her moans grow louder as she moves her other hand to her pussy and delves inside.

My cock is hard. Too hard. Pulling it from my pants, I

join her, stroking myself while watching her. There's nothing more I want than to stride into that bathroom, pin her against the cool tile wall and fuck her senseless.

It would be heavenly to feel her tight cunt spasming around my dick as I wring every ounce of pleasure from her body.

The problem is she's stubborn, and so am I. Until she begs for me, I won't give her it. Her surrender and submission will be so much more satisfying when she gives it to me freely.

You don't get to my position in life without having control over your wants and desires, but Blake is seriously testing them more than anyone ever has.

And I know that she's tempted by the darkness. She was tempted to give in and submit to her deepest, depraved desires. But her stubbornness is the only barrier at the moment.

For now, I'll watch her come and come right along with her. My cock is leaking as I hold out, sensing she's getting close as she begins to shudder and moan louder, arching her back. "Gaston," she groans, and my cock jerks, my release coming so fast and hard I can't stop it. Cum coats my desk, making a mess.

I'm sure she's about to come when a frustrated growl tears from her lips. "No," she breathes, shaking her head and stopping.

My brow furrows and I stare intently at the screen, watching as she tilts her head back under the stream of water, eyes squeezed shut. I can see the rapid rise and fall of her chest as she pants, her body wound tight. What is she doing? She was right on the edge of orgasm.

Why did she stop?

And then it hits me. She's denying herself release because she's fantasizing about me. Even in the privacy of her own mind, she doesn't want to give me that power. She doesn't want to come with my name on her lips or have her pleasure be about me in any way. Her stubbornness knows no bounds.

I lean back in my chair, a satisfied smile spreading across my face. If she's fantasizing about me already, that's the first step.

She turns the water off and steps out of the shower, wrapping a towel around herself. I switch cameras, following her as she enters the bedroom and starts rifling through the lingerie I've provided for her. She selects a lacy black bra and panty set, dropping the towel without an ounce of modesty.

Soon I'll have her wrapped around my cock, screaming my name. I want to run my hands over every curve and discover all her secret places.

For now, I close the feeds and tuck my still semi-hard dick into my pants before cleaning up the mess I made. There's a more important task at hand. Estrada. It's clear he won't back down over my land, which he wants for his drug smuggling operations.

I straighten my tie and smooth my hair back. And then I get to work hacking into Estrada's personal servers to learn his plans. I built my tech company from nothing so hacking a criminal like Estrada will be a piece of cake.

My fingers fly over the keyboard, probing into Estrada's personal servers. This man clearly has no idea how to properly secure his data. It's almost too easy for someone like me to slice through his meager defenses and access everything he wishes to keep private.

A few more keystrokes, and I'm in, browsing through Estrada's files and emails. Most of it is innocuous—schedules, memos, mundane business matters. But eventually I stumble upon a encrypted folder marked 'Operation Green Gold.' Now, this looks more promising.

I crack the encryption in minutes. Really, Estrada should invest in better security professionals instead of showy cars and women. Inside the folder are schematics and plans for his smuggling operation in Mexico City, including detailed maps marking transportation routes and storehouses. Jackpot.

I lean back in my leather chair, steepling my fingers together while I ponder this new information. Estrada wants to use my land to move his drugs from his production facilities to distribution hubs across the country. Clever in its simplicity but unacceptable. I refuse to allow my assets to enable this man's criminal enterprise.

My land won't become a highway for poison, corruption, and moral decay. Even if I myself have a questionable moral compass. Estrada wants my land but how would that make my corporation look if I sell land to criminals? QuantumTech Solutions obeys the letter of the law, even if at times I choose to operate in the gray areas, there are lines I won't cross.

I close the files, wiping away all traces of my digital footprint as I withdraw from Estrada's system. The man needs to drastically overhaul his security protocols if he wishes to keep his operation hidden.

But that's not my concern. I know what I need to do. Estrada cannot be allowed to use my land as part of his smuggling route. I'll be firm in refusing any offer he may put forward.

My mind drifts to the security feed and I bring it up, drawn like a magnet to the image of Blake lying on our bed. Even in casual clothes, she ignites a hunger in me I've never known before her. Watching her, I notice the way her thighs squeeze together, and she bites her lip. The girl is desperate for release but denies it to herself.

If she carries on like that, it'll only make it easier to seduce her. To lure her to the dark side. I cannot wait to make her wholly and irrevocably mine. To strip away her layers of resistance until only raw need remains.

There's a battle raging within my Blake between her defiant spirit and her dark, hidden cravings. Soon, her mind will surrender to what her body already knows—she was made to serve me.

10

BLAKE

*E*ach day stuck in this apartment feels like hell. I pace the floors like a caged animal, my mind racing with no outlet. Gaston keeps me trapped here with my spiraling thoughts as my only company. I need to get out and do something.

I make my way to Gaston's home office, knowing he's gone for the day. Maybe I can find something useful in here, anything to occupy my mind. I jiggle the handle and find it's locked, of course. I search the apartment for a key. After a while I find a set in a kitchen drawer.

Returning to the door, I try the keys until I find the right one. The room is meticulously organized, not a paper out of place. I make my way to the sleek desktop computer on the desk. It whirs to life with a click of the mouse.

He obviously forgot to log out the last time he was on. I search through his files and emails first, looking for anything incriminating. If he has any shady dealings, I could get him arrested or something and then flee back to the states. However, I find nothing beyond monotonous business communications.

My eyes catch on a folder labeled "Security Feeds." I open it to find live camera feeds from all over the apartment. The foyer, kitchen, living room, bedroom, and even the bathroom. My hands tremble with anger. He could've been watching me this whole time.

And then I see a file called "Saved Footage." There are video feed recordings of me. In the shower, cooking, sleeping.

Motherfucker.

This bastard is practically stalking me when I'm living under the same roof as him. Nothing screams psychopath more than that. Returning to the feeds, I select the one labeled "Office." And there I am, sitting at his desk.

What if he can view these at work?

My stomach churns because even if he doesn't see me breaking into his office if he checks the recorded footage, he'll know. Leaning back in his chair, I glare up at the camera. A part of me wants to smash his computer to pieces as well as every camera in here. It's very tempting, but God knows what he'd do to me if I did. And something tells me the sadistic part of Gaston would enjoy seeing me lose control of my rage.

The bedroom and adjoining bathroom were the one place I thought I had total privacy. Turns out privacy doesn't exists in this apartment.

Returning to his "Saved Footage" folder I delete every

video in there, since it's a violation of my privacy. And then I click out and turn off the monitor, my mind racing with how I'm going to make him pay for this.

Glancing at the clock on the wall, I realize he'll be home in an hour and a half, and I haven't started dinner. My cooking skills have improved, but I'm no Gordon Ramsay. So I leave the office the way I found it, shut the door, and lock it before entering the kitchen, where I stow the keys in the drawer.

And then I grab one of the cookbooks and decide to make Chicken Alfredo. It looks simple enough. Chopping the vegetables, I start to have violent thoughts of stabbing the bastard who bought me and has been watching me with the knife. He could be watching me right now.

Slowly, I add the ingredients together, stirring the creamy sauce and sprinkling in spices. The aroma fills the kitchen, rich and enticing. Maybe I'm not so hopeless at this cooking thing after all.

While I sprinkle shredded cheese over the finished dish, the door to his apartment opens. Gaston strides into the kitchen, briefcase in hand.

I force a smile. "Welcome home. I made Chicken Alfredo."

He raises an eyebrow, looking genuinely impressed. "It smells delicious, beautiful." He moves behind me and grips my waist with his large hands, making me stiffen. "You're getting good at cooking for us." His lips tease against the back of my neck, and instantly, I'm disarmed.

Part of me wants to blow up at him and reveal I've

found the footage, but another part knows I've got to bide my time.

We carry our plates to the dining room table and sit across from each other. I take a bite of the pasta, relieved to find it's actually really good. We eat in silence for a few minutes.

"This is impressive, Blake. Thank you."

"I'm full of surprises," I reply lightly.

He smirks. "It would seem like it." There's an odd glint in his eyes, and I wonder if he knows that I've been in his office.

Throughout dinner, he hardly speaks, which isn't like him. And then, when he's finished, he stands abruptly. "I've got work to do in my office. I'll see you later."

I nod and clear the table while he disappears down the hall. How long will it take for him to realize his saved footage of me has been deleted? Once I hear the click of his office door, I release a shaky breath I didn't know I was holding.

That's the moment I make a decision. He wants me to beg him to fuck me, but I won't. Instead, I intend to tease him into being the one to beg me. Put on a live show for him. So, I head toward the bedroom and close the door behind me. My heart is racing at a million miles an hour. I strip out of my clothes, standing naked in front of the mirror.

Taking a deep breath, I climb onto the bed and position myself so Gaston will have a perfect view of my pussy.

Hopefully, this will make his resolve snap and force him to come to me.

I slide my hand slowly down to my clit and circle it, groaning because I'm so sensitive. Ever since Gaston bought me, I haven't allowed myself to come because every time I touch myself, his face appears in my mind. But now I'm like a fucking atom bomb ready to explode.

"Gaston," I moan his name, in part to fit in with my act, but it feels right to call his name.

I push three fingers inside myself and imagine it's his cock, shutting my eyes and picturing his beautiful face in my mind's eyes. Before I know it, I'm lost to the sensations, writhing on the bed.

Once I'm on the brink, I don't stop. I can't. My pussy clenches around my fingers, and then I come apart.

"Fuck, Gaston!" I cry out his name again the moment my climax hits me, and a flood of liquid squirts from my pussy. The release is intense, almost painful. Finally, I've come apart thinking of him, and I hate how good it feels to submit to him, even though it's only in my mind.

Once the afterwaves subside, I sit up and glance at the camera, hoping he'll come for me now. Until I hear the creak of the bedroom door and freeze. Before I even see him, I know he's there.

11

GASTON

*B*lake's delicate fingers caress her body as she lies on our bed, positioned at the perfect angle for my cameras. Her luscious lips part, releasing a breathy moan. She thinks she's so clever, trying to manipulate me with her seductive display. But I see right through her.

She found the cameras. I already knew that after watching her break into my office this afternoon. The naughty girl deleted all my saved footage of her, but I guess I'm partially to blame for not logging out of my computer. And now, she thinks she can lure me in like a fish on a hook, but the thing is, I'm one step ahead.

My cock is hard while I watch her little show. God damn, her body is the most exquisite piece of art I've ever seen.

Blake's hips undulate sensually while she pleasures herself, her back arching in ecstasy. The sight of her writhing in pleasure is enough to make my blood boil. If she thinks this is going to make me fuck her, she's mistaken. All she is doing is priming herself, ready to beg me for my dick.

Tapping my fingers on the armrest of my office chair, I study her face. It's flushed with arousal. Time to turn this little game of hers against her.

Slowly, I rise from my chair and make my way toward the bedroom, keeping my footsteps silent. I pause in the doorway, drinking in the sight of Blake's tight little cunt making a mess of our comforter.

Damn it.

I missed the main event. My beautiful girl just came for me. She slumps backward and shuts her eyes, enjoying the blissful afterglow of her climax.

"Enjoying yourself, are we?" I purr.

Blake freezes, her eyes snapping open. The look of fear and defiance in her gaze only serves to heighten my arousal.

"Gaston," she breathes, her voice trembling.

I step closer to the bed and stop a foot away, looming over her naked body. "You thought you could outsmart me, didn't you?"

Blake scrambles backward on the bed, trying to use the comforter to cover her beautiful body. Her eyes dart around the room as if searching for an escape, but she knows it's futile. I've got her right where I want her.

"I heard you call my name. Does that mean you're finally ready to beg me?" I grab the thick bulge in my pants, forcing her gaze to follow the movement.

Her throat bobs as she swallows, and some of that defiance in her stunning blue eyes ebbs away. "I won't beg you, Gaston."

I tsk softly, shaking my head in mock disappointment. "When will you learn that resistance is pointless?" I take a step closer, my predatory gaze pinning her in place. "I hold all the cards here."

There's hunger in her eyes when she stares at me, her body tense with barely restrained desire. She's trying so hard to resist and cling to that rapidly crumbling facade of defiance. Unzipping my pants, I free my cock from the restrictive fabric.

Blake's eyes flash, and she licks her lips at the sight, making me leak on my hand when I wrap it firmly around my cock. Lazily, I stroke myself without breaking our eye contact. A low guttural groan of pleasure comes from my chest, and I watch her thighs clench at the sound.

"You want my cock, don't you?" I ask. "I know how wet you are and how badly you're aching to be filled and fucked. Just beg me, Blake, and I'll give you everything you desire."

A delightful shiver runs through her body, and she digs her nails into the bedsheets as if physically anchoring herself in place. But the hunger in her eyes only grows more intense.

"I know you're imagining all the things I could do to you." I move so that my knees are pressed against the edge of the bed. "How I could force you onto your back and devour that sweet pussy of yours. The way I could overpower you and slam every inch of my cock into you, and you couldn't do a thing about it."

A breathy moan escapes her lips while I continue stroking myself.

"Just think of how much fun we can have, baby girl." My gaze dips to her nipples, which are hard peaks. "Beg for it, Blake," I demand, my commanding tone making her whimper. "Beg me to fuck you. And I promise you won't regret it. I'll take you to heights you never knew existed."

"Gaston," she says my name, and it sounds so fucking hot.

"Yes, baby girl?" I wait, wondering whether she's going to continue to deny herself what she wants. She's close to cracking. I know that. Our gazes lock, and at that moment, I see her defenses come crashing down. Her stubborn resistance is washed away by a tidal wave of desire. She needs this, needs me, just as badly as I need her.

"Gaston, please," she finally gasps, her voice thick with lust. "I need you so badly. Please, do whatever you want with me. Just fuck me, I'm begging you."

A grin crosses my lips, and I lean down to kiss her neck. "Good girl," I growl into her ear. I pull back, my gaze drinking at the sight of Blake's flushed, trembling skin. "You've kept me waiting, though," I murmur. "Now it's your turn to wait."

I trail my fingers teasingly along the soft skin of her inner thigh, relishing the way she squirms. "Did you really think you could manipulate me so easily with your little show?" I chuckle darkly. "You've got much to learn about the depth of my control."

Gripping her chin, I force her to meet my gaze. "Even so, you've tested me more than most. My cock is throbbing just thinking about fucking your cunt and imagining how tightly you'll squeeze around me." I move my lips to her neck and bite. "I can't stop thinking about how you'll whimper and moan when I push deep inside you."

Blake is gone now, moaning and panting like the dirty girl she is deep down.

"You want me to take you hard, don't you? Want me to make you scream my name until your throat is raw?"

She sinks her teeth into her bottom lip and nods eagerly. "Yes, please, sir."

"I'm afraid you'll have to be patient." I release my hold on her, stepping back to admire her body. "I'm going to play with you, baby girl. I'm going to tease and torment you until you're begging for release."

Moving with slowness, I strip off my clothes and toss them aside.

Blake's moan when she finally sees me naked is ego-boosting, to say the least. Her eyes drink me in, and I like her looking at me like that.

Reaching out, I trail my fingertips along the curve of her hip, relishing the way she shudders at the light touch. "I'm going to enjoy watching you squirm. Watching you unravel as I push you to the edge, repeatedly only to deny your release."

I press a feather-light kiss to the sensitive skin of her

neck, smiling against her as she arches into me. "And when I finally decide to grant you your release," I whisper, "it's going to be earth-shattering."

Stepping back, I admire the sight of her, flushed and panting, her eyes dark with desire. "On the floor," I demand.

Her brow furrows slightly, but she does as she's told, kneeling on the floor. I move to the other side of the room, holding her gaze. "Now be a good girl and crawl to me," I purr.

Her jaw falls open. "What?"

Has my angel underestimated how much I like to dominate? It would seem so from the shocked expression on her stunning face. "I said, be a good girl and crawl to me."

Indecision enters those azure blue eyes. A battle commences between her stubborn pride and the unmistakable desire she harbors within. We both know which will win in the end.

"I won't—" she starts, her eyes flashing with defiance.

I raise a hand, silencing her with a sharp look. "It wasn't a question. Now do as I say, or there will be consequences."

Her gaze lands on my hard cock, and I sense desire beginning to win the war. "Gaston, I—" she tries again.

"Blake." I cut her off, my tone brooking no argument. "I won't ask you again."

Slowly, reluctantly, she begins to move. Initially, her movements are stiff. However, less than halfway across, I can see her eyes flooding with desire as she eases into her submissive position.

A flood of pride hits me, seeing the girl who was so defiant now crawling to me like the good girl she is deep down. I memorize this moment. The way her hips sway as she crawls, the delicate curve of her spine and the wild tangle of her beautiful blonde hair.

When she reaches me, I extend a hand, tangling my fingers in those silken strands and tugging sharply. Blake gasps, her eyes widening, and I yank her head back, exposing the long, elegant column of her throat.

"Good girl," I murmur, crouching down and brushing my lips across the sensitive skin just beneath her jaw.

A strangled whimper escapes her lips, and she shivers at the light touch.

"Do you want to know what I'm going to do with you?" I demand, pushing back to meet her gaze.

"Yes, sir."

Fuck.

Blake has rarely addressed me in that way despite me demanding she call me sir from the start. And it sounds so fucking right when she's naked and before me like this.

"I'm going to make you scream, make you cry, make you come so hard you'll forget your own name. When I'm done with you, you'll be nothing but a quivering, whimpering mess at my feet."

"Oh God," she gasps, pleading me with her eyes. "Please."

I smirk. "Are you begging, baby girl?"

Blake's eyes are dark with desire as she stares up at me, her lips parted. "Yes, Gaston," she breathes. "I'm begging you. Please, I need you so badly."

I tighten my grip on her hair, eliciting a sharp gasp from her. "That's what I want to hear." Slowly, I release my hold and trail my fingers down the side of her face. "Tell me, baby girl, what is it you want me to do to you?"

She leans into my touch, her eyelids fluttering. "I want you to fuck me," she murmurs. "I want you to take me hard and fast until I can't think straight." Her gaze darts down to my cock, which is standing to attention. "I want you to fill me up and make me scream."

A low, guttural groan rumbles in my chest. "That can be arranged." Grabbing her by the shoulders, I haul her to her feet and toss her back onto the bed. She lands with a soft thud, her hair splaying out around her like a golden halo.

"Spread your legs for me," I command, watching her.

Blake obeys without hesitation, her eyes locked on mine. I take a moment to admire the view of her flushed, trembling body open and ready for me.

I get onto the bed and lower my head between her thighs. Blake's breath hitches as I blow air against her clit. "Gaston, please," she whimpers, her hips shifting restlessly.

I chuckle darkly. "Patience, baby girl. I intend to savor every moment."

Flattening my tongue, I take a long, languid lick along

her slick folds, savoring her sweet taste. Blake cries out, her back arching.

"You like that, don't you?" I murmur against her skin. "Tell me how much you want my mouth on you."

"God, Gaston, I want it so badly," she gasps, her fingers tangling in my hair. "Please, don't tease me. I need you."

Humming in approval, I lap at her clit, drawing tight circles around the sensitive bundle of nerves. Blake's grip on my hair tightens while she writhes beneath me, her thighs trembling.

"You're so fucking wet for me," I growl, nipping lightly at her inner thigh. "I could do this all day and never get enough of your sweet pussy."

"Then don't stop," she pleads. "Make me come. I need it so badly."

I chuckle, the vibration sending a shiver through her. "Not so fast. You won't be coming until my cock is deep inside of you. And I'm afraid I'm going to make you wait quite a while."

Blake's eyes darken with frustration as she glares at me. "That's not fair. You can't just tease me like this."

I chuckle, trailing my fingers up the insides of her thighs. "I can. And I will. The anticipation is half the fun, don't you think?"

"No, I don't think!" she snaps, trying to clench her legs shut, but I hold them firmly in place. "This is pure torture."

"Exactly what you've been putting me through with your stubbornness." I push up so that I'm looming over her and brush my lips against hers in a fleeting kiss before returning between her thighs.

"Stubbornness?" she rasps, looking frustrated. "Are you serious?"

I continue licking and sucking on Blake's sensitive flesh, reveling in her gasps and moans of pleasure. She's squirming beneath me, torn between the desire for release and the frustration of my teasing.

"Gaston, please!" she cries out, her voice strained. "I can't take anymore, I need you inside me!"

I pull back slightly, gazing up at her flushed, desperate expression. "Not yet, baby girl. I'm going to make you beg for it."

Blake lets out a frustrated growl, her hands fisting in the bedsheets. "I hate you for this."

I chuckle darkly. "Don't lie, baby girl. You don't hate me. And you love what I'm doing to you." Dipping my head, I suck her clit into my mouth, flicking my tongue against the sensitive bundle of nerves.

Blake's back arches off the bed, and a strangled cry tears from her throat. "Fuck!" She's trembling now, her thighs clamping around my head.

I hum in satisfaction, the vibrations sending shockwaves of pleasure through her. Just as I feel her tensing, signaling her impending orgasm, I pull away completely.

Blake's eyes fly open, her gaze wild and desperate. "No, no, no! Don't stop, please!"

I shake my head, tsking softly. "Ah ah ah, not yet. You don't get to come until I say so."

Tears of frustration well in her eyes as she glares at me. "You're a sadistic bastard, you know that?"

"Maybe." I shrug, trailing my fingers along the insides of her thighs. "But you tormented me for a week by being headstrong." Leaning in, I brush my lips against hers in a searing kiss, swallowing her muffled whimpers.

When I pull back, her lips are swollen, and her eyes are hazy with desire. "Please," she whispers, her voice barely above a breath. "I need you so badly. I'll do anything."

I quirk a brow, intrigued. "Anything, hmm?" Trailing my fingers up her thigh, I pause at the juncture between her legs. "Tell me what you're willing to do."

Blake's breath hitches. "I-I'll be good," she stammers. "I'll do whatever you say, just please, please fuck me."

Gripping her hips, I yank her to the edge of the bed. "Then get on your hands and knees."

Blake's eyes widen, but she quickly complies, turning over and assuming the position I've demanded. I take a moment to admire the view of her ass in the air, her glistening pussy on display.

I run my hands along the curve of her back. "Now stay just like that for me." Positioning myself behind her, I grip her hips and slowly guide the tip of my cock through her slick pussy. Her strangled whimper is music to my ears, but then she fucking begs me again.

"Please," she begs, her voice ragged. "I want you to fill me with your thick cock. I want you to claim me, to make me yours. I want you to fuck me until I can't remember my own name."

Fuck.

"That can be arranged." I spank her perfect red ass. "But first, I think it's time we discuss your punishment."

I need to satisfy our hunger, but the need to punish her for making me so damn horny this past week and holding out on me is too intense. Not to mention, she tried to fucking manipulate me with my own cameras that can't go unpunished.

She will be filled with my cock at some point, but I'll decide when. And it won't be tonight.

12

BLAKE

"*P*unishment for what?" I ask, trying to keep my voice steady.

Gaston rubs the head of his cock through my folds again, bumping my clit in the process. I'm so desperate and mindless right now.

He tightens his grip on my hips painfully. "For trying to use my cameras against me. For trying to manipulate me."

"I wasn't trying to manipulate you," I lie, knowing it's futile. "I was just..." My voice trails off because I don't know how to explain what I am doing. He's right. I was trying to manipulate him.

Gaston grabs the back of my neck, forcing me to arch my back. "Don't lie to me or you're punishment will be worse."

Grinding my teeth, I nod. "Fine. I was trying to manipulate you."

He spanks my ass, making me gasp. "Well done for

telling the truth." Suddenly, I feel the tip of his cock pressing at my entrance. "You want it so badly, don't you, Blake?"

This man is a fucking sadist.

"Yes," I breathe, trying to push back against him.

The tip slips in just about, and Gaston groans. "Fuck, you feel so good even with just the tip of my cock in your tight pussy." His voice is raspy and a little shaky. "But you don't get what you want tonight."

"Gaston, please," I beg, trying to push back, but he's too strong.

He pulls away, leaving me so unsatisfied I squeal in frustration.

"What the fuck?"

"Watch your language, baby girl." He spanks my ass again before forcing me onto my back. "Now, don't move while I get ready to punish you."

I watch as he disappears into the walk-in closet, wanting nothing more than to run into the bathroom and lock myself inside. Unfortunately, I don't trust my legs to be able to support me if I stand because they feel like jelly.

When he returns, he's got some sex toys in his hands, making me tense. He's going to torment me to fucking tears at this rate.

"What are you going to do with those?" I ask, despite already knowing the answer.

Gaston chuckles and stops before me. "No questions." He trails a sleek black object along my spine, making me shiver at the contact. "I'm going to have so much fun with you, beautiful."

Grinding my teeth, I try to school my reactions. However, it's no use the moment he presses the slick black toy against my pussy, I gasp. I'm so sensitive.

"Just relax and let me play with you."

Let him play with me? He's been playing with me since the moment he bought me, and despite my attempt to remain strong and defiant, somehow, he's unraveled me already. It's embarrassing.

Gaston pushes the toy inside of me, and I arch my back, groaning as it feels so good to have that ache quenched. Even if I was hoping for something thicker and longer inside me. I rock back against it, fucking myself on the toy.

"That's it, baby girl," Gaston purrs, his voice dripping with approval. "You're doing so well."

My stomach flutters, hearing his validation. Why the hell do I even want it? Slowly, I feel my release building again. A warmth pooling low while he continues to fuck me with it. When I think I'm close, Gaston removes it.

A half whimper and half growl tears from my lips. "Patience," he breathes, gazing into my eyes with those cool gray ones of his.

He sets the rubber dildo aside and picks up a vibrator. My thigh shakes in anticipation, knowing he could truly torture me with that.

"No, please—" I start, but Gaston silences me with a firm look.

"This is part of your punishment, remember? Now be a good girl and take your punishment quietly."

I swallow hard, my mouth suddenly dry. "Gaston, I—"

He doesn't let me finish, turning it on and pressing it against my clit. My entire body jerks violently because I've never been so sensitive before. A deep moan escapes me.

Gaston leans in, his breath ghosting my lips. "That's it, bonita. Let me hear you moan."

The pleasure is too much to bear. I try to squirm away, but Gaston holds me in place with his powerful body.

"Stay still," he demands.

I clench the sheets beneath me, trying to find something to ground me. All the while, Gaston reads me like a book, using the vibrator to send me toward the edge, only to back off when I'm teetering on the precipice.

A cry of frustration tears from my lips when he removes the vibrations entirely. "Please," I beg, tears of desperation trickling down my cheeks. "I'm so fucking desperate, Gaston. Please."

"Not yet, beautiful. You don't get to come until I allow it." And then he moves his lips to mine and kisses me, his tongue sliding into my mouth and tangling with my own. Fuck. It's the best kiss I've ever had. Instead of clutching the sheets beneath me, I claw my fingers in his hair, desperate for more from him. I need everything he can give me.

He growls into my mouth and pulls back, nipping my bottom lip. "Fuck, you really are needy for me, aren't you, beautiful?" The look in his eyes suggests he's struggling to maintain control right now. He wants to fuck me, but perhaps he's more stubborn than me, hellbent on proving a point.

I try to pull his lips back to mine, but he shakes his head and forces my arms down. "Who is in control?"

God damn it.

"You are, sir," I reply, my voice cracking slightly.

"That's right," he breathes, eyes flashing with a dangerous spark. "Now be a good girl and lie still for me." He moves the vibrator over my nipples, slowly trailing it lower and lower until it's hovering over my clit.

Gaston watches me, a dark look in his eyes. "Do you want it?"

I nod in response, hardly able to speak right now.

He pushes it against my clit and then suddenly turns the setting right up to maximum. "Now come for me. I want to hear you come apart. I want the whole of Mexico City to hear what I do to you."

My back arches, and I scream out in pleasure. Before I have time to process what's happening, my orgasm slams into me with the weight of a freight train. And I squirt everywhere, making a mess of the bed. I'm shuddering and shaking so violently while my vision blurs at the intensity.

I collapse against the sheets, panting and trembling, coming down from the most intense orgasm of my life. Every nerve in my body still thrums with pleasure, and I feel almost delirious.

Gaston strokes my hair, murmuring praise. "Such a good girl. You took your punishment so well." And then he kisses me softly, lazily. His tongue explores my mouth as I moan into it. A mere kiss is all it takes to light me back on fire as I lace my fingers in his hair.

When we break apart, I look into those gorgeous gray eyes. "Please."

He arches a brow. "Please, what?"

"I need you to fuck me."

He chuckles and pulls back, shaking his head. "No chance. You don't get my cock yet, beautiful. Not after holding out on me and trying to manipulate me." He grabs a hand full of my hair and yanks me forward so I'm kneeling in front of him. "Suck it."

I nod and lean forward, opening my mouth for his thick cock. Gaston hisses as I take him in, my tongue swirling around the head. He grips the back of my head, holding me in place while I start to bob up and down his length.

"Fuck, that's it," he groans, rolling his hips. "You're such a good little cocksucker, aren't you?"

I moan around him, the vibrations making him shudder. Hollowing my cheeks, I suck him hard and take him deeper into my throat. My eyes water, but I refuse to gag.

Gaston grabs the back of my neck and takes control, thrusting into my throat so hard I have no choice but to gag. Tears prickle my eyes while he takes what he wants from me.

He groans, his hips snapping forward. "Fuck, you feel so good, baby girl. Taking my cock in that throat like a good little slut."

His grip tightens, and I can tell he's close. He doesn't slow. "I want you to swallow every damn drop, understood?" His gray eyes gleam with an intensity that makes me shudder.

I can't speak, but I give him a small nod.

Gaston lets out a guttural groan when his climax hits him, and he spills down my throat, his grip on the back of my neck tightening. I swallow every drop, just as he demanded.

When he's finally spent, he pulls my mouth off his softening cock, a satisfied smirk on his face. "Good girl. I think you're finally learning your place, aren't you?"

I lick my swollen lips, my eyes downcast. Speaking right now isn't a good idea. I'll either spit venom at him or beg him for more. Neither option seems wise at the moment.

Gaston tsks at my lack of response, gripping my chin and forcing me to meet his intense gaze. "I asked you a question, Blake. I expect an answer."

"Yes," I finally whisper.

His lips curve into a satisfied smile. "Yes, what?"

"Yes, sir."

"Good girl." Gaston presses a kiss to my forehead before releasing me from his grip. "Go get yourself cleaned up."

My body revolts at the idea. This can't be over? Surely he's going to fuck me now. And then I realize that's his ultimate punishment. He's going to deny me what, deep down, under all the shame and disgust, I really want. This man taking me and showing me who truly owns me in the most primal way.

I take a deep, shaky breath and force myself to stand on wobbly legs. Gaston watches me intently, his gaze burning into me while I make my way to the bathroom.

Once inside, I turn on the faucet and splash cold water on my face, trying to clear the fog in my mind. My body is still humming with need, desperate for Gaston's touch. But I know better than to beg. He'll only deny me further.

I quickly clean myself up, wincing at how sensitive I still am. Gaston really worked me over.

Why do I want him so badly?

It's so fucked up.

While I gaze at myself in the mirror, determination wells up within to fight this. To fight the dark part of me that longs for Gaston. Despite the determination, a small voice in the back of my head tells me it's only a matter of time until I'm on my knees before him again, begging for his exquisite torture.

13

GASTON

The Mexico City skyline outside my windows draws my attention while I sit on the sofa in the living room, waiting for my angel to wake.

All I can think about since last night is how fucking far she pushed me. Further than any woman ever has. God damn. I was so close to fucking her, but that would make her think she was in control. Something I can't allow to happen.

I need to be careful with Blake. She's like a wild mare that needs to be broken in slowly. My cock has been hard since the moment I woke beside her. And the memory of her moans and pleas while I edged her over and over only makes me harder. I release a low groan and adjust myself.

Blake will be the death of me.

Tonight I've got an event to attend and Pablo will be there. I don't show up to events without a date, and there's this part of me that wants Blake by my side. However, I don't know that she's ready. Her stubbornness knows no bounds.And I can't have her cause a scene or worse, try to escape.

Originally, I'd set a date with Jasmine, who's always eager to be seen on my arm at events like this. She is a socialite who drives me nuts, but she looks pretty enough. Luciana asked if I had a date only last night, and picking to go with her would send Estrada a message not to mess with me. Her family owns half the city.

Irritation coils through me as there's only one woman I want by my side tonight. And that's the little vixen asleep in my bed. I'd love to parade Blake around in a gorgeous fucking dress, showing everyone she belongs to me.

Anticipation thrums through me. I stand and walk toward the bedroom, pushing open the door carefully and step inside, my eyes immediately drawn to Blake sleeping peacefully beneath the comforter. The gentle rise and fall of her bare chest where the comforter has slipped down is mesmerizing.

It's hard not to admire her like this. Her lips are slightly parted, looking so fucking kissable. Grinding my teeth together, I push that thought from my mind since kissing isn't something I ordinarily indulge in, but with Blake, it feels like it's a necessity. As though I can't get enough of her unless my mouth is against hers, drinking her in.

There's something odd about my beauty. In sleep, she's so peaceful. However, whenever she's awake, she's restless and erratic. I've noticed the way she can't focus on one task for too long and flits about from one thing to the next. Initially, I assumed it was anxiety in her new surroundings, but I can't help but wonder if there's something more to it.

Lowering myself to the edge of the bed, I reach out and tuck a stray lock of golden hair behind her ear, allowing my fingers to ghost the soft skin of her cheek. Blake stirs slightly, a soft sigh escaping her lips and her brow furrowing a little. She's dreaming. I wonder what her dreams are filled with.

Does she dream of me? And why do I ever care?

There's one thing for sure, this girl is dangerous.

"Blake," I say her name softly.

Her eyes flutter open. Those gorgeous bright blue eyes. And when she sees me, there's a flash of deep desire in them that makes my heart skip a beat. She yawns and stretches her arms above her head, forgetting she's stark naked. The movement draws my gaze to her beautiful breasts. This woman is under my skin like no other.

She blushes and pulls the comforter up to hide herself.

I grab her wrist. "Don't hide from me, beautiful."

Releasing the comforter, she clears her throat. "What time is it?"

"Eleven," I murmur, reaching out and dragging my finger along the swell of her breasts. "Did you sleep well?"

Her eyes dilate further. "I did, actually. I feel rested." There's a hint of surprise in her voice.

Finally getting her release after denying herself it since

she arrived here no doubt helped her sleep. She was exhausted after she washed and fell fast asleep before I returned to the bedroom.

"Good. I have something I want to discuss with you."

Her brow furrows. "What is it?"

"There's an event tonight that I'm expected to attend." I pause, gauging her reaction. "I'd like you to be by my side."

There's a flicker of excitement in her eyes, no doubt because she's been begging me to let her out of this apartment since she arrived. "Really? I'd get out of this apartment?"

"Yes, however, I'm not sure I can trust you yet."

She bites her lip. "You can. I'll be on my best behavior."

"There'll be important people there. If you make a scene, it'll reflect badly on me."

"I promise, Gaston." She leans toward me and places a hand on my thigh, way too close to my cock, which is still solid. "I'll be good. All I want is to get some air and come with you."

I can't help but chuckle. "Alright, beautiful. But I mean it, no causing a scene and no trying to run off." I cup her chin, tilting her face upward. "Understood?"

"Understood, sir," she breathes, her eyes shining with determination. "I'll be on my best behavior."

If Blake is trying to play me, I don't detect it in her eyes. "Very well. We leave at seven o'clock tonight. Ensure you're ready and pick a ball gown out of the dresses in the closet."

Leaning closer, my breath ghosting against her lips. "And Blake?"

"Yes, sir?"

My cock swells every time she calls me that. She's already being so submissive, and I love it.

"Make sure it's not too revealing. Your body is for my perusal only, understood?"

"I understand," she breathes, nostrils flaring as she inches closer to me.

Our lips are so close. And I can't help it. I grab the back of her neck and pull her lips to mine, kissing her passionately.

Blake moans into my mouth the moment my tongue breaks through her defenses. And suddenly, she's clawing at me. Her arms wrap around my neck while I pull her into my lap. A groan escapes me as she rocks her hips, finding friction on my cock.

Within a minute, I can feel her wetness soaking into my pants. I haven't got time for this. There are some matters at the office I need to take care of before tonight. Reluctantly, I break the kiss, looking at my angel, all flushed and breathless. Her eyes are hooded with desire. "Careful, baby girl. You're playing with fire and might get burned."

She licks her lips. "Maybe I want to be."

Chuckling, I force her off my lap. "As much as I'd love to play with you, I've got to get to the office. I'll be back before the event to pick you up." I kiss her once more. "See you later."

I should change my pants after she made a mess of them, but I don't bother. The idea of having Blake's arousal on me for the rest of the day excites me. Instead, I exit the bedroom and head out of my apartment. Tonight is going to be interesting, but if my baby girl is good, maybe I'll finally give her what I know she's gagging for.

14

BLAKE

*S*moothing my hands across the silky material of the emerald green gown I chose from the closet, I wonder how my friends are doing. They're in that horrible, dank basement being subjected to God knows what. And here I am going to fancy parties and living a life of luxury. It makes me feel so guilty.

Hopefully Gaston will be happy with my choice of dress. It's low cut but not too low and hugs my curves before flaring out at the hips into a mermaid style skirt. My hair is swept up into an elegant updo, drawing attention to the diamond necklace Gaston left on the kitchen counter with a note to wear.

I apply a coat of red lipstick before taking in my appearance. Gaston made me promise I'd behave, but if an opportunity arises for me to make an escape, then I will.

This lavish prison may seem glamorous, but I'm still

his captive. The diamond choker around my neck may be worth a fortune, but it's a collar. A sign of his ownership, and I know if I don't get out soon, I'll be completely lost to him. Because it's getting more and more difficult to remember what the dynamic is between us. He's a slaver, and I'm his slave. Simple.

No amount of luxury can make up for my lack of freedom. And my friends need my help. Tonight could be my one chance to get away from him. If I can slip away and find an exit, maybe I can disappear into the busy streets of Mexico City and then find my way from there. The necklace around my neck should be worth something at a pawn shop. At least enough to buy my way home. I have to be patient and wait for the right moment.

The ding of the elevator signals Gaston is home. Taking one final look in the mirror, I turn and head into the living room.

He steps out of the elevator and halts when he sees me, eyes dragging down my body. Fire ignites in them, and he growls softly, marching toward me. "You looking fucking exquisite. Like a goddamn piece of art," he purrs, grabbing my hips and yanking me into his muscular body. "Are you trying to kill me, baby girl?"

I force a smile. "Don't tempt me," I jest, because there have been many times since I met this dominant, enigmatic man that I've wanted to murder him with my bare hands.

He arches a brow. "I'd like to see you try," he breathes,

placing his lips over the pulse at my neck and kissing. "I've got to shower quickly and change. I won't be long."

I watch him walk away and disappear into our bedroom. Sighing, I sit down on the sofa and gaze out of the windows while the sun begins to dip behind the skyline. This place can be surprisingly beautiful despite the lack of nature. After less than twenty minutes, Gaston returns looking sharp and pristine in a form-fitting tux.

"Shall we?" he asks, holding his arm out to me.

I stand and take it, nodding. Gaston calls the elevator, and when it arrives, we step inside together. All the while, I'm pondering how tonight will go. Will I get a chance to make a run for it? Will I escape my gilded cage?

Gaston's hand slides onto the small of my back and he keeps me close. The masculine, heady scent of him overwhelms me in such a confined space. And I hate how it ignites an ache deep within. An ache only he can quench.

A soft ding breaks the tension, and the elevator doors slide open to the building's grand lobby. He steers me toward the exit, and I can't believe how good it feels to step out of the building and away from my prison.

"Good evening, Mr. Marques," the man on the door greets.

"Evening," he says, guiding me toward an idling black limousine parked right out front.

The chauffeur opens the door the moment he sees us.

"After you, baby girl," Gaston murmurs.

I slide inside, smoothing my gown beneath me. Gaston

settles in beside me, sliding a hand onto my thigh. His touch shouldn't have such a violent effect on me, but I visibly shudder, which he notices. The smirk on his face is irritating.

"I can't get over how fucking gorgeous you look," he murmurs, moving his lips to my neck and kissing me. "I can't wait to get you home later."

Pulling back, I glare at him. "Why, so you can punish me?"

He clears his throat. "That all depends on whether you're a good girl for me tonight or not."

Suddenly, the limo hits a pothole, and Gaston's hand slips higher onto the edge of my panties, making me gasp. I'm already on edge. Wound tighter than a coil by his touch.

"So responsive. I love that, baby girl," he murmurs, moving back to lean against the leather of his seat. "Be a good girl for me tonight, and you'll be rewarded."

I'm so torn between arousal and revulsion it's insane. There's one part of me that wants to slap his hand away. Another part that wants him to slip his fingers under my panties and stroke me to climax. While I hate this man, I crave him with as much ferocity.

The limo slows, and Gaston reluctantly withdraws his hand.

"We're here," he says briskly, back to business. "Be a good girl for me." His eyes bore into mine, full of warning.

I nod mutely while the chauffeur opens the door.

Cameras flash wildly as Gaston takes my hand and helps me out of the limo. I paste on a smile, pushing down my turbulent feelings.

Tonight, I'm a trophy on his arm. And as much as I despise it, a part of me relishes playing this role and being the object of his obsession and desire.

He guides me down the red carpet and into the fancy gala. His firm and possessive grip on the small of my back grounds me as I walk by his side. And I find myself leaning into him, drawn to him. It doesn't matter how hard I fight it. I'm under his spell.

A small gasp escapes me when we step into an opulent ballroom. The kind you only see in movies. The vaulted ceilings are dripping in crystals and gold accents. Intricate ice sculptures adorn every table while waiters in crisp white suits weave through the crowds carrying trays of champagne flutes or canapés.

"Quite a party, huh?" Gaston murmurs in my ear. "Only the finest for Mexico's elite."

I resist the urge to roll my eyes. The extravagance seems absurd, especially for a charity event.

As if reading my mind, Gaston continues, "I know what you're thinking. Does any of the money actually make it to the cause?" He pauses, surveying the room. "These things are mostly about appearances. The donations are pennies compared to what gets spent on the soirée itself."

"Well, that makes me feel so good about attending," I replied drily.

Gaston lets out a genuine laugh, the sound rich and warm. I'm momentarily taken aback. Since we've met, I've never heard him laugh like that, but it gives me goosebumps.

"Perhaps I should throw my own charity gala and make it more basic, more about the charity."

"What a novel concept," I shoot back.

The corner of his mouth twitches. "Come on, let's go and get a drink." He leads me toward the bar, keeping his arm around me. "What would you like?"

I chew on my lip. "A margarita?"

He smiles. "Good choice."

"What can I get for you, Mr. Marques?" The bartender asks.

"A Macallan on the rocks and a margarita."

The bartender nods and goes to fetch our drinks. Gaston watches me like a hawk, making me feel self-conscious.

"What are you staring at?" I ask.

"You," he breathes. "Because you're the only thing in this room worth staring at."

My stomach clenches, and I clear my throat. "Don't be ridiculous." He's making me feel things I shouldn't be feeling toward him.

Thankfully, the bartender returns with our drinks, and Gaston turns away from me to pay him. He passes my drink into my hand and our fingers touch, sending shockwaves of electricity through me. I know he feels it, too, as his nostrils flare.

We drink in silence while people chatter around us. Once we've both finished our drinks, Gaston moves closer to me, his lips a few inches from me. "Dance with me, baby girl."

Damn it. This event is making me feel all the wrong things toward this man. As if he's just a charming, gorgeous guy I'm on a date with, which couldn't be father from the truth.

"Okay," I breathe.

He takes my hand and steers me toward the dance floor. The live orchestra are playing a waltz and couples swirl around in their elegant attire.

"I'm not sure I know how to dance the waltz," I say.

His hand rests on the small of my back, and he smirks. "Don't worry, just let me take the lead." And then he moves me into the steps and I do let him lead. Allowing him to guide me across the polished marble.

For a moment, I forget about my escape. Forget that this man purchased me. I lose myself in the music, in the feeling of his strong arms guiding me effortlessly. The rest of the room fades away until it's just the two of us, spinning and gliding.

The song ends, and Gaston dips me back gracefully. When he pulls me upright, our faces are mere centimeters apart. For a split second, I think he might kiss me. Instead, he simply smiles and says, "Not bad, beautiful. You're a natural."

Before I can respond, he takes my hand and leads me off the dance floor. The spell is broken, and I shake off the unsettling emotions swirling within me. This event is another smoke screen. I can't forget who he is.

Gaston may be dangerously charming, but he's a beast beneath a beautiful facade. There's still a chance I can slip away unnoticed at some point tonight. And when that opportunity comes, I've got to be ready.

15

GASTON

*B*lake's hand feels small and delicate in my own as we make our way through the crowded ballroom. Mexico's elite are all drawn here, but everyone pales in comparison to the beauty on my arm. Her nearness is a constant thrill—addictive, in fact.

Suddenly, I feel eyes on us and my attention moves to Pablo standing across the room. His lips curl into a sly smile when our eyes meet. No doubt he wants to speak to me about my land again. I've got nothing to say to him.

"Let's get some air," I suggest, leading her toward the balcony.

She follows, but I don't miss the way her eyes dart around the room. Something tells me she secretly hopes for a chance to slip away and escape. There's no chance I'm letting her go anywhere.

It's a cool night. Below us, the city sprawls out in an expanse of lights. Blake walks away from me toward the railing, gazing out at the skyline. This girl is something else. I approach her and place my hands gently on her hips, making her tense. "I can't get over how utterly breathtaking you are," I murmur into her ear.

She turns to face me so I've got her caged in my arms against the railings, her beautiful lips parting temptingly. Her eyes look even more striking as they reflect the lights around us. "A breathtaking possession that you own," she says flatly.

I grip her chin between my fingers. "You're far more than that, nena."

She jerks her face away. "Stop it."

I tilt my head. "So spirited. I do love that about you. What exactly is it you want me to stop?"

"Acting like a charming human being when deep down you're a monster," she spits.

She's conflicted over her feelings for me. It's natural. And now, she's lashing out. "It may surprise you, but I have the capability to be a human being. In fact, I care about your well-being."

Blake scoffs. "You don't care about anything but yourself. You bought me!"

"I saved you," I correct. "From a far worse fate." It's the truth. Blake wouldn't like to know where her friends might end up. But I know from past auctions that Ileana has held that some of the men who would purchase those girls would subject them to fates far worse than Blake's. A few of the men Ileana invites are gang leaders, and they like to make the girls they buy fuck all of their men at the same time. Often, they end up discarded in a ditch, practically fucked to death.

Blake opens her mouth and then closes it, conflict passing through those beautiful eyes. There's no denying the truth; while I might punish her like last night, with me, she's protected. Not used and tossed aside like a piece of trash.

"Let's enjoy the gala. There's no need to continue this discussion."

When I turn to leave, my stomach dips. Pablo is in the doorway to the balcony, watching us. His eyes flick between me and my girl. I stiffen when I see his eyes dilate with desire. He won't be going anywhere near her, or I'll be committing third-degree murder right here in a public gala.

"Gaston," he purrs, reaching for my hand. His grip is crushing. "So good to see you again."

I force a tight smile. "And you, Pablo."

His attention shifts to Blake, looking her up and down. "And who is this lovely creature?"

Blake inches closer to me.

Good girl.

I place an arm around her back, pulling into my side. "This is Blake," I reply through gritted teeth. "My date."

Pablo continues to leer at her like she's a juicy steak. Clearly he assumes she's just another one of my playthings who I won't care about him objectifying, but Blake is so much more. The thought angers me.

"She's quite lovely, Gaston," Pablo purrs. "I don't

suppose you'd be interested in sharing? I could make it worth your while."

My hands clench into fists. How dare he ask me that?

There's no world in which any man is ever going near Blake. I feel her nestle closer to my side and it makes pride swell in my chest. Such a good girl.

"Careful, Pablo. My girl belongs to me and me alone," I growl, knowing that getting physical with a drug lord at a charity gala would be a bad idea. But my muscles are so tightly bunched. I want to murder him for even suggesting it.

Pablo quirks an eyebrow. "Come on, Gaston. I know that you aren't possessive over your playthings. And I could show her things even you haven't thought of."

Red clouds my vision, and for the first time in my life, I'm very close to losing control. Releasing Blake and pushing her behind me, I get into his face. "Let me make this clear once and only once," I growl. "She's off limits. Completely and utterly mine. She's not a whore to be passed around. And if any fucking idiot even thinks of placing a finger on her, I'll murder him with my bare hands. Got it?"

There's a flash in Pablo's eyes and he smirks, holding up his hands in mock surrender. "My mistake. I meant no offense."

It's at that moment I realize I've shown him my cards. Blake means something to me, and I've just declared that to a very dangerous man who wants my land. Even so, I can't back down now.

"If I ever discover you so much as look at her the wrong way, you'll learn exactly why people fear crossing me."

Pablo stares at me, undeterred. "Duly noted."

I stare him down coldly before turning and guiding Blake away, my hand returning to her hip.

"I'd reconsider my offer if I were you," Pablo calls after me. "Two can play at this game."

I whirl around, hands clenching into fists. "Don't threaten me!" I hiss. "You've got no claim on that land. Don't test me, Pablo."

With that, I steer Blake back into the ballroom. She's glancing at me curiously. Perhaps surprised at my show of rage at him objectifying her. "You're mine," I explain, pulling her to a stop and gazing into her eyes. "Never forget that. And anyone who tries to touch what's mine will die at my hands."

Blake's eyes flood with a mix of fear and arousal. The darkness within me scares her as much as it excites her.

We move through the ballroom and Blake pulls me to a stop to grab a canapé, popping it into her mouth. "Would you like one?"

I nod, and she picks it up, giving me a sensual look as she brings it to my lips. Fuck. This girl needs to become mine tonight in every sense of the word. I'm done waiting to claim her.

Blake's attention shifts behind me and I see Pablo has also returned to the ballroom, his gaze raking over us. "Who is that man?"

"It's none of your concern."

She clenches her jaw, and I know she's going to demand answers. Stubborn, as always.

"His name is Pablo Estrada," I reply. "He's the leader of a cartel that operates primarily outside the city. But lately, he has been trying to gain more territory within Mexico City itself."

Blake frowns. "I thought I read somewhere the cartels stay out of Mexico City."

"They do. Which is why Estrada's actions are concerning. He seeks to disrupt the balance of power."

"Why?" Blake asks. "What does he want?"

I hesitate before answering. "His main aim is to end the reign of the red queen."

Her brow furrows. "What?"

"The woman who was holding you. Ileana Navarro. She's known as the Red Queen and is a psychopath in the truest of forms. The other cartels want her gone and believe gaining control of Mexico City will give them that." I rub a hand across the back of my neck. "Unfortunately, Pablo is greedy. He intends to take it all once they succeed. He believes this city and trade routes around Mexico should belong to him."

Blake shakes her head. "He seems like a snake the way he looked at me."

Anger flares within me at the memory. "He is a snake. And I will carve his eyeballs out and make a keepsake of them if he ever looks at you like that again."

Blake pales slightly. "That's pretty dark."

I grab her and pull her against me. "I'm dark, beautiful. Can you handle that?"

Her throat bobs as she swallows. "I think so."

"Good girl," I purr, kissing her softly. "Now I'm already bored of this event, aren't you?"

She shakes her head. "I'm not ready to return to my prison yet."

Prison.

Is that what she views it as?

"If you give me your loyalty and prove I can trust you, it doesn't have to be a prison, baby girl."

She sinks her teeth into her bottom lip. "But what exactly is the endgame? What happens when you tire of me and go to buy a new girl?"

The mere suggestion drives me insane. And I grab the back of her neck possessively, yanking her toward me. "There won't be a new girl because I want your loyalty, your obedience, and your submission. But not just physically. I want your mind and soul to submit to me." My lips linger within an inch of hers. "I want all of you, Blake. To belong only to me. Forever."

She inhales at my words, eyes widening. I can tell my possessiveness thrills and frightens her. There's a heavy weight behind my words because never before have I felt this way about anyone.

"I'll never let anyone touch you or harm you," I continue. "You're mine. My treasure, to protect and keep. No one will ever take you from me."

Blake swallows hard. "Gaston..." she begins softly.

But I silence her with a soft kiss. "Hush now. No more talk of prisons or anything else. Let us enjoy this night together and get another drink."

Blake nods wordlessly. I offer her my arm, and she takes it, letting me guide her toward the bar. There's an odd shift within me as I know Blake is just as dangerous to me as I am to her. She makes me possessive. A character flaw I've never once possessed for another person.

Not to mention, I was so close to violence when Estrada suggested I share her. But what I told him and her is the truth. No one will ever take her from me, and I'll murder any man who dares try.

16

BLAKE

*T*houghts of escape have moved to the back of my mind by the end of the night. Completely eradicated now while we sit in the back of the limo on the way back to the apartment. I softened toward him tonight, witnessing the way he stood up to Pablo for me. It helped that he treated me like a princess the entire night, too.

It's odd that his hands aren't on me now. I'm so used to him being close to me, but he's sitting with a foot between us, gazing out the window.

"Gaston," I murmur his name, placing a hand on his thigh.

He turns his attention to me, his eyes conflicted. "Yes, nena?" His voice is low and husky, sending a shiver through my spine.

"Thank you for defending me tonight." I let my hand inch slightly higher up his thigh. "When Pablo asked you to share me."

His muscles are tense beneath my hand. "Always, baby girl." Suddenly, his eyes darken as they meet mine. "Why are you touching me?"

I bite my inner cheek. "Why not?"

A whisper of a smile graces his lips. "What do you want, beautiful?"

This feels like a crossroads. We've had a nice evening together. And the truth is, I want him more than anything. After everything, I want to feel him inside me. I want to be taken and claimed by this powerful, gorgeous man, even if he did buy me. "You," I breathe.

He kisses me softly. "You've had me since the moment I met you."

I swallow hard. Tonight has changed things between us. I can feel it in the charged air, in the way his eyes blaze into mine. The limo pulls up outside the apartment building, but neither of us makes an effort to exit.

"Gaston..." I begin, but he cuts me off with another kiss.

His lips are demanding, claiming mine in a way that steals my breath away. I grasp his shoulders while he pulls me onto his lap, my dress riding up my thighs. His hands grip my waist, holding me firmly in place while his tongue explores my mouth.

A deep moan escapes me, which spurs him on. His kisses grow more urgent and passionate. His cock strains against my pussy, and I grind against him, searching for friction.

He growls into my mouth, his fingers digging almost painfully into my hips.

"Gaston," I gasp his name as he breaks away from my lips, trailing them down my neck.

He nips me with his teeth. "I want you too, Blake," he murmurs, his voice a deep rasp that sends heat flooding through me. "But not here. Inside."

Before I can respond he's lifting me and pushing open the door to the limo, carrying me out of it and into the building.

We barely make it into the elevator before his mouth is on mine again, kissing me deeply as his hands roam my body.

I cling to him, consumed by the fire raging inside.

Somehow, we make it to the apartment. Gaston kicks the door shut behind us, pressing me up against it. His eyes blaze with unrestrained desire.

"Please," I whisper, not even sure what I'm asking for. But Gaston understands. With a wicked grin, he spins me around, pressing my front into the cool wood of the door. I gasp at the sudden movement, my pulse thundering in my ears.

Slowly, he drags the zipper of my dress down. I tremble in anticipation, wanting him more than I've ever wanted anyone or anything. The dress pools at my feet, and I step out of it, clad only in my lacy underwear.

Gaston's hands caress my bare back, and I arch into his touch, needing more. He dances his fingers along my spine, leaving goosebumps in their wake. My palms remain flat against the door, bracing myself.

"So beautiful," he murmurs. His hands slide around to cup my breasts, and I bite my lip. My nipples harden instantly under his touch, and he rolls them between his fingers.

"I've wanted this since the day I saw you, baby girl." His words are like velvet against my ear. "To have you trembling and begging to be taken."

I let out a soft gasp when one hand slips lower, fingertips brushing over the lace covering my cunt. He applies enough pressure to have me writhing, desperate for more.

"Tell me what you want, Blake." His voice holds a note of command.

I hesitate only a moment before the words spill out. "I want you. Please."

He rewards me by pushing the lace aside and stroking through my wet pussy. I cry out, pushing back against him shamelessly. His other hand keeps working my aching nipples while he continues his sweet torture between my legs.

"You're so wet for me already," he growls. "Is this how you pictured it, Blake?" His chest presses against my back as he teases his lips against my earlobe. "Fucked senseless by me against the door?"

My mind is too consumed with my desire for him to respond. All I can do is focus on his fingers expertly stroking my clit. The pressure builds steadily inside me and I know I'm close, so close…

Suddenly, he stops.

I whimper in protest but then feel him turning me to face him. His eyes are dark with unrestrained lust. Deftly, he unzips his pants, freeing his thick, hard cock. The sight ignites that deep ache inside.

Gaston grips my chin. "Kneel for me, beautiful."

I drop to my knees, gazing at him for the next instruction.

"Such a good girl. Open that pretty mouth."

Opening my mouth, I move forward and take him into the back of my throat, gagging slightly. I pull back and swirl my tongue over the silky head of his cock, tasting his delicious precum.

He lets out a guttural groan, grabbing a handful of my hair.

"That's it, take it all right into the back of your throat." He guides himself deeper.

I relax my jaw, allowing him to use my mouth as he pleases. As I pleasure him, I feel myself growing impossibly wetter. I need him to fuck me more than I need anything else. Before long, I'm moaning around his cock like a dirty whore.

Gaston's eyes flash when he notices I'm playing with myself. "Did I tell you that you could touch your pussy?"

I stop instantly, eyes wide as I shake my head.

He slips his cock out of my mouth and yanks me to my feet roughly, wrapping his large hand around my throat and squeezing. "I can't hold back any longer, Blake," he gasps, sounding overcome. "Tell me what you need."

"I need you to fuck me."

He growls and kisses me one more time before forcing me roughly face-first against the door. Anticipation makes my thighs quiver as I feel the tip of his cock pressing against my soaking-wet cunt.

"Please, Gaston. Fuck me. I need you inside me."

His hands grip my hips tight. "You want my cock, my little slut?"

"Yes, sir!" I cry out.

With one powerful thrust, he slams inside me. Finally, I see stars stretched and filled so perfectly. It feels better than I imagined. The sting of his size coupled with the pleasure of finally having that ache quenched.

Gaston has lost control as I glance at him over my shoulder. He's beast-like as he ruthlessly pounds into me, forcing me to claw at the door for support. I've never felt anything so intense, so all-consuming.

"You feel incredible," he growls. "So fucking tight." A sharp smack on my ass makes me gasp. "How's that feel, baby girl?"

"S-so full," I gasp, my voice shaky. "So good," I add.

My palms slap against the door as he drives into me from behind, his fingers digging bruises into the soft flesh of my hips. I relish the exquisite mix of pain and pleasure, pushing back wantonly to meet his urgent rhythm.

"You're mine, Blake," he growls, emphasizing his words with a sharp thrust. "No other man will ever have you like this."

I know it's true. Gaston has ruined me for anyone else.

He's awakened something primal within me, an aching need I never knew existed.

"You like that, don't you?" he growls, his voice strained with the effort. "Taking my cock like the greedy little slut you are."

I cry out in response, the pleasure bordering on pain. "Yes, yes! Harder, sir, please!"

He obliges, his thrusts becoming more erratic and savage. The sound of skin slapping against skin fills the air, punctuated by my desperate moans.

"You feel so fucking good." He leans in close, his hot breath fanning across my neck. "I'm gonna make you come so hard."

My peak builds steadily with each plunge of his thick cock inside my soaked pussy. I'm wound tight as a coil, right on the cusp of blissful release. "Then do it," I pant. "Make me come, Gaston."

He chuckles darkly. "As you wish."

One hand snakes around to rub furious circles on my clit while the other grips my hair, yanking my head back. The dual sensations are overwhelming while I teeter on the edge.

"Come for me, Blake," Gaston commands. "Show me how much you love my cock."

His words are my undoing. I shatter. My orgasm crashes over me in waves of blinding pleasure. My walls clench around him, milking his cock.

"Fucking hell, that's tight," he groans, fucking me

through every wave and aftershock, prolonging the most intense orgasm of my life.

When the last tremors subside, I go limp against the door, spent. Gaston is still rock-hard inside me, and I know he hasn't come yet.

Slowly, he withdraws, forcing me around to face him and lifting me so my back is against the door now. I meet his heated gaze, chest heaving.

And then he kisses me, tongue swirling around my mouth as if he's trying to suck out my soul.

Gaston's kiss leaves me breathless, my head spinning. He carries me effortlessly, forcing me to wrap my legs around his waist. The apartment is dark but he doesn't bother to switch the lights on while he carries me to the bedroom.

My back hits the cool sheets of his massive bed, and he hovers above me. Those gray eyes almost gleam in the low light. He's so beautiful. I reach for him, but he catches my wrists, pinning them to the mattress.

"Ah ah, I'm in charge," he rumbles.

Anticipation thrums through me. I ache to feel his hands on me again and his cock filling me up. But I force myself to be patient. To surrender.

Gaston's gaze rakes over my naked body possessively. Slowly, he releases my wrists and trails his fingers down between my breasts, over my stomach. I shiver at the barely-there touch.

"So beautiful," he murmurs. "And all mine."

His hand slips lower, fingers grazing my sensitive flesh. My hips buck instinctively, and he chuckles.

"So eager, aren't you?"

I bite my lip and nod. He rewards me by stroking my clit until I'm squirming. But just as I near the edge, he withdraws his hand, denying me release.

A whimper escapes my lips. Gaston grips my chin firmly. "You'll come when I allow it. Understand?"

"Yes, sir," I whisper. My heart pounds with exhilaration.

Slowly, he leans down until his lips brush my ear. "I'm going to ruin you for any other man, Blake. After tonight, you'll only ever crave my touch for the rest of your life."

A shudder ripples through me. Some distant part of my mind knows I should resist, but it's too late now. I need him in a way I don't fully understand.

Gaston trails hot, open-mouthed kisses down my neck and across my heaving chest. When his tongue swirls around one hard nipple, I cry out, arching off the bed. He lavishes attention on my breasts until I'm mindless with want.

"Please, Gaston," I gasp.

He silences me with a searing kiss before flipping me onto my stomach effortlessly. I grasp the sheets in anticipation as he maneuvers my hips up. I feel his hard length brush my entrance and wiggle back eagerly.

Gaston chuckles darkly. "So eager for my cock." He punctuates his words with a sharp slap to my ass that makes me yelp. "Such a good little slut."

Before I can respond he drives into me in one smooth stroke. I cry out at the sudden fullness, the exquisite stretch of him inside me again.

Gaston fucks me hard and deep at this new angle, making my eyes roll back in my head. I grasp the sheets desperately, overwhelmed by the pleasure.

"You feel incredible," he growls above me. "Taking my cock so well."

I can only moan in response, drunk on the feeling of him rapidly building that pressure inside me once more. Sensing how close I am, Gaston reaches between us to rub tight circles on my throbbing clit. The added stimulation is my undoing, and I shatter around him.

"Oh, fuck! Gaston!"

"That's it, baby. Come for me. Milk my cock just like that," He growls, fucking me through every pulse and aftershock, drawing out my climax until I'm spent and limp beneath him."I'm going to fill you up so full with my cum that you'll feel it dripping out of you for hours."

The idea drives me wild. All I want is to feel his cum deep in my cunt. A deep roar tears from him the moment he finds his release. A hot rush of cum fills me deep. He pumps his thick cock in and out of me repeatedly until every drop is drained.

And then he rests on top of me, his solid weight pinning me to the mattress. We lay there gasping for several moments, our slick bodies still entwined.

He withdraws, and I whimper at the loss of him.

Gaston maneuvers himself so he's lying on the bed

before pulling my back tight against his chest. His lips press against the back of my neck.

"You're mine now, Blake," he murmurs, already growing hard against my ass. "I'll never let you go."

Exhausted yet sated, I find myself drifting off in his embrace despite sensing he's nowhere near finished with me. But in that moment, I feel the most at peace I've felt since I was kidnapped. Tonight, I'm his. And while I drift off, I hope I'll still be his come morning light.

17

GASTON

*T*he contract I've been staring at for the last hour is a blur of words. I pinch the bridge of my nose and sigh heavily, forcing my gaze away from it.

All I can think about is Blake. That woman has gotten under my skin like no one else ever has.

I shouldn't have let things get so intense last night. The way she begged for my cock, the way she surrendered to my domination—it was intoxicating.

But she's a distraction I can't afford. The reason I buy women in the first place is because I don't have time for entanglements or relationships. I'm a busy man with a multi-billion dollar company to run and rivals to outmaneuver.

Falling for someone has never been an option for me, yet here I am, obsessed with her. Blake is not like anyone I've ever met. Her defiance and steel are admirable in her position. I love how she challenges me. It only makes me want her more.

Tossing the contract aside, I rub a hand across my face. There's no use trying to work right now because all I can see is those blue eyes sparkling with defiance and desire. Somehow, I've got to get her out of my head.

That's when I notice the time, realizing the board meeting starts in five minutes. They can't see me distracted, so I've got to pull myself together.

With a deep breath, I stand and straighten my tie. Time to go put on a show. Even ahead of the board meeting, my mind wanders to Blake. I wonder what she's doing. The desire to check the cameras has been clawing at me, but I disconnected them after she asked me to.

Straightening my shoulders, I stride into the boardroom. The shareholders are already seated around the long mahogany table, their gazes sharp and assessing while they track my entrance.

"Good morning, gentlemen," I say briskly, taking my seat at the head of the table. "Shall we get started?"

The expressions on their faces are solemn. They mean business today. Ordinarily, these meetings are little more than a formality—a periodic update for the major shareholders before they go back to their golf games and mistresses. But today, there's an undercurrent of tension in the room. They're out for blood.

Rodrigo speaks first, his reedy voice cutting through the heavy silence. "Perhaps you could start by explaining these rumors we've been hearing about a rather interesting new acquisition of yours."

I keep my face impassive, betraying none of the irritation I feel at his probing. They could only know about me buying Blake if Pablo tipped them off.

"I'm a collector of rare, beautiful things," I reply smoothly. "Surely the nature of my personal acquisitions is no business of this board."

"It is when it impacts the value of our shares," snaps Eduardo, his meaty fist thudding the table. "Your illegal indiscretions reflect poorly on all of us."

Leaning back in my chair, I regard them individually before speaking. "Then let's discuss business, shall we? Profits are up 22% this quarter..."

The facts and figures roll effortlessly off my tongue, but my thoughts keep straying back to Blake. Is she thinking of me right now as I am of her? Does she feel the same magnetic pull and addictive thrill?

Once I've finished giving them the numbers, I wait for their response.

Rodrigo shakes his head. "Your focus seems to have strayed from the company lately, and there are concerns about where your priorities lie."

My focus has only strayed for a couple of weeks after spending most of my life laser-focused on this fucking company. They're vultures eager to exploit any perceived weakness. I built QuantumTech Solutions from the ground up.

"I can assure you, my priority is, and will always be, the

success of this company," I reply evenly. "I founded this empire through blood, sweat, and sacrifice. No one wants to see it prosper more than I do."

Eduardo scoffs. "Yet your attentions appear divided, and you are being sloppy in your personal life."

Michael clears his throat. "While no one can prove you purchased a woman and supported illegal trafficking, the rumors don't help matters."

I've been doing so for years, and no one has batted an eyelid. Pablo is behind the rumors that I'm certain of. "And who exactly is spreading these rumors?"

Carlos clears his throat. "That's not important. Even if they aren't true, the weight rumors have is surprising."

I shake my head. "You're all listening to a criminal spreading rumors about me because he simply wants to shake our company down for real estate he desires," I state.

They bristle a little at that.

"It would be wise not to listen to gossip, especially when it can be unfounded and untrue."

Instantly, the tension in the air shifts. My denial about involvement in trafficking has appeased them a little, even though it's a lie.

Rodrigo nods. "Fine, but what assurances can you give us that your extracurricular activities won't become a distraction? We all saw you with that woman at the gala, and she's different from the other women you parade around."

Fuck.

Am I that obvious with my infatuation?

My jaw tightens because these stuck-up bastards inherited their money. They know nothing of the long nights and endless grind to build this company from the ground up.

"You have my word that my personal affairs will never impact business," I state firmly. "I've led this company to record profits for seven straight years. My track record speaks for itself."

Meeting each of their gazes in turn, I assert my authority. The board may have some power, but they know they can't eliminate me.

After an extended silence, Rodrigo sighs. "Very well, we'll take you at your word for now," he says. "But the board will closely monitor things moving forward."

I give a curt nod. "If there's nothing else, gentlemen?"

Their expressions are stony, but no one speaks, so I gather my notes and stand swiftly. "Good day to you all," I say crisply before striding from the boardroom.

Those lazy pieces of shit dare to question me as if I haven't given my whole life to this company. As if I'm not solely responsible for their cushy dividends and inflated share prices. The entitlement is astounding.

My hands clench into fists when I step into the elevator. It would be so satisfying to crush each of them, leaving them destitute and begging at my feet. One day, I will. For now, damage control is key. Pablo is trying to mess with me, but he's made a big mistake. I built this empire from nothing, and I'll be damned if I let it slip away now.

I dial Damien's number, tapping my foot impatiently on the elevator floor as I wait for him to pick me up.

"Gaston," he answers briskly. "What can I do for you?"

"I'm sending over a file with some interesting information about our friend Pablo Estrada," I say. "I want it leaked to the press immediately."

Damien chuckles. "I take it Mr. Estrada has gotten on your bad side?"

"You could say that. He's making trouble, sticking his nose where it doesn't belong. I want him publicly ruined."

"Consider it done," Damien assures me smoothly.

I end the call and attach the incriminating files I hacked from Estrada's servers, detailing some of his connections to the Sinaloa cartel in Columbia and money laundering operations. Once this gets out, his public reputation will be destroyed overnight. Not to mention the scrutiny it will bring down on his enterprises from the government.

The ding signals my arrival at the ground floor of QuantumTech Solutions headquarters, and I stride toward the exit. It's early for me to leave, but there's no use sitting in my office staring blankly at paperwork when I could be home with my angel.

Pablo Estrada will be put in his place tomorrow. And from there, I'll deal with him. I tried to warn him, but he won't back down. Now, he'll pay the price for crossing me. No one fucks with me and gets away with it.

Estrada will serve as an example to anyone stupid

enough to challenge me. The board will fall back in line. I always win in the end.

Striding into the afternoon sun, I step toward the town car, waiting to take me home to Elysium. Time for me to get to work on securing my most important acquisition. Last night was the first step to making Blake mine in every sense of the word. She's torn between her desire to submit and her nature to fight, but her submission wins. And when she finally surrenders herself completely and utterly it will make it so much sweeter when she falls for me.

The thought quickens my pulse with anticipation. I loosen my tie, my mind filling with vivid images of how I intend to claim her. To possess every inch of that luscious body and make her scream my name in pleasure.

Then my phone dings, and I pull it out of my jacket. Damien has pulled Blake's medical records for me after hacking into a few institutions. I open them, and my stomach drops when I read through them. All this time, I was sure there was something amiss with the way my girl couldn't focus, and I was right. The question is, why didn't she tell me she needed meds?

I press the button on the intercom. "Andre, I need to make a stop on the way home. Take me to a pharmacy."

"Of course, sir."

Sitting back, I pinch the bridge of my nose. A guilt coils through me because I hate that she's been suffering in silence. I could have gotten her the meds the moment I bought her, but she didn't trust me enough to tell me. I can't understand why it makes me so sick to my stomach.

18

BLAKE

*B*utterflies flutter to life in my stomach when I hear the door open. This is the first time since he bought me that I've been excited about his return.

Last night was electric. Gaston is a beast in bed. And it's the only thing that has given me any real excitement or pleasure in this gilded cage he's trapped me in.

Hurrying into the kitchen, I put the finishing touches on my prepared meal. Gaston loves traditional Mexican cuisine, so I've made beef barbacoa tacos with all the fixings.

I straighten my dress when I hear soft footsteps approaching. A form-fitting pink dress that finishes just above the knee and accentuates my curves. The desire to look my best for him is odd, yet after last night, I'll do anything to get a repeat.

Gaston's eyes light up when he sees me, gaze dropping

appreciatively down my body and back up. "Fuck, you look delicious." He sets a bag on the counter.

Heat floods me as I clear my throat. "I made tacos," I point out, waving at them.

He stalks toward me, not once taking his eyes off me. "They smell good, but I'm hungry for something else." Once he's before me, he grabs me hard and presses his lips to mine, thrusting his tongue into my mouth.

I melt for him, clawing my fingers through his dark hair. "Gaston," I breathe his name as he peppers kisses down my neck.

"Yes, baby girl?"

"The food will get cold," I gasp, arching into him. "It took me quite a long time to prepare."

I'm surprised when he listens to me, straightening up. "Of course, sorry, you're just so irresistible."

He forces himself away from me and turns to sit at the table in his normal chair. There's a shift in the atmosphere tonight. It's different, perhaps because we fucked last night, but Gaston can't take his eyes off me.

"Are you going to eat?" I ask, my cheeks blazing with heat.

He tilts his head. "Of course, I'm just admiring a piece of art."

God damn it. This man could charm anyone, and when he's looking at me like that, it makes me want to strip all my clothes off and ride him right here at the dinner table.

No, I need to get a handle on my urges around him.

Clenching my thighs together, I tear my eyes from his and serve myself some food.

Gaston follows suit and does the same. Even as I focus on my taco, I can feel his eyes on me. Finally, he takes a bite of the barbacoa tacos and groans. "Mmm, absolutely delicious."

They are good.

My cooking has really improved, and I'm proud of myself, especially since it's really hard to focus on tasks without my meds. We eat in silence for a short while before Gaston breaks it. "I know this whole situation for you has been difficult," he says gently. But I hope in time you'll come to appreciate the opportunities being here affords you."

Opportunities? What opportunities could he talk about? I'm his prisoner.

"I don't understand." I glance into his gray eyes. "What kind of opportunities could I have here?"

Gaston takes a sip of wine. "You're free from that disgusting prison and no longer forced to degrade yourself for Navarro's profit. As you can tell, I will care for you and lavish you with anything your heart desires."

Materialistic pig.

I clench my jaw, a flare of anger rising within me. "So I've traded one cage for a better one," I snap. "Some opportunity."

"Blake..." Gaston begins, his voice edged with warning.

I hold up my hand. "No, I know. You saved me from a

much worse fate," I concede begrudgingly. "At least here I'm not being sold off to someone more savage and despicable or used by anyone and everyone who walks through the door." A pang of guilt pierces my heart as I think of Kali, Luna, and Alice, wondering if they've already been sold into worse fates or are still prisoners of the Navarro Cartel.

Gaston nods. "You'll appreciate all I can provide for you in time."

It's true that I could have landed in a worse situation—I've got no doubt about that. My appetite is gone, and an uncomfortable silence settles between us.

"On that note, Blake," Gaston says, breaking the silence. "Why didn't you tell me you suffer from ADHD?"

My eyes widen, and my head snaps to meet his gaze. How does he know about my diagnosis? I never mentioned it to him.

"I..." I falter, grasping for words. "How do you know about that?"

He draws in a deep breath. "I suspected it was something like that from the way you're always pacing around the apartment, how you struggle to sit still for any length of time," he explains, taking a sip of wine. "And the way you flit from one thing to another, unable to focus. I could've gotten you your meds if you'd told me." He nods toward a bag on the counter. "They're in there."

My cheeks flush with embarrassment. Clearly, Gaston is more observant than I give him credit for, and my symptoms are more noticeable than I realize.

"I didn't think it was relevant to mention," I say defensively, glancing at the bag. "How do you know what meds I take?"

"My man hacked into your medical records to confirm my suspicion. I found out from your file."

Anger and embarrassment slam into me. He doesn't have the right to access my private medical records, yet he did it anyway.

"You what?" I ask. "That's a total invasion of my privacy. You had no right to look into my confidential medical information."

Gaston remains cool, watching me over the rim of his wine glass. "I have every right. You belong to me. Everything about you is my business."

I clench my fists under the table, barely resisting the urge to throw the rest of my wine glass in his arrogant face.

"I don't belong to anyone," I spit out. "Especially not you."

Gaston's eyes darken dangerously. "Need I remind you that, strictly speaking, you're my property now? Bought and paid for."

"Not legally. You can't own me in the eyes of the law," I challenge.

He sets his wine glass on the table. "No, that's true, but the fact is I do own you. And it's only a matter of time until I own every part of you. Not just your fucking stunning body, but that beautiful mind of yours and that pure soul."

I sit there stunned, unable to find the words to respond

to Gaston's chilling declaration. His intense gaze pins me in place, making me feel utterly powerless.

"And if I want to check your medical records to ensure that I know everything about you and your well-being, then I've got a right to do so."

"Why did you feel the need to invade my privacy by looking into my medical records? Why not just ask me?"

He arches a brow. "Would you have told me if I had?"

Probably not. After all, I didn't want him to know about my condition and try to use it against me. "I don't know," I murmur.

"And to answer your first question, I wanted to understand you better. I need to be fully informed about who I'm living with."

"So now you know all about my ADHD," I say coldly. "Does that help you understand me better? Give you more power over me?"

Gaston smiles. "In a manner of speaking. Knowledge is power, after all."

Pushing my plate away, I stand abruptly. "I'm not hungry anymore."

Gaston's eyes follow me as I move around the table. "Where are you going?"

"I need some air." I head for the balcony, desperate to put some distance between us.

The cool night breeze is a welcome relief as I step outside, wrapping my arms around myself. I take a few deep breaths, trying to calm my racing heart.

Gaston appears in the doorway, leaning against the frame. "You're upset."

"Of course I'm upset!" I whirl around to face him. "You invaded my privacy and accessed my medical records without my permission. That's a violation of trust."

He nods slowly. "I understand why you feel that way. But as I said, I must be fully informed about you to take care of you properly."

"Take care of me?" I scoff. "Is that what you call this? Imprisoning me in your gilded cage and treating me like your personal property?" I can't really understand why I'm so angry. Now that Gaston knows, he got me my meds, which I need, despite wishing I didn't.

We stand there at a stand-off, glaring into each other's eyes. And I hate how turned on I am right now. My body is highly strung whenever I'm in his presence. And maybe that's why I'm lashing out because it's so fucking irritating.

Gaston closes the distance between us with two strides and yanks my body against his. "I've missed you today," he breathes.

Goosebumps rise over my skin at his declaration. And I hate that I've missed him too. It's been hard to think of anything else. "Missed me?" I ask, shaking my head. Before I can say another word, he yanks my lips to his and kisses me with so much passion I go weak in his arms.

It consumes me, his tongue sliding against mine in a desperate, hungry exploration. I can't help but melt into him, the anger and frustration fading when his strong arms wrap around me.

When he finally breaks the kiss, we're both breathless. He rests his forehead against mine, his eyes searching my face.

"I never want you to keep something like that from me again," he says sternly. "I don't want you to suffer because you're too proud or stubborn to tell me you need medication."

I open my mouth to protest but Gaston presses a finger to my lips.

"No arguments," he says. "Your health and well-being are my responsibility now. So no more secrets about things like this. Understood?"

I nod. "Yes, sir," I murmur.

"Good girl," he murmurs.

A shiver races through me when he calls me that. It's the same every time, as though I crave his validation.

"Now come back inside." I allow him to pull me back into the kitchen, sinking sink into my chair to finish the rest of my food.

Gaston grabs my meds and a glass of water and puts them in front of me. "Take them."

It's an order the way he says it, but I willingly comply. Thankful to finally have them because it will make the itch beneath my skin less apparent.

Once we're both finished, I stand and clear the dishes. All the while, I feel his gaze burning a hole in my back. It excites me.

When finished, I find him lounging in his chair with one leg crossed over the other. His steel gray eyes are flashing with unmistakable desire. "Come here, nena."

I hesitate briefly before crossing the room to stand before him.

"That was delicious, thank you. You did so well." Gaston uncrosses his legs and leans forward. "Now, what shall I do with you?"

My cheeks are hot as I try to avoid his gaze.

"Look at me, Blake," he demands.

I meet his gaze and wish I didn't because I'm so turned on.

"Answer my question."

"Whatever you want, sir," I reply, meeting his gaze.

He groans and grabs my hips suddenly, forcing a gasp from my lips. "Sit on my lap."

I go willingly as he eases me to straddle him. His arms encircle my waist, and I relax into him, my heart fluttering excitedly.

Gaston's fingers trail up and down my spine. "That's my good girl," he murmurs, his lips brushing against my neck.

He's hard and ready beneath me, making me moan. I grind against him, desperate for friction. Gaston's tongue dances along my bottom lip, and I open for him with a soft gasp. The kiss deepens and grows more heated as his hands trail up my back, fingers tangling in my hair. I rock my hips harder, eliciting a low groan from him, which sends heat pooling low in my belly.

"That's it, baby girl," he rasps, his lips trailing down my throat. "Take what you need from me."

I grind harder against the ridge of his cock, making his breath come out faster against my skin. Emboldened by his groans, I roll my hips fast and moan at the delicious friction between us.

"Fuck, I've been thinking about your perfect little cunt all damn day, nena."

I grind harder against him, chasing that delicious friction. His grip on my hips tightens, guiding my movements.

"Please," I gasp, needing more.

The sound of his zipper coming down makes my heart rate spike, followed by him pulling his thick, hard cock out so it's pressed against my lace-clad pussy.

Gaston groans and grips my hips tighter, guiding me as I rock against his hard cock. "Fuck, that feels so good," he growls.

I whimper, heat pooling low in my belly as I chase that delicious friction. "Please, I need you," I beg breathlessly.

With a low rumble, Gaston slips his hand under the lace of my panties, fingers gliding through my slick folds. I gasp and jerk against him, my nails digging into his shoulders.

"So wet for me," he murmurs, circling my clit. "That's my good girl."

I moan and press into his touch, the familiar coil of tension building. "Don't stop," I pant.

Gaston's mouth finds mine in a searing kiss as his

fingers pick up their pace. I grind against his hand desperately, chasing my release.

Just when I'm on the verge, he stills his movements. I whimper in protest, my hips rocking futilely.

"Please," I beg, "I need to come."

Gaston chuckles lowly. "Not yet, baby girl." He tears the fabric of my panties so that there's nothing between us. The hard press of him against my soaking wet entrance.

Gaston grips my hips tightly, lifting me just enough to line up the thick head of his cock with my slick entrance. I whimper in anticipation, my body aching to be filled.

"Look at me," he commands, his voice rough with desire.

I meet his smoldering gaze, my heart pounding as he slowly lowers me down onto his rigid length. The stretch and fullness have me gasping, my fingers digging into his shoulders.

"That's it, take it all," he growls.

He pauses once he's buried to the hilt, allowing me to adjust. I clench around him, savoring the delicious sensation of being so perfectly, completely filled.

Gaston's hands roam my body, caressing and kneading. "Such a good girl for me. So tight and wet."

Experimentally, I roll my hips, drawing a groan from deep in his chest. "Fuck, you feel incredible riding my dick." Gaston begins to guide my movements, lifting me up and down his thick length. I moan, my walls clenching around him.

"That's it, ride me hard," Gaston growls.

I pick up the pace, chasing my release like an addict. Gaston's mouth finds mine in a bruising kiss, his tongue plundering my mouth. I whimper into the kiss, the sound muffled by his lips.

Gaston's hand slides down to palm my ass, encouraging me to move faster. I oblige, grinding down on him desperately. The new angle has me seeing stars, a strangled cry tearing from my throat.

"Fuck, you feel so good," Gaston rasps, nipping at my bottom lip. "Come for me."

His words, combined with the relentless pace of his hips snapping up to meet mine, send me hurtling over the edge. My orgasm crashes over me in waves, my inner walls fluttering and clenching around Gaston's cock.

"Ah, fuck!" Gaston groans, his hips stuttering as he chases his own release. With a few more deep, powerful thrusts, he stills, spilling himself deep inside me.

We stay locked together, both of us panting and trembling from the force of our climaxes. Gaston's grip on me gradually loosens as he presses tender kisses to my face and neck.

"My good girl," he murmurs, nuzzling into my neck. "So perfect for me."

I bask in the afterglow, my body tingling with satisfaction. But even while I revel in the feeling of Gaston's arms around me and his still semi-hard cock inside me, a nagging sense of unease begins to creep in. My passion for this man is becoming too deep.

He's my captor, my owner. I can't start having feelings for him. But I could spend the rest of my life wrapped up in him. And that's a very dangerous feeling to have.

19

BLAKE

*E*ver since we fucked at the kitchen table three days ago, I've tried to keep my distance from Gaston. We haven't had sex since. It's clear from my desperation that I was getting in too deep. And now I'm back on my meds. I'm seeing things a little more clearly.

Gaston is nothing more than a monster who believes in slavery, and I can't see him as anything else but that. Thankfully, it's a Monday, so he should be in the office today.

Once dressed, I head into the kitchen, only to freeze when I see him sitting at the kitchen island with a cup of coffee and a newspaper.

"Don't you have work today?" I ask.

Gaston glances at me. "I'm the CEO. I can go in when I want." He returns his attention back to the newspaper.

Instantly, I regret wearing my yoga pants and tank top. I thought he'd be out and intended to workout in the home gym for an hour. "Okay, I'm going to grab something to eat and then work out," I say, walking past him.

There's a soft rumble in his chest when my back is turned to him. I know these pants hug my curves like a second skin. Damn it. I should've changed after I ate because I feel his eyes on me.

And the ache between my thighs is undeniable. I grab a bowl and spoon, but I'm shaking so much I drop the spoon on the floor. "Damn it," I murmur under my breath before bending over and picking it up.

"You shouldn't bend over in those pants in front of me," Gaston warns.

I straighten and glare at him. "I dropped my spoon."

He smirks, eyes smoldering with a heat that makes my thighs clench. "I know, but you're making me so fucking hard." Gaston's eyes darken, his grip tightening on his mug. "You're asking for trouble, dressing like that."

"I'm dressed to work out. And I didn't know you were here." I turn my back on him and grab the cereals from the cupboard, pouring myself a bowl. And then I open the fridge and pull out the milk, all while trying to ignore him.

When I turn around, my breath hitches. He's right there, inches from me. His eyes are dark with desire as he grabs my hips. "Put down the milk."

No, this is the last thing I wanted to happen.

It was only a matter of time until he wanted me again, but I'd hoped my terrible outfits had put him off.

"Why?"

He tilts his head. "Because I need you. And I'd assumed

your baggy attire the past few days was because you were on your period. Were they?"

My brow furrows as my period has been irregular ever since I got the implant. "No."

"Just know, when you're on your period, I'll fuck you regardless." He moves his lips close to mine. "I don't mind the blood. And my need for you surpasses it, but I was respecting that you weren't in the mood for it with how you dressed." He grabs my throat, squeezing softly. "Why were you dressing like that?"

I can't tell him why. I can't tell him that I'm scared of my feelings for him. Or that I crave him constantly.

"Just felt like it," I lie.

"You're not a very good liar, baby girl."

Gaston's grip on my throat tightens ever so slightly. "I asked you a question."

I swallow hard, my heart pounding. I was trying to avoid...this." I gesture between us.

"Avoid this?" He arches a brow. "Avoid me?" His lips quirk up in a humorless smile. "That's not possible, baby girl. Not anymore." His thumb brushes my bottom lip. "I'm under your skin. In your head. In your body." His eyes darken. "You can't escape me."

The desire to argue and tell him he's wrong dies on my lips when he crushes his mouth to mine. It's a desperate, hungry kiss that leaves me aching for more.

When he finally pulls away, we're both panting. "Gaston, please..." I don't know if I'm begging him to stop or continue.

"Please, what?" His grip on my hips tightens. "Tell me what you want."

I avert my gaze, ashamed of the truth. "I want you."

He lets out a low, rumbling chuckle. "I know." His hand slides down to cup my ass. "And I'm going to take you right here, right now. Turn around."

I do as I'm told and turn my back to him. He bends me over the kitchen counter and yanks down my yoga pants and panties in one swift move, running a finger through me. "Are you ready for me to breed this pretty little cunt?"

I hesitate, the words caught in my throat. "I...I don't know."

Gaston chuckles darkly. "Oh, but I do." He grabs my hips and yanks me back against him, his hard length pressing against my ass. "You want me to fuck you. To fill you up with my cum."

I whimper, hating how my body reacts to his touch and how the ache between my thighs intensifies. "Gaston, please..."

"Please what, nena?" he murmurs, his lips brushing my ear. "Tell me what you want."

I squeeze my eyes shut, unable to look at him. "I want..." My voice trails off, the admission too shameful to voice.

"That's what I thought." Gaston grips my hips tighter, his fingertips digging into my skin. "You want me to take you, to claim you." He grinds against me, the friction sending sparks of pleasure through me. "And that's exactly what I'm going to do."

He yanks down my pants until they're around my ankles. Gaston runs his fingers through my slick folds, a pleased rumble escaping him. "So wet for me, baby girl. You're aching to be filled, aren't you?"

I bite my lip, holding back the moan that threatens to escape.

"Answer me," Gaston growls, his grip on my hips tightening.

"Y-yes," I breathe, hating how needy I sound.

"Good girl." He kisses the side of my neck, his teeth grazing my skin. "Now beg me to fuck you."

I take a shaky breath, the words caught in my throat. "Please, Gaston...I need you to fuck me with your big cock."

He rubs the head of his dick between my thighs, bumping my clit and sending sparks of pleasure through me. Without warning, he thrusts into me, filling me to the hilt. I cry out. The sensation is both painful and pleasurable. Gaston pauses, giving me a moment to adjust, his breath hot against the back of my neck.

"You feel so good," he murmurs, his voice rough with desire. "The perfect fit for me." He pulls out slowly, then slams back in, setting a punishing pace.

I brace myself against the counter, my knuckles turning white as I grip the edge. The sounds of our bodies meeting fill the air, mingling with our harsh breathing and the constant moans that tumble from my lips.

Gaston's grip on my hips is bruising, his thrusts deep and relentless. I can feel the familiar heat coiling in the pit of my stomach, the pressure building with each thrust.

"That's it," Gaston growls, his voice strained. "Take my cock. You love the way I fill you, don't you?"

My response is a whimper, the pleasure bordering on pain as he drives into me.

"Answer me," he demands, punctuating his words with a particularly hard thrust that steals the breath from my lungs.

"Y-yes," I manage to gasp out. "I love it, Gaston. I love the way you fuck me."

"Good girl." Gaston's thumb finds my clit, and I shudder. Expertly, he strokes me in time with his thrusts until I'm writhing and moaning against the counter.

"Please," I sob, so close to the edge I can taste it. My vision blurs as I glance over my shoulder, seeing Gaston's face twisted in pleasure and concentration.

Gaston leans in, his breath hot against the back of my neck. "Now come for me. Let me feel you clench around my cock."

I whimper, the coil of pleasure tightening with each snap of his hips. Gaston's fingers rub in tight, relentless circles over my clit.

"That's it, baby girl," he murmurs. "Let go for me."

The sensation is overwhelming, the pressure building until it finally crests, washing over me in waves of blinding ecstasy. His next stroke sends me hurtling over the cliff edge. I cry out, my walls fluttering and clenching around Gaston's thick length as my orgasm tears through me.

Gaston growls, his hips slamming forward as he chases his own release. "That's it, beautiful. Milk my dick. Fuck, you're amazing." He buries himself to the hilt and spills himself inside me.

We stay like that for a long moment, both panting and spent. Gaston presses a kiss to the back of my neck, his grip on my hips loosening.

"That's my good girl," he murmurs, his voice low and rough. Gaston pulls out slowly, a trail of our combined fluids dripping down my thighs.

I wince at the sensation, my body trembling from the force of my orgasm. Gaston chuckles, his fingers tracing the curve of my ass. I feel a pang of guilt, knowing that I've given in to him once again. But the afterglow of our encounter makes it hard to regret.

He grabs a towel off the counter and gently wipes me clean, his touch surprisingly tender.

Once he's finished, Gaston pulls me into his arms, cradling me against his chest. I can't help but melt into his embrace, the familiar ache between my thighs a constant reminder of what transpired.

Gaston presses a kiss to the top of my head. "You're mine, baby girl. Body and soul."

I want to argue, to tell him that he's wrong, that I'm not his to claim. But the words die on my lips because I know he's right deep down. I am his, whether I like it or not.

HOURS LATER, I can only stare at the ceiling while sleep evades me. Gaston's arm is draped over my waist, my back against his chest, and his breath caresses my neck. I'm hyperaware of his presence.

In the stillness of the night, guilt, doubt, and shame overwhelm me. How can I willingly fuck this man? Allow him to hold me. Feel anything other than hate toward him?

It's at times like this I wish I could psychoanalyze myself because this is fucked up. Is it Stockholm Syndrome? Maybe. I couldn't say, but I felt this powerful connection with him when we met.

I shift carefully, trying not to wake Gaston. But his arm tightens, holding me in place. "Where do you think you're going?" he murmurs sleepily.

I freeze. "Nowhere. Just can't sleep."

Gaston nuzzles the sensitive spot below my ear. "Relax. You're safe here with me."

I nearly laugh. Safe? I'm trapped here, at the mercy of this powerful, dangerous man. A gilded cage is still a prison. When I don't relax, he pulls me around to face him and props himself up to look at me. His eyes gleam even in the darkness.

"You know you belong here now. With me." His tone brokers no argument.

"Belong with you? I've got no choice. Just because I've fucked you a few times, it doesn't mean anything."

"No?" Gaston smiles, but it's wolfish. "Are you sure it doesn't mean anything?"

I'm not sure. I fear it means too much, so I'm so torn up. "What are you suggesting?"

He moves his lips to within an inch of mine and then kisses me softly. "I'm suggesting that you feel like you belong here, wrapped in my arms. And that scares you."

Goddamn it.

How is he so perceptive?

Or am I just really fucking obvious?

"I don't know what you're talking about," I reply.

He smirks. "Deny it all you want, mi reina. You're meant for me." He kisses me once again before pulling me tightly against his chest so my head is just above his heart. "Now sleep."

My Spanish isn't great, but I know that one. My queen. Is that how he sees me? Is it possible that Gaston actually cares for me?

The thought makes butterflies take flight in my stomach and my heart pound harder. I can't help but think of my friends while I lie here, wrapped up in my captor's arms. Are they okay? Are they even still alive?

The thought of harm coming to any of them makes my heart clench. I need to find a way to help them, to save them.

Gaston's breathing turns rhythmic behind me, warning me he's fallen asleep. And as I feel the rise and fall of his chest beneath my head, sleep eventually claims me again. But my dreams are filled with stormy gray eyes and the feeling of strong, greedy hands claiming my body. And I know that I'm already too deep in his trap.

20

GASTON

The engine of the town car has lulled my angel to sleep.

Blake didn't seem too excited to leave the apartment this time, possibly because I wouldn't tell her where we were going.

I gently tuck a stray lock of hair behind her ear. She's been such a good girl, and I've decided to treat her.

"Blake," I murmur, gently shaking her. "Wake up, mi reina. We're almost there."

She groans, and then her stunning blue eyes open, meeting mine. "Gaston?"

"We're here."

"Where is here?" she asks, stretching her arms and sitting straight. Her brow furrows when she sees the port.

"Acapulco," I reply. "I thought a little getaway would do us both some good."

She tenses, looking angry. "I don't want a getaway. Take me back to your apartment," she demands.

I love that she's still got that defiant streak.

"Why would I do that? This is a treat, baby girl. Not a punishment."

She bites her lip, looking uncertain. "We can't keep doing this."

"Doing what?" I demand.

"Acting like this is normal. Like we're a couple just going on a last-minute vacation or something."

Ah, that's why she's angry. I've noticed her trying to pull away from me since we started sleeping together. She's falling for me, just like I've fallen for her, but she's resisting. Natural, but futile. Ultimately, she'll come to accept we're meant for each other.

I reach out and cup her face, tilting it so she has to look me in the eye. "This is normal, mi reina. You and I, we're special. We belong together."

She shakes her head, tears welling in her eyes. "No, Gaston. This isn't right. I'm not—"

I press a finger to her lips, silencing her. "Shhh. Don't fight it, mi amor. Just let it happen."

She stares at me, fear and uncertainty swirling in her gaze. I can see the conflict within her, the desire warring with the need to pull away.

"I don't want to," she whispers.

"Yes, you do," I murmur, leaning in to kiss her forehead softly. "You want this as much as I do."

She turns her head away, breaking the contact. "Take me back to the apartment. Please."

I sigh, my hand dropping from her face. "Blake, you're being unreasonable."

"I'm being reasonable," she snaps. "You bought me, for fuck's sake. You can't just act like I'm your girlfriend when you're my fucking owner."

"Watch your language." I grab her throat, squeezing in a warning. "And stop being so defiant."

Blake opens her mouth to protest, but I silence her with a firm kiss. Initially, she's tense against me. Until she begins to relax, her lips opening to welcome my tongue. And then we're clawing at each other, desperate.

When we break apart, I press my forehead against hers. "Now, no more dramatics. Let's enjoy our getaway." With that, I release her throat and open the car door, signaling for her to step out.

She slides out, and I follow her, offering my hand. I see the hesitation in her eyes before she takes it. My girl is being cautious, and I don't like it.

"Here we are," I say, nodding at my yacht docked at the port.

Blake carefully steps onto the luxurious yacht, her blue eyes widening as she takes in the gleaming teak deck and state-of-the-art amenities. A part of me thrills at the chance to impress her, to lavish her with the kind of lifestyle few ever dream of. But something tells me Blake's above all that.

Blake stares at the yacht, her lips parted slightly in awe.

I can see the longing in her eyes, the temptation of the luxurious life I'm offering her. Still, there's also a shadow of fear and uncertainty.

"It's beautiful," she murmurs, almost to herself.

"It is," I agree, stepping beside her and placing a hand on the small of her back. "And it's yours now, mi reina." I can't understand why Blake is different from the other girls. All I know is that I've been sure I won't be purchasing another girl again for a while now. Blake is it for me.

She tenses at my touch, then slowly turns to face me. "Gaston, I can't keep doing this. I don't want to be here. I want to go home."

I frown, my grip tightening ever so slightly. "This is your home now, Blake. With me."

"No," she says firmly, shaking her head. "No, it's not. I don't belong here with you. I belong in America, finishing my degree. This isn't right."

I let out a soft sigh, pulling her closer. "You're being stubborn. Can't you see that you and I are meant to be together? I've given you everything, and all I ask in return is that you accept it."

"Accept it?" she scoffs, her eyes flashing with anger. "You bought me, Gaston. You didn't give me anything. You took me."

"Enough talk of that. Let me give you a tour," I say, ignoring her pleas for me to let her go home. She doesn't know what she's asking. Letting her go home would be like ripping my heart from my chest.

Forcing her into step beside me, I show her the kitchen,

dining area, living room, and the luxurious master suite, where I intend to ravage her multiple times a day. The mere thought makes my cock harden.

"We'll be sailing up the coast," I tell her. "The yacht is stocked with everything we could need." I gesture to where the crew is preparing to cast off. "I've also hired a full crew, so you won't have to lift a finger if you don't want to."

Blake is quiet, her jaw hard set. She's angry. But it won't last.

"Why don't we have a drink in the lounge?" I suggest. "We can relax and watch the coastline slip by while we set sail."

Her glare is piercing. "I'd rather retire and get some rest."

"Nonsense, you slept the entire journey here." I place my hand on her back, leading her up the roof deck lounge. While Blake may be scared of getting too close to me because her feelings are confused, I've got no illusions; making Blake fall for me will be the greatest challenge of my life.

"Take a seat, and I'll grab us a drink."

She sits on the cream leather built-in couch and glares at me, arms crossed over her chest.

"What can I get you?" I ask, moving behind the polished mahogany bar. The crew is too busy preparing to sail, so no one is manning the bar.

"Just a club soda, please," Blake replies.

I fix her a club soda over ice and splash a few dashes of lime into it before pouring myself a glass of aged tequila.

And then I sit beside her, passing the soda into her hands. Our fingers brush together, and I'm drawn to how her lips part.

The tang of citrus mingles with the woody aroma of the liquor as I take a slow sip, watching Blake over the rim of my glass.

I drape my arm across her shoulders when I feel the boat beginning to move. To my surprise, Blake doesn't pull away. She leans into me. And I feel my heart flutter.

I'm supposed to be a ruthless, cold-hearted billionaire. Love isn't meant to be in the card for me. Hell, it's why I bought women. Keep it like a business transaction. No fear of feelings getting in the way. And look at me now—smitten over a woman I paid millions of dollars for. I want to give her the world. I want to be her whole fucking world, but is it even possible considering everything that has happened between us?

When the last sliver of sun disappears below the horizon, she finally breaks the silence. "I've always loved the sea," she says softly. "Ever since I was a little girl. My parents used to take me to the beaches near our vacation home in California. I felt free, standing with the water lapping at my feet and the salty breeze in my hair."

Considering she has never told me anything about her family or friends, I am captivated by this unexpected glimpse into her past. I wait silently, not wanting to interrupt and break the spell.

"Surfing became my passion," she continues after a moment. "I started competing when I was thirteen. Those early morning sessions with the swells rising to meet me were the only time I truly felt at peace."

Blake would hate me if she learned I already know everything she told me. I made it my business to learn everything I could about Blake's background. But I don't let on that I'm aware of her competitive surfing career. It would only anger her if she realized how thoroughly I've investigated her.

"I didn't know you were a surfer. You'll have to show me your moves while we're sailing the coast."

She chews on her lip. "Maybe, if the conditions are right."

I clink my glass lightly against hers. "To good waves then."

The corners of Blake's mouth quirks up ever so slightly. It's the closest I've seen to a real smile from her today. I find myself transfixed by the way it lights up her delicate features.

We lapse into a comfortable silence while the yacht motors through the darkening waters. I've got a feeling this trip may prove to be a turning point for Blake and me. Only time will tell, but I intend to be patient. With this wild, fascinating creature by my side, I'm in no rush to get to the destination when the ride is so thrilling.

21

BLAKE

The gentle rocking of the yacht is so peaceful. Slowly, I come to, stretching out my limbs as memories of my evening with Gaston return. He didn't fuck me last night. Instead, he held me until I fell asleep. It's like he's slowly trying to deconstruct my walls and make me fall for him with everything he does, and I'm losing the battle to resist.

Glancing at the other side of the bed, I find him lying beside me, his features softened in sleep. My feelings toward him are ever-evolving, from hatred to lust to something far more complex.

Shifting onto my side, I study him. The strong line of his jaw, the dark sweep of his lashes against his cheeks. Even asleep, there's this dominant, hard air about him. It's both intriguing and terrifying.

I have this horrible desire to trace the contours of his

face with my fingers, but I resist. Instead, I drink in the sight of him. So beautiful and yet so dark and dominant.

Suddenly, his eyes flutter open, and he catches me gazing at him. Those unique gray eyes instantly on mine. "Good morning, mi reina," he murmurs.

"Morning," I breathe.

He reaches out and trails a finger along my cheek gently. "Did you sleep well?"

"Yes," I admit, cursing my honesty. I should be putting up more of a fight. And yet, in this quiet moment, I find myself wanting nothing more than to bask in his attention.

Gaston's lips curve into a beautiful smile. "I'm glad." His hand slides down, cupping the back of my neck, and he pulls me close to give me a quick kiss. "There's something I want to discuss with you."

I swallow hard, my heart pounding. "What is it?"

"It's about our future." His gaze is intense, burning into me. "I think it's time we discussed where this is going."

Where is this going? He's my captor. It's going wherever the fuck he wants it to.

I stare at Gaston, my heart hammering in my chest. What if he's fed up with me and wants a new woman? And why the hell does that make me feel so fucking jealous.

"Our future? Are you fed up with me now? Do you want to buy a new girl?"

He growls like an animal, grabbing my throat. "Never."

God. That declaration makes my heart flutter.

"I want to discuss what you want," he says.

"What do I want? Since when does it matter? You've made it very clear that you own me since we met."

He sighs, releasing my throat. "Indeed, but I don't want it to be that way. I want you to choose this life with me because you want it."

"You're giving me a choice?" I ask hesitantly.

Gaston nods. "I want you to want this. I want you to want...me."

It's clear what he's saying, even if he's not saying the words. He cares. He has feelings for me.

After a long moment, I find my voice again. "Gaston, I don't know if that's possible."

His eyes darken, lips pressing into a thin line.

"It's not that I don't appreciate what you're offering. But as long as I'm your captive, I'll never be able to make that choice freely." I meet his intense gaze unflinchingly. "If you really want me to want this, to want you, then you've got to let me go. You've got to set me free."

Gaston is silent, his expression unreadable. "If I were to free you, would you want me then?"

Freedom is the only thing I need right now. My feelings for this man are too mixed up, and I don't know what's real and what isn't. Space would let me sort through everything that has happened. I'd probably need to see a shrink, too.

"I don't know," I answer. "Too much has happened between us. My feelings are so complicated." I sigh, sitting up in bed. "But if you freed me, I could try to move forward.

I could figure out what I want without being under your control."

Gaston nods, considering my words. I think he might agree to let me go for a wild moment. But then his expression hardens. "We'll discuss this more when we return to the city."

"But—"

Gaston silences me with a finger against my lips. "No more talk of this on our trip, okay? At least let me have that."

I let out a resigned sigh, watching Gaston's muscular, beautiful body while he slides out of bed. "Come on, get up and get dressed," he says briskly. "I want to explore the town we've docked near. I think you'll find it charming."

Gaston senses my hesitation, sitting on the edge of the bed, his hand resting on my thigh. Despite myself, I feel a spark of electricity at his touch.

"Don't look so worried, mi reina," he says, his voice gentler now. "We will just spend the day together and get to know each other better. I promise to be on my best behavior."

I nod in response, forcing myself to get out of bed and donning a breezy sundress and sandals. I can feel Gaston's eyes on me the whole time, watching my every move.

Once I'm ready, he offers me his arm. "Shall we go explore?"

I hesitate momentarily before slipping my hand into the crook of his elbow. As we make our way onto the deck,

I'm struck again by the beauty of the crystal blue waters surrounding us.

We disembark onto a rib boat since, due to the size of the yacht, we can't get closer to the town. It bounces over the waves as we approach the picturesque seaside town.

Despite my lingering unease, I can't help but enjoy the salty breeze tousling my hair and the dazzling aquamarine water all around us. Gaston looks perfectly at home behind the wheel, exuding an air of casual command.

We dock at a tiny pontoon and disembark. The town is as charming as Gaston promised, with cobblestone streets, pastel buildings, and lush tropical foliage everywhere.

Gaston takes my hand. "Beautiful, isn't it?"

I nod in response as he leads me away from the dock and into the center of the town. It should feel weird being out in public hand in hand with him, but it doesn't. Nothing has felt more natural as Gaston points out sights.

On occasions when we stop to look at something, Gaston's arms settle around my waist. Anyone would think we're a normal couple on vacation.

"Are you hungry?" he asks after a few hours of sightseeing.

I nod. "Starving."

"Good. I know the perfect place." He leads me down toward the beach, where there's a delightful little beach restaurant.

Gaston speaks to the host in Spanish, and hearing him speak Spanish is alluring. Then, the host leads us to an outdoor table shaded by palms. It's got a spectacular ocean view. Never before have I had a meal in such a picturesque setting. Gaston orders fresh seafood, ceviche, shrimp skewers, and grilled fish. It's all delicious.

"How do you like the town?" he asks.

"This place is beautiful."

"I'm glad you think so. When I saw it on the map, I thought you might appreciate the charm."

"You were right. Thank you for bringing me here." Despite my reluctance to go on this trip with him, it beats being cooped up in that apartment.

"Tell me more about your interests," Gaston says after a while. "What do you enjoy doing in your free time besides surfing?"

It feels strangely intimate to discuss my hobbies and passions with him. Still, the earnest curiosity in his gray eyes compels me to open up.

"I like being outdoors and active," I begin slowly. "Hiking, swimming, and surfing whenever I get the chance. I find it freeing, being out in nature away from everything."

Gaston smiles. "No wonder you were so impatient stuck in the apartment. I'll have to take you out more."

The idea sends an unexpected thrill through me. To cover it, I take another sip of wine before continuing. "I also enjoy painting and creative things. Always have, ever since I was young. The only problem is that I often find I don't finish projects. The difficulties of ADHD, I admit." I tilt my head. "What about you?"

He arches a brow. "What about me?"

"What are your hobbies?" I ask.

His lips press together, and he shakes his head. "Unfortunately, I don't have time for hobbies. All I do is work."

Gaston's words give me pause. All he does is work? That doesn't sound very fulfilling.

"Don't you ever take time for yourself? For relaxation or enjoyment?" I press.

He shakes his head. "Not really. My work is my life."

I frown, unable to hide my disappointment. "That's a shame. Everyone needs balance, Gaston. All work and no play..."

His lips curve into a wry smile. "I suppose you have a point. But my work is what's most important to me." Then his expression turns serious, and his eyes darken. "Or at least, it was."

Goosebumps rise over every inch of my skin at what he's implying. I ignore the comment and focus on my food, finishing it off.

The sun-dappled waves, the swaying palms, the delicious food—it all feels so peaceful. And yet, I'm acutely aware that I'm here as Gaston's captive, not as his willing companion.

I glance at him, studying the strong line of his jaw and the intensity in his gaze as he watches me. There's an almost predatory quality to him, even in this tranquil setting. I shiver slightly, my appetite waning.

"Is everything alright, mi reina?" Gaston asks, reaching across the table to cover my hand.

I nod, offering him a small smile. "Yes, it's all wonderful. The food is amazing."

"I'm glad you're enjoying it." His thumb caresses my hand, and I find myself inexplicably leaning into his touch. "You seem a bit pensive, though. Care to share what's on your mind?"

I hesitate, unsure of how much to reveal. "I was just thinking about...everything. About us." I meet his gaze, my heart pounding. "Gaston, I meant what I said this morning. If you want me to ever be truly yours, you've got to let me go."

His expression darkens, and for a moment, I fear I've pushed him too far. But then he sighs, squeezing my hand gently. "I know, mi amor. And I promise we'll discuss it further when we return. But for now, I want to enjoy being with you."

I nod, not entirely satisfied but willing to let it go. We finish our meal in relative silence, the tension palpable between us. When the plates are cleared, Gaston stands and offers me his hand.

"Come, there's somewhere I want to take you."

I place my hand in his, allowing him to guide me through the quaint streets and back toward the coastline. We eventually reach a small, secluded cove, the sand pristine and the water a breathtaking shade of turquoise.

"This is my favorite spot in the whole town," Gaston murmurs, leading me to the water's edge. "I come here when I need to think, to find a moment of peace."

I gaze out at the serene scene, the gentle lapping of the waves soothing my frazzled nerves. "It's beautiful."

Gaston steps behind me, his arms encircling my waist. "Just like you."

I stiffen momentarily, then relax back against him. At this moment, with the sun warming my skin and the sound of the ocean surrounding us, I allow myself to just...be.

We stand there together, silent, for what feels like an eternity. Too soon, the sun dips low over the water. "We should head back before it gets dark," Gaston says regretfully.

I let him take my hand, hyperaware of the warmth of his palm against mine. While we stroll leisurely back to the boat, I can't ignore the niggling thought that maybe, just maybe, I've glimpsed the man behind the monster today.

GASTON

*W*hen we return to the yacht, it's dark. As I requested, the chef has prepared us a light meal.

"Dinner? I thought we ate enough at lunch," she says, holding her stomach. "Are you trying to fatten me up?"

I laugh. "No, but I requested a light meal be prepared. Nothing heavy." I pull a seat out. "Sit."

She eyes me warily before taking her seat.

The chef brings a light salad with fresh crab and avocado while I pour Blake a white wine.

I raise my own glass. "To a lovely day."

She clinks her glass against mine.

"Tell me more about your surfing in competitions. It sounds thrilling."

The moment I ask her about that, I see her guard slip. Surfing really is her passion. Her eyes light up as she tells me about competitions she's been in and how she won nationals when she was sixteen.

"Did you never want to do it professionally?"

Blake's expression turns sad. "It was my dream, but my parents wouldn't let me pursue it." She sighs. "Not to mention, it's tough. Being a pro surfer isn't easy at all."

I wish her parents hadn't dashed her dreams like that. My baby girl should do whatever makes her happy. If I had her willingly, I'd support every dream she held, even nourishing them.

God, what the hell is happening to me?

I don't care about anyone but myself normally.

"I'd love to see you surf someday," I tell her sincerely.

She looks surprised. "Maybe you will."

The chef returns and clears out plates before placing a dessert of chocolate soufflé in front of us.

Blake groans in appreciation. "This looks amazing."

The chef smiles. "Enjoy."

Once we're alone again, Blake's attention fixes on me. "So tell me about your business," Blake says after a bite of the decadent dessert. "Did you start the company yourself or inherit it?"

"I started it from nothing," I reply. "I had the vision for the software and slowly built up the company over the past fifteen years."

She nods, looking intrigued. "That must have taken a lot of hard work and dedication."

"It certainly wasn't easy," I say with a small laugh. "There were many long days and sleepless nights in those early years. But the satisfaction of building something from the ground up made it worthwhile."

Blake takes a sip of wine, her bright blue eyes fixed on me. "What gave you the idea for the software in the first place?"

I remember those early days when I was in college with big dreams. "I saw a need that the technology wasn't addressing at the time. I knew I could create something better, something that would really help businesses operate more efficiently. My professors told me I was chasing a pipe dream, but I believed in my vision."

"And clearly, you were right," Blake says, gesturing at the luxurious yacht.

I nod. "It took perseverance and determination, but my work paid off in the end."

"That's really impressive," she says. For the first time, I detect a hint of admiration in her voice.

After a short silence, Blake speaks again. "So, do you have a big family? Any brothers or sisters?"

I tense up. My family is the one subject I never discuss. The wounds are too raw, even after all these years.

"I'd rather not talk about my family," I snap, taking a large sip of wine.

Blake looks surprised by my abrupt tone. "Oh, I'm sorry, I didn't mean to pry."

An awkward silence descends. I debate internally whether I should open up to her. Blake is the first person I've felt any real connection with for a long time. And her kind eyes and genuine interest make me want to confess things I've never told anyone.

But I can't because I know how she'll look at me—with pity. And I don't need anyone's pity. My parents and sister died when I was eight in a car crash, and somehow, I survived it, but it doesn't take away from who I am.

"No worries, I just don't talk about it." I clear my throat. "Are your family close?"

Blake hesitates, swirling the wine in her glass. "It's complicated," she finally says.

"How so?"

She sighs. "Well, my dad is a top surgeon back in Atlanta. He's the head of cardiothoracic surgery at Emory University Hospital. My mom is a surgeon, too. She specializes in neurology."

"Impressive," I say. "They must be thrilled to have a daughter following in their footsteps."

Blake gives a hollow laugh. "Thrilled might be stretching it. They've always valued achievement above all else. I'm expected to be the best, to carry on the family legacy."

"And your brother?" I ask. "Does he feel that pressure, too?"

"He's the golden child," Blake says bitterly. "He went to Harvard Medical School just like my dad and is already a hotshot cardiothoracic surgeon. My parents adore him."

I reach across the table, taking her hand. "I'm sorry, that must be difficult."

She nods. "They've never thought I was good enough

despite everything I've accomplished. And they remind me that I wouldn't have gotten this far without their connections."

"That's unfair," I say. "You've worked hard and earned your achievements."

"Try telling them that," Blake says with a sad smile.

"Well, you've got a bright future ahead of you," I tell her. "You're about to graduate medical school."

"And my father has secured me a position as a psychiatrist at Emory University Hospital," she confirms. "Just like he planned for me years ago. I don't know if it's what I want, though." She laughs. "Although none of that matters now, does it? I'm your captive."

"What do you want to do?" I ask intently.

Blake looks into my eyes. "I'm still figuring that out."

I give her hand a gentle squeeze. "I don't want to stand in the way of your studies." The idea of letting her go terrifies me. I'm still not sold on the idea. "Maybe you can transfer to a university here in Mexico."

"Maybe," she breathes. "Or you can let me go like we discussed, and I'll return to Brown."

My heart aches at the idea. I've fallen deeply and irrevocably in love with this remarkable woman during our time together.

I know what I need to do as much as it pains me. If I hope to win Blake's heart, I need to set her free. The problem is, I don't know how to let go.

"It's a lovely evening. How about a dip in the hot tub on the lower deck?" I suggest changing the subject.

"Sure, why not?" she says.

I lead the way down the stairs to the spacious hot tub area. Soft jazz music plays over the speakers, setting the scene. I turn on the jets in the tub, and Blake walks to the edge and slowly slips off her sundress, revealing a sexy black bikini beneath. It was torture not fucking her last night, but I sensed she needed me to back off a touch.

I swallow hard, peeling off my shirt and shorts and getting in naked. Blake's eyes are drawn to my semi-hard cock, making it leak as I sink beneath the water. I sit on one side, Blake on the other. The tension between us is palpable.

"This is nice," Blake says.

"It's relaxing," I agree.

I need her close more than anything.

"Come sit on my lap," I demand.

Blake gives me a hesitant look, her blue eyes searching my face. Slowly, she rises from her spot across from me and steps through the swirling water. I hold my breath, pulse-quickening in anticipation.

Blake straddles me, placing her hands on my chest. "Like this, sir?"

Fuck. The way she looks at me, so innocent and yet so seductive, sends a jolt of desire straight to my groin. I pull her closer, my hands sliding down to grip her hips.

"Perfect," I growl, my eyes locked on hers. And then I grab a fistful of her hair and yank her lips to mine. My tongue thrusts in and out as if trying to fuck her with it, and she moans, clawing at me.

And then she reaches down to stroke my cock, moaning as she slides her hand up and down my shaft. "Do you want it?" I ask.

"Yes, sir," she murmurs, grinding against me, her hips moving in rhythm. The feel of her hot, wet cunt through her biking bottoms pressing against my cock drives me mad with lust.

"Fuck, baby," I growl. "You're going to make me lose control."

Blake leans in, her lips brushing my ear. "Then lose control. I want you to."

I don't need to be told twice. I stand up, Blake's legs wrapped around my waist, and carry her out of the water to the nearby chaise lounge. I lay her down gently, hovering over her.

"You're so beautiful," I murmur, trailing kisses down her neck. "I'm going to fuck you so hard that everyone on this boat will hear your scream." I undo the ties of her bikini bottoms and toss them aside.

Blake arches into me, her nails raking down my chest.

I kiss her deeply while I slowly push my cock inside her. We both groan at the sensation, our bodies joining as one. I start to move, my thrusts slow and deep.

Blake meets me stroke for stroke, her hips undulating in perfect sync with mine as I fuck her into the chaise lounge beneath her.

"Gaston," Blake moans, her voice thick with desire. "You feel so good."

I pick up the pace, pounding into her harder and faster.

Blake wraps her legs tightly around my waist, pulling me in deeper.

"That's it, baby," I growl. "Take it all."

Blake's eyes flutter closed, her head thrown back in ecstasy. Her back arches to take me deeper with each stroke. I trail kisses along her neck, savoring her soft skin and the sweet sounds of her pleasure.

"Gaston," she breathes, her nails raking down my back. "I need more."

I growl possessively, gripping her hips to fuck her harder.

Blake cries out, her body trembling while she clings to me. I can feel her inner muscles fluttering, her orgasm building. I slow the pace, determined to draw this out.

"Not yet," I command, pulling my cock from her.

She whimpers in protest, but I silence her with a bruising kiss.

When I finally slam back inside her, she's shaking with need. "Please, I need to come," she begs.

"Not until I say so." I capture one of her nipples between my teeth, tugging gently. "You belong to me, remember? I control when you get to come."

Blake moans, grinding against me with desperation. I slip a hand between us, finding her swollen clit and rubbing it in torturously slow circles.

"Gaston, please!" she pleads. "I can't...I need..."

"Shh," I soothe, kissing her deeply. "I've got you, mi amor. Come for me." With a few more well-placed strokes, I push her over the edge. Blake's back arches as she comes undone, her walls clenching around me in delicious spasms.

When the last tremors of her climax have subsided, I pull out of her and lift her in my arms. "I've got something special planned for tonight, beautiful. Let's take this to the bedroom."

"What've you got planned?" she asks, her blue eyes searching mine.

I chuckle. "If I told you, it wouldn't be a surprise now, would it?"

She pouts playfully. "Not even a little hint?"

"Let's just say it's something I think you'll enjoy."

"Hmm, you've got me intrigued now," Blake says.

"Good, that's the idea."

I kick the door to our bedroom shut and carry her to the bed. Placing her down on the soft bedding, I smile. "Tell me, beautiful. Has a man ever popped your anal cherry?"

She gasps at the question, eyes flashing and thighs clenching. "No."

I gaze into Blake's eyes, my hands caressing her soft skin. "Would you like me to be the first?"

Her breath hitches, and I can feel the tension radiating from her body. "I don't know," she stammers.

I tighten my grip on her hips, pulling her closer. "Because ever since I saw it, I've wanted to fuck that tight little asshole of yours. I want to lick it, finger it, and then when you're begging for it, slide my thick cock inside.

You'd feel so full, so used. And you'd love every second of it, my dirty little slut."

Blake bites her lip, arching her back. Slowly, she nods.

"Good girl," I praise, kissing her neck. "On all fours for me."

Blake whimpers, flipping over and baring her tight virgin asshole to me. I dip the tip of my finger inside, eliciting a sharp gasp.

"So tight," I groan, circling her puckered entrance. "You're going to take me so well, aren't you?"

I probe the tight ring of muscles with my tongue. Before long, Blake is moaning and pushing back against it, seeking more. Reaching over to the nightstand, I grab a bottle of lube and squirt some on her before working my finger inside slowly, steadily, feeling her muscles gradually start to yield.

Slowly, I add another finger and then another until she slams her hips back against my four fingers. "Fuck, your ass looks beautiful being stretched." When I feel her body has sufficiently adjusted, I withdraw my finger and stroke my ridiculously hard cock. "Are you ready?"

Blake glances over her shoulder at me and nods shakily, her eyes wide. "Yes, sir."

Squirting more lube into her stretched hole, and on my cock, I position it at her gaping entrance. Gripping her hips firmly, I press forward, inch by agonizing inch.

Blake's breath hitches, her body tensing. "That's it, good girl," I croon, loving how her tight muscles cling to me. "You're doing so well." Inch by inch, I slip deeper.

She's clutching the comforter beneath her and whimpering beautifully, her back arched. At the same time, I stretch her ass around my cock for the first time.

"Gaston," Blake gasps, her voice thick with emotion.

I feel my balls resting against her clit once I'm all the way inside. "How does it feel to have my cock filling your virgin ass?"

She trembles, glancing at me over her shoulder. "Like heaven."

I take a moment to let Blake adjust to the sensation, stroking her back soothingly. "That's my good girl. You're doing so well."

I move, slowly withdrawing before pushing back in. Before long, I can't help but pick up the pace, pounding into her tight ass with deep, relentless strokes.

"Gaston!" Blake cries my name, her voice a mix of pain and pleasure. "It feels so..."

I cut her off with a sharp slap to her asscheeks. "So what? Tell me how it feels."

"Intense!" she gasps. "So full, I can't..."

I lean down, my chest pressed against her back. "You can, mi amor. Take it all." I punctuate my words with a particularly hard thrust.

Before long, she's moaning and panting. "Oh God!"

"That's it, call for your God. Because that's me, now." I spank her firm ass cheeks, groaning as I watch my thick cock get swallowed by her greedy ass. She clings to me like she never wants me to leave, and God damn it, I don't ever want to.

I pull out of her gaping ass, making her whimper in protest. Quickly, I flip her onto her back and then slide all the way back in, making her cry out at the new position, which allows me to drive even deeper. "That's it, baby. Let me fuck that ass the way it deserves to be fucked."

She claws her fingers into my hair and pulls my lips to hers, kissing me hungrily. At this moment, I can pretend that she loves me, too. That, despite everything, she can fall for a monster like me. That's all I really want.

The bed squeaks loudly beneath while my pace quickens. I lean into her ear, my hot breath fanning her neck. "You like that, don't you? My big, thick cock stretches your tight little asshole. You were made for this, weren't you?"

"Gaston!" she screams, her body tensing. I know what's coming and quicken my pace. I feel her ass muscles clamp around my cock as she orgasms hard. "Oh God!" she sobs. Her body shudders uncontrollably underneath me.

I lean down and capture one of her nipples in my mouth, sucking hard. With a final thrust, I come deep inside her, my entire body shuddering with the force. I groan into her breast. "Fucking hell, Blake. Take my cum in that perfect little ass."

The intensity of my climax is insane. I fall onto her, kissing her neck and pumping my hips as I breed her ass. Claim it as mine. Once I've spent every drop, I pull out of her, my cock still hard and aching for her, but I need to let her rest. Reluctantly, I grab an anal plug from the nightstand and oil it up, preparing it to take the place of my cock inside her.

I spread her legs and slip the plug in, filling the void left by my cock. "You'll sleep with that in so that my cum stays in your ass, okay?"

Her gaze is sleepy and satiated as she nods. "Yes, sir."

I'm about to slip out of the bed to clean up, but she grabs my hand to stop me. Her blue eyes beg me. "Stay a moment."

My stomach flips, and I know I can't refuse. Climbing onto the bed, I pull Blake into my lap and hold her close. She buries her face in my chest. I tighten my grip on her, knowing we're both falling too deep into this. She wants me to let her go, but how can I when she's all I want?

I'll fight for her and love her until the end of time.

Getting under the sheets with her cradled against me, I drift asleep, dreaming of a future where she's mine, forever, our love unbreakable, our bond indestructible. And for now, that's enough. Even though deep down, I know I have to let her go.

23

BLAKE

*W*e've only been back one day from our vacation, but I feel suffocated here. Gaston sits beside me on the sofa in his plush penthouse apartment. The brief taste of independence has left me longing for more.

Our vacation only made my feelings more confusing. Gaston has this way with words. He's a charmer, that's for sure. Our connection has deepened and I find myself craving his touch, his affection.

Just as I'm about to break the silence, the shrill ring of the house phone shatters it. Gaston's brow furrows slightly, but he rises to answer it.

I watch him intently, trying to discern clues from his expression or body language. Is it business-related? A call from one of his associates? Or something more personal? My mind races with the possibilities because that phone hasn't rang since I've been here.

Gaston's features shift, hardening into an unreadable mask. I hold my breath, waiting for him to return and share whatever news he's received.

Finally, Gaston turns and makes his way back to the sofa.

"Who was that?" I ask.

Gaston's jaw clenches. "A guest in the lobby. He'll be up in a moment." There's an odd tension surrounding him.

"Oh, a friend of yours?"

He shakes his head. "Not exactly."

My brow furrows as his once easy demeanor is completely shifted. I bounce my foot up and down, eager to meet this 'guest' he speaks of.

My heart leaps into my throat when the elevator dings and the doors slide open. There stands Taren and Alice. "Alice! What are you doing here?"

Gaston glares at me. "Quiet, beautiful."

My jaw clenches, and I fall silent.

"They're here to save you, aren't you?" Gaston asks, looking between Taren and Alice.

Save me. Of course, the pact we made.

Taren walks toward us with Alice by his side. "Is there anything I can give you to encourage you to part with your purchase?"

A weird twisting sensation ignites in my gut. Do I even want to be saved anymore?

Gaston rubs his jaw. "What do you think, beautiful?" he asks, looking at me. "Do you want to leave?"

Indecisions slam into me the moment I gaze into those gray eyes I've come to adore. And yet, I know I must leave and take this opportunity if he'll allow it because it was true what I told him on the yacht. I can't love him, not unless I'm free.

I lean toward him. "If I say yes, will you tell me I can't go, anyway?" I murmur. "Because if this is a genuine question, then yes, I want to go."

Gaston's eyes flood with an anguish that takes my breath away. He straightens, still holding my gaze. "You can go, beautiful." Gaston's eyes remain fixed as if begging me to change my mind.

The moment I stand and his hand drops from my thigh, I grieve the loss of his warm touch. An ache ignites in my chest, but it doesn't matter. He bought me. I can't stay of my own free will, not after everything.

I turn and look back at Gaston, my heart pounding in my chest. This is what I wanted, isn't it? To be free from his control, to return to my old life. So why does the thought of leaving him behind fill me with such sadness?

Gazing into his stormy gray eyes, I see a raw vulnerability that catches me off guard. The usual confident, domineering facade has crumbled, revealing the man beneath—a man who cares for me.

"Thank you for letting me go," I murmur, my voice thick with emotion.

Gaston remains silent, his expression unreadable, but I can sense his turmoil. I want to reach out, to comfort him, but I can't. This is the moment I've been longing for, the chance to reclaim my freedom.

Turning away, I force myself to walk toward Alice, my steps heavy with indecision. I can feel Gaston's eyes burning into my back, willing me to stay. But I know I have to go for my own sanity.

When I reach Alice, she wraps me in a tight hug, her relief palpable. "Oh, Blake, I'm so glad you're okay," she whispers.

I nod, my gaze drifting back to Gaston. He stands there, unmoving, his hands clenched at his sides. I want to run to him, to throw myself into his arms and beg him to come with me. But I know that's not possible after everything that's happened. Instead, I get into the elevator and ride it down to the bottom with Alice and Taren, wondering why he's here. The man who 'trained' us.

When we get to the sidewalk outside of Elysium, we're stopped by a chauffeur. "Mr. Marques has arranged for me to take you to the airport."

"Why?" Taren asks.

The chauffeur's jaw clenches. "Mr. Marques doesn't explain himself to me."

"Because I'm coming with you," a deep, velvet voice says, sending heat through me. Part of me is relieved to hear it, and another part is horrified.

Taren turns to Gaston. "What the fuck?"

I step closer to him. "What do you mean you're coming? I thought you said—"

"I'll win you over back in your country. Where you feel

most comfortable." There's a flicker of darkness in his eyes. "I love a challenge, as you know, baby girl." He tilts his head. "Not to mention, you look pretty torn over parting with me anyway."

Alice shakes her head. "She's upset because of the trauma you put her through!"

Gaston ignores her. "Is that what she said?"

"She doesn't need to," Alice says.

"You coming wasn't the deal," Taren points out.

Gaston smirks. "I didn't make any deal. I merely said Blake is free to go, and she is, but I'm going too."

"You're unbelievable," I growl.

His smirk widens. "I know." And then he gets into the back of the limo, looking at us expectantly.

Alice shakes her head. "Can't we ignore him and go in a taxi?"

Gaston clears his throat. "Do it. I dare you. See what happens."

"You better not be threatening my girl," Taren growls.

Gaston's smirk grows and around people, I see that darkness resurfacing. "I knew you had a thing for the gringa when I was looking at them. I must admit, I was tempted to mess with you and buy her." He shrugs. "But I couldn't resist my beautiful angel. Get in," Gaston demands.

We all exchange glances before reluctantly getting into the car with him. I try to sit as far away from him as possible, but he grabs my wrist and forces me next to him. He firmly grips my thigh. "Don't worry, beautiful. I had no intention of really letting you go. You're too damn addictive."

"And you're a cocky asshole," I reply.

"A cocky asshole who owns you." Gaston's grip tightens on my thigh.

I swallow hard, not breaking his gaze. "I don't belong to anyone since you just let me go."

He chuckles, his pale gray eyes gleaming under the dim light. "We shall see."

And just like that, all the irritation and anger toward him returns. He's so cocky it's infuriating.

The moment we pull away from the curb, the reality of my situation begins to sink in. I'm finally free from Gaston's control, no longer trapped in his lavish prison. Yet despite my regained freedom, I can't deny the thrill that courses through me, knowing he intends to pursue me back home.

While his cocky arrogance infuriates me, I know it masks his true feelings. Our time together has shown me glimpses of the man behind the beast. I know he cares for me. And now, the tables have turned. For once, I'll have the upper hand on my home turf.

Gaston's hand remains on my thigh for the entire drive to the airport. I don't bother trying to remove it. Let him grasp and grope while he still can. Soon I'll be back among familiar streets, my friends, my life at Brown. Back where I belong.

Gaston may be powerful, but he doesn't intimidate me. I won't be controlled or dominated, not anymore. If he wants me, he'll have to earn it. And I intend to make him work for it.

Perhaps I shouldn't indulge these dangerous thoughts. I should focus on recovery and healing from my ordeal. But I can't deny the tantalizing thrill of the chase, of having Gaston's singular focus fixed upon me. Let him try to seduce me on my turf. I'm more than ready for that challenge.

Gaston leans in, his breath hot against my ear. "You won't escape me easily, beautiful. I'll have you begging again for me soon enough."

I turn and fix him with a defiant stare. "Careful, Gaston. Don't make promises you can't keep."

His eyes blaze with lustful intent. Good. Let him burn for me. I'll stoke those flames, leaving him smoldering in frustration, a victim of his desires.

This time, I'm the one in control. And I intend to savor every minute of it.

24

GASTON

"Damien, I'm not going to argue about this. I'm in the States for as long as I need to be and that's final," I reiterate firmly into the phone.

I can practically hear Damien fuming on the other end of the line. "Have you lost your mind? You've just been on vacation and been back one day. And now you've taken off without warning and have no idea when you're back. The board is going to riot when they find out. What the hell is going on?"

I pinch the bridge of my nose, already exhausted by this conversation. "I've got some personal affairs to attend to. That's all you need to know."

"Personal affairs? What could be so important that you'd leave everything behind in Mexico?" Damien demands.

I hesitate, unsure how much to reveal. While I trust

Damien, this situation with Blake is complicated. The less he knows, the better.

"It's confidential," I respond. "I've got something I need to take care of here. I can't discuss it."

Damien sighs heavily. "You know I can't keep the board at bay forever. They're going to want answers."

"Just tell them it's a family emergency. I had to leave immediately." It's vague enough to give me some cover for now.

"I hope you know what you're doing, Gaston," Damien says warily. "This isn't like you to take off so suddenly. Does this have something to do with that girl?"

I stiffen. Damien is too damn perceptive sometimes. "Like I said, it's confidential. Don't ask questions you don't want the answers to."

"Fine, have it your way. But you better get this sorted quickly. I can only hold off the board for so long before they start moving to oust you as CEO," Damien warns.

"I understand. Just do what you can, and I'll be back as soon as possible," I confirm. "I've got to go now. I'll be in touch soon."

Before Damien can object further, I end the call. I know he'll have a hundred more questions, but I don't have time for them now.

Blake glares at me, sitting in the seat opposite. Lifting my whiskey, I raise my glass to her. "To America," I toast.

Taren and Alice are on the other side of the plane, looking uncertain. I notice them cast glances over and talk in hushed voices now and then.

"How exactly is this going to work?" Blake asks arms crossed over her chest.

I take a slow sip of my whiskey, contemplating how to respond. Blake is back to her fiery-as-ever self, her blue eyes flashing with defiance. It's one of the things I admire most about her. She's a fighter.

"It's quite simple," I begin. "I intend to properly court you here in America. Flowers, romantic dates, the whole nine yards."

Blake scoffs. "You must be joking. You think you can swoop in and pretend to be Prince Charming after everything?"

I set my glass down and lean toward her, meeting her gaze directly. "I understand your hesitation. But I'm quite serious. I want to prove to you how deeply I care. I want you to choose me of your own free will, not because I've forced you into submission."

Blake scoffs, shaking her head. "So you're just going to live in America for as long as it takes? And what happens if I never feel that way."

I smirk. "You will, that I don't doubt. And I'm in it for the long haul, however long it takes."

"If your phone call was anything to go by, it doesn't sound like you can leave Mexico for the long haul," she goads.

I stare out the jet's window, watching the clouds drift below us. I know it won't be easy. Blake's as stubborn as a mule and has plenty of reasons to despise me, but I cannot back down from a challenge.

"I don't know what kind of fantasy you're living in if you think you can just sweep me off my feet now," she says.

I meet her gaze. "I don't expect it to happen quickly. But I'm a patient man. And persistent."

She rolls her eyes. "Right. Because buying me from captivity in Mexico was just the first step in your grand romantic plan."

I sigh. "Why don't we start over?" I suggest. "Pretend we're meeting for the first time."

Blake looks incredulous. "Seriously?"

"Humor me," I say with a small smile, extending my hand to her.

She's silent for a moment, then extends her hand tentatively. "Blake."

I take it in mine. "Gaston. A pleasure."

We shake.

"See? Not so bad," I say lightly.

The corner of Blake's mouth quirks up into an almost smile.

Progress.

I decide not to press further for now. Baby steps. We have a long flight ahead of us. Blake stands and walks over to Alice, whispering something to her. They both get up and head toward the back of the plane, likely to use the restroom.

Every instinct in me wants to follow them, to keep Blake within my sight. But I know I need to give her space if I ever hope to gain her trust. So I refrain, taking a sip of whiskey instead.

A moment later, Taren comes over and sits down opposite me. I brace myself for whatever is coming next.

"What made you so soft, Marques?" he asks. "The great and powerful Gaston Marques, chasing after a woman across borders like a love-sick fool."

I take a slow breath, keeping my voice even. "I wouldn't exactly call it 'soft,'" I reply. "More like tenacious in achieving my goals."

Taren snorts. "Call it what you want. But I've never seen you act this way over a woman. She must really have her claws in you deep."

My jaw tightens. "Careful, Taren. That's dangerous talk."

He holds up his hands. "No offense meant. Just an observation. We've known each other a while, no?"

I nod slowly. Taren has been by Illeana's side for years, and I've gotten to know him. "People change," I say with a shrug. "What matters to us shifts."

Taren appraises me for a moment. "Just don't lose yourself chasing this girl. She won't make you happy, not really. A man like you gets bored quickly."

I meet his gaze evenly. "I appreciate the concern, but I know what I want."

Taren stands. "Fair enough. Never thought I'd see the day when Gaston Marques fell for a girl."

I clear my throat before he walks away. "Heard you cut

the head off the snake. Congrats." Illeana's death was the talk of the city. No one was upset she was gone.

Taren's expression darkens at the mention of his former boss. "Yes, I finally put that snake in the ground where she belongs," he says bitterly. "Should have done it years ago and saved myself a lot of misery."

He pauses as if debating how much to say. I wait patiently, sipping my whiskey. His hands clench into fists briefly before he forces them to relax. "The things she made me do over the years..."

"The past is done," I say quietly. "Nothing changes what she did. But her reign of terror is over now."

Taren nods slowly. "For that, I'm grateful." He glances toward the back of the plane where Alice and Blake disappeared earlier. "Maybe now there's a chance for something better ahead. If we choose to take it."

I follow his gaze, thinking of Blake. "Yes. Perhaps there is."

We remain silent momentarily, two monsters contemplating redemption, or at least the closest we may ever come to it.

The moment ends when Blake and Alice reappear. But the glimpse of humanity I've seen in Taren lingers, and I find myself hoping, despite everything, that he's right. Even beasts like us can find some small piece of light ahead if we dare to seek it.

He returns to his seat, leaving me to my thoughts again. I know Taren means well in his own warped way.

But he's wrong about Blake. She's not just another conquest to me; I intend to prove it, no matter what it takes.

25

BLAKE

*a*s I walk through our apartment door, Kali and Luna rush over and pull me into a tight group hug. We hold each other close, the three of us clinging to each other.

"I missed you so much!" Kali says, squeezing me tight.

"Me too!" Luna chimes in. "We were so worried about you."

That's when Alice enters and joins in. Now, all four of us are here, reunited at last.

I feel tears pricking at my eyes as we stand there, wrapped in each other's arms—my three best friends, whom I was terrified I might never see again. We stay huddled together for a long moment, breathing each other in.

Finally, we separate, and I get a good look at them, assuring myself they're here and okay.

We all have tears in our eyes. So much pain and fear is

behind us now, but also so much joy at being together again.

"I can't believe we all made it through that," Kali says.

Luna nods, wiping at her eyes. "I never thought we'd see Blake again."

"Me either," Alice whispers. She looks pale and drawn like the experience took a heavy toll on her.

I feel a swell of emotion rising in my chest. We endured so much, but we survived. We're together again.

Then the door opens again, and Taren walks in. We all fall silent, tensing instinctively at the sight of him. But before I can react, Gaston follows behind, strolling into my apartment like he owns the place.

Kali and Luna glance between Gaston and me, confusion etched on their faces.

"What the hell is he doing here?" Kali asks bluntly.

I let out a weary sigh. How can I even begin to explain this mess?

"It's complicated," I say evasively. I'm not ready to get into the twisted details of my relationship with Gaston. Not now, when I've just been reunited with my best friends.

Gaston smirks at me.

I avoid looking in his direction, unsure what kind of game he thinks he's playing by coming here, but I want no part. After everything he put me through, how can he possibly think he can just waltz into my life and try to win my affections?

One thing is for sure, I'm done being under his control.

Kali and Luna look at me expectantly, but I smile and pull them both in for another hug. "It doesn't matter," I say firmly. "He's leaving now. Let's just focus on the four of us being together again."

Gaston opens his mouth like he wants to protest, but I silence him with a glare. Whatever twisted game he's playing, I won't let him interfere with this long-awaited reunion. He has no power over me or my friends.

And to my surprise, he nods in response and turns away. I watch him walk toward the door, looking back over his shoulder at me one last time. "I'll see you soon, Blake," he says with a sly wink before disappearing from the apartment.

I let out a breath I didn't realize I was holding. Having Gaston here, even briefly, put me on edge.

"Good riddance," Kali mutters once he's gone. She puts a protective arm around me. "Let's have a seat."

I sink down onto the couch, my three best friends surrounding me. Kali and Luna squeeze in on either side while Alice settles into the armchair across from us.

"I can't believe you're really here," I say, my voice thick with emotion. "I was so scared I'd never see any of you again."

Luna reaches over and gives my hand a gentle squeeze. "We were terrified too. But Taren... he saved us."

I glance over at Taren, who's busying himself in the kitchen. "Taren?" The name feels foreign on my tongue. The last time I saw him, he was one of our captors.

Alice nods. "He helped us escape. He promised to help me save you, too."

I furrow my brow, trying to make sense of it all. "But why? After everything he's done..."

Kali sighs. "It's a long story. But the short version is, he's in love with Alice." She shoots a teasing grin at her.

Alice blushes and takes a sip of her coffee. "He's been trying to protect us in his own twisted way."

I shake my head in disbelief. "I can't believe this." My gaze drifts back to Taren, and I study him carefully. There's a tension in his shoulders, a haunted look in his eyes. Whatever he's been through, it's clearly taken a toll.

"It's a lot to process, I know," Luna says gently. "But he really did save us. Without him, we wouldn't be here right now."

I nod slowly, my mind racing. So much has happened since we were torn apart. I feel like I'm barely catching up.

"And what about you?" Kali asks, her voice laced with concern. "What happened with Gaston?"

I suck in a shaky breath. "It's... complicated." I don't even know where to begin. The whirlwind of emotions I've felt, the way Gaston has managed to burrow his way under my skin—it's all so overwhelming.

"We're here for you, Blake," Alice says, leaning forward in her chair. "Whatever happens, we're not going anywhere."

I look around at my three best friends, feeling a lump rise in my throat. Somehow, against all odds, we're all alive.

"Thank you," I whisper, my voice trembling. "I don't know what I'd do without you.

Kali wraps an arm around me, pulling me into a tight hug. "You'll never have to find out again. I'm sorry you got split from us."

I melt into her embrace, letting the comfort of my friends wash over me. For the first time in weeks, I feel safe. Whatever lies ahead, I know I don't have to face it alone.

"There's something else," Luna says.

"What is it?" I ask.

Kali shuffles next to me uncomfortably.

Luna clears her throat. "Matias and Thiago are here in Providence."

I stiffen at the mention of Matias. The man who took advantage of me in those cells. "What? Why?"

"Taren has assumed control of the Navarro Cartel, and Thiago and Matias are helping oversee the operations Stateside," Alice says.

"Great," I say.

"That's not all... I'm dating Thiago, and Kali is seeing Matias," Luna says.

I can't believe what I'm hearing. Kali and Luna are dating Matias and Thiago? The very same men who tormented us during our captivity? My stomach churns at the thought.

"How can you be with them?" I ask, my voice laced with disbelief. "After everything they did?"

Kali shifts uncomfortably on the couch. "I know, it's... complicated."

"Complicated?" I scoff. "Kali, those guys are psychopaths! They get off on hurting people."

Luna places a hand on my arm, her eyes pleading. "Blake, please try to understand. Thiago is not like his brother. He's been good to me."

I shake my head vehemently. "Good to you? Luna, he's the one who—" I stop myself, the memory of Thiago forcing himself on Luna that day seared into my mind.

Kali bites her lip. "Matias... he's been different since we got out. He's trying to make amends."

"Make amends?" I practically shout. "How could he make up for what he did to us?" The memory of that man dragging me into a cell at night will forever haunt me.

The room falls silent, the tension palpable. I can feel Taren's eyes on me from the kitchen, but I refuse to look in his direction.

Finally, Kali speaks again, her voice barely above a whisper. "He protected me. And looked after me."

My heart sinks as the implication of her words hits me. "Kali, what did he do to you?"

She shakes her head quickly. "No, it's not like that. He kept me safe in his own way."

I want to scream, to shake some sense into her. Because I know he took her to that cell at night, too. How can she possibly defend him after what he's done? But one look at her face tells me she's already struggling with this herself.

"I'm sorry," I say, my voice softening. "I just can't understand how you can be with him after everything."

Kali reaches over and takes my hand, giving it a gentle squeeze. "I know. Believe me, I'm still trying to figure it out myself."

I want to argue, to tell her she's being naive. But the pain and conflict in her eyes stops me. This can't be easy for her, and I can't talk when I'm confused over Gaston.

"I just want you to be safe," I murmur. "All of you."

Kali nods, a small smile tugging at the corners of her mouth. "We are. I promise."

I wish I could believe her. But the memories of Matias' cruel hands on my body, the way he took pleasure in my pain, they haunt me. How can I ever trust him to treat my friend right?

BLAKE

I take a deep breath, approaching the dean's office. I've been summoned to explain myself since I missed the first few weeks of my senior year of college.

My hand shakes slightly as I stop in front of the door. I have no idea what I'm going to say or how I'm going to explain my absence, but I don't have a choice if I want any chance of staying in school.

Knocking on the door, I await the reply of the dean.

"Come in," He calls.

I open the door and freeze. Sitting across from Dean Richardson with a glass of fucking whiskey is Gaston. The reason I missed the first few weeks of school. His gray eyes meet mine, and there's a flash of dark triumph in them that makes my blood boil.

"Ah, Ms. Carter. Just in time," the dean says, smiling,

oblivious to the undercurrent of tension between me and the man opposite him. "Please come and sit. I believe you know Mr. Marques?"

I nod mutely, wondering what kind of story Gaston has spun about how we know each other. Sinking into the chair next to Gaston, I wait for the dean to speak.

What the hell is he playing at.

"I was telling the dean, Blake, you had a bit of a vacation from hell after losing your passport, but you sure as hell made up for it doing psyche evals for some of my staff."

I stare at Gaston in disbelief while he spins an elaborate tale to explain my absence to the dean. Lost passport? Psyche evals for his staff? It's complete fiction that surely no one would believe.

"I'm so sorry to hear about your passport troubles, Ms. Carter," the dean says, shaking his head. "It sounds like you've been through quite an ordeal these past few weeks."

He's not buying this shit, surely?

I open my mouth, but no words come out. What can I say? No, that's not what happened; the charismatic and charming man next to me actually purchased me from the cartel and then proceeded to hold me captive.

Likely story.

The dean checks his watch. "Well, I appreciate you both coming to explain the situation. I'm willing to make an exception so you can resume your studies, Ms. Carter. But I expect you to meet with your advisor to get caught up on missed work."

"Yes, of course," I manage to say. "Thank you, I really appreciate it."

Gaston stands and buttons his suit jacket. "Wonderful. Well, I should be going. But Blake, please don't hesitate to call." He hands me a business card. I take it without looking at him.

"Thanks again for your help, Mr. Marques," the dean says as he escorts Gaston out.

And then I'm alone, sitting in shocked silence. I glance down at the business card: Gaston Marques, CEO. Once the shock wears off, I also stand and walk out of the dean's office.

Gaston still keeps me trapped despite thinking I'd escaped his grasp. Somehow, he has this power over people, even in the States. Forcing my mind away from him now is as good a time to visit my advisor's office and start catching up on the coursework I've missed.

Glancing around the corridor, I make sure there's no sign of Gaston before turning left and walking toward the advisor's office. Only a few moments later, I sense him. "Wait a minute, Blake."

I freeze at the sound of his deep, husky voice. And when I whirl around, he's standing right behind me. "What do you want?"

He smirks at me. "A thank you would be a good place to start."

"I don't have time for this," I say through gritted teeth. "I have to see my advisor."

I try to step around him, but he sidesteps, blocking my path. "That's no way to thank someone who helped you."

"Thank you?" I scoff. "You call spinning a ridiculous story to cover for me 'helping'? I never asked for your help."

"But you needed it," he says. "Admit it, you'd be in serious trouble if it wasn't for me swooping in to save the day."

"The only reason I was in trouble in the first place was because of you," I shoot back. "Now get out of my way."

I try to push past him again, but he grabs my hips and yanks me against his warm, hard body. Instantly, I'm on fire. My body floods with an electric current while I gaze into those cold, gray eyes. "I may have let you go, Blake, but you know I don't like being talked to that way." He brushes the hair from my neck and kisses me softly. "I miss you in my bed, beautiful." The feel of his lips on my neck drives me crazy, and I arch toward him, knowing I've missed his touch too, despite myself.

Part of me wants to melt into his embrace, claw at and kiss him. But it's ridiculous. He can't just do this. Waltz into my life and expect me to fall in line for him. Using all my willpower, I push him away.

Gaston doesn't try to keep hold of me, allowing me to step back. "Stay away from me," I say, my voice shaky. "I don't want anything to do with you."

"I'm afraid that's not possible, beautiful. Getting you to fall in love with me requires proximity, doesn't it?" He steps toward me again.

I hold up my hand, stopping him in his tracks. Fall in love with him? He really is crazy if he thinks that's going to happen. "I told you to stay away. I want nothing to do with you, not after everything you've put me through."

He steps closer, a flash of challenge in his eyes. "Come on, Blake. We both know that's not true." He takes another step toward me. "You can't deny what's between us. I felt it on that yacht, and I know you did, too."

My cheeks get hot at the memory, and I clench my thighs. A movement that Gaston instantly notices as he smirks, stepping even closer and grabbing me for the second time.

"Admit it, baby girl," he purrs into my ear. "You can't help but get turned on when I'm around. And all those times you gave yourself to me, you fucking loved it."

It's true, but it means nothing. "So what? Sex is just sex. It means nothing."

He growls softly. "It means everything. And you better not go near another man on this campus unless you want him dead at my hands," he hisses, making my heart skip a beat. "I took your anal virginity. And I wish I'd taken your pussy for the first time too, but if any man goes fucking near you." He shakes his head, anger sparking in his irises

"You're insane," I breathe.

"Just remember how good it felt when I fucked you all those times." He kisses my neck. "How good it felt when I slammed into your ass for the first time."

His words affect me too much, and I need to get away.

So, I do something out of character. I slap him sharply, skin meeting skin, echoing in the empty hallway.

Gaston's eyes flash dangerously. For a moment, I think he might retaliate. But he simply rubs his cheek where I struck him, an amused smile on his lips. "Feisty as ever. I do love that fire in you." His voice drops to a silky purr. "Just imagine how incredible we could be together if you finally embraced us."

A dark part of me wants to relent, but I shake my head. "That's never going to happen," I say coldly. "Now get out of my way."

Gaston searches my face to ascertain whether I really mean it. After a moment, he steps back, smoothing down the fabric of his suit jacket.

"Very well. I'll leave you be for now." He smiles. "But this isn't over. I always get what I want in the end."

With that ominous promise hanging in the air, he turns on his heel and strides away down the hall. I watch him go, my heart pounding against my ribs. I've got no doubt he'll be back to torment me again soon. But I know I can't let him get to me. I won't be his plaything again, not willingly, because what does that say about me?

Taking a deep breath, I turn and continue to meet with my advisor, trying to focus on getting my life back on track. But my thoughts keep straying back to Gaston and his dark, addictive presence.

If he keeps trying to reel me back into his web of control, I know I won't be able to resist forever. I can only hope I'll be strong enough to withstand him when he returns to pursue me again. Because deep down, I know he will. And deep down, there's a part of me that doesn't want to resist. A part of me that wants to free fall into the darkness with him.

BLAKE

*A*n irritated sigh escapes me when I open the apartment door and find another extravagant flower bouquet on the welcome mat.

Since returning from Mexico, these flower arrangements have appeared on my doorstep daily. He seems convinced that throwing flowers and expensive gifts at me will win me over, but it's having the opposite effect. I don't want fancy flowers or jewelry—I want him to leave me alone.

I scoop up the roses more forcefully than necessary, the thorns scratching my fingers. A stupid man can't take a hint. Storming into the kitchen, I chuck the bouquet in the trash with a satisfying thud, not caring that the crystal vase shatters.

The nerve of him, acting like I'm some commodity to be bought again. I'm not interested in his bribes. No amount of flowers or jewelry will make me change my mind.

"Hey girl, this came for you," my roommate Luna calls out, emerging from her room. She holds out a sleek black box tied with a silky white ribbon. I don't have to guess who it's from—the fancy packaging screams Gaston.

"Ugh, just put it over there," I say with a dismissive wave. No doubt it's some gaudy piece of jewelry that costs more than my tuition. As if I'd ever wear anything that came from him.

Luna sets the box on the counter, giving me a sympathetic look. "Still trying to win you over, huh? You've got to give him points for persistence."

I roll my eyes in exasperation. "Yeah, well, he's wasting his time. I already told him I want nothing to do with him."

But even as I say the words, I feel a twinge of doubt. I know how determined Gaston can be, and a part of me misses him. That grieves the addictive feeling of being with him.

I tense up when I hear the knock, my gut telling me exactly who it is before Luna opens the door. Gaston breezes right in without waiting for an invitation, acting like he owns the place.

"Blake, I've come to ask you to dinner at La Paloma," he says smoothly, flashing me that infuriatingly handsome smile.

I scowl, crossing my arms over my chest. "I already told you I'm not interested."

Luna's eyes widen because La Paloma is one of the most exclusive places in town. I can tell she's practically drooling over the thought of their famous roasted duck entrée.

"Oh, Blake, you have to go!" she gushes, ignoring the daggers I'm staring at her. "I heard it takes months to get a reservation there!"

I shoot her a withering look. Whose side is she on anyway? Releasing an exasperated sigh, I throw my hands up in defeat. As much as I hate to admit it, the lure of La Paloma's famous cuisine is too tempting to resist. I've dreamed of eating there since I moved to Providence. And Luna has a point—scoring a reservation there is nearly impossible. Only someone like Gaston could get a table on such short notice.

"Ugh, fine," I mutter through gritted teeth, avoiding looking directly at Gaston. I can feel his eyes burning into me. Great, now he thinks he's won.

"Excellent choice, mi reina," he purrs, stepping closer and trailing a finger along my jaw.

I jerk my head away, glaring at him. "This is just for the food," I snap, slapping his hand away. "It's not a date, and it doesn't mean anything."

Gaston simply chuckles, clearly not believing me. "Of course. I'll send a car for you at 8."

He turns and strides out, no doubt feeling pleased with himself. Once the door shuts behind him, I groan and rub my temples. I already have a headache.

"What did I just get myself into?" I mutter under my breath.

Luna bounces on her toes, clasping her hands together excitedly. "Oh, who cares? You're going on a date at La Paloma!"

"It's not a date!" I argue, but Luna just giggles and dances off to my room, no doubt already digging through my closet for something for me to wear.

I flop down on the couch, cursing myself for giving in so easily. But if I'm being honest, a tiny part of me is thrilled at the thought of an evening at La Paloma. And maybe a part of me is also a little curious to see where this thing with Gaston could go.

"What kind of dress do you want to wear? La Paloma's dress code is pretty strict."

"I've got no idea!" I call back, my mind racing. "Just nothing too revealing. I don't want Gaston getting the wrong idea." What does someone even wear to a place as fancy as La Paloma? I've never been anywhere remotely close to that level of upscale. I stand and walk into my bedroom, shaking my head when I see Luna practically buried in my closet.

She finally emerges, holding the most stunning cream maxi dress I didn't even know I owned. The fabric flows in elegant gathers, and the neckline plunges slightly in a tasteful yet alluring way. I can't believe I own something so exquisite.

"Oh my god, it's perfect!" I breathe out, gingerly taking

the dress from Luna's hands to admire it. "Where on earth did I get this?"

Luna grins, clearly pleased with herself for finding it buried in my closet. "I knew you'd have something amazing for La Paloma. This dress screams elegance and class."

I carefully lay the dress on the bed, still in awe of its beauty. The fabric looks luxuriously soft, and I can't wait to wear it. I trail my fingers over the intricate beading on the straps, feeling a flutter of anticipation in my stomach at the thought of wearing this to dinner with Gaston tonight.

"I don't even remember buying this," I muse aloud. "How did I not know this was in my closet?"

Luna shrugs. "Who cares? It's going to look incredible on you."

I nod in agreement. The dress seems custom made for a place like La Paloma with its timeless glamor. I try to tamp down the excitement rising in me at the thought of Gaston seeing me in this dress, but I can't deny I'm looking forward to the look on his face.

"Alright, I guess I better start getting ready then," I say, gathering the dress carefully.

Luna grins and gives me an encouraging push toward the bathroom. "Go take a bubble bath and relax. I'll do your hair and makeup before the car gets here."

As much as I hate to admit it, a part of me is curious to see what the evening has in store. Wearing a dress this beautiful, it's bound to be a night to remember. Whether that's a good thing or not remains to be seen.

GASTON

*G*lancing at my watch for the tenth time in as many minutes, I tap my foot impatiently against the marble floor and sip the wine I ordered. The din of laughter and clinking glasses fades into the background while I scan the entryway for any sign of Blake.

I insisted on arriving early to ensure everything was in order, but now I regret that decision. Each minute that I'm left waiting only increases my agitation.

Checking my appearance in the mirror again, I adjust my bow tie and smooth back an errant lock of hair. I look impeccable in my tailored Armani tuxedo, but I want to be perfect for her. This night needs to be flawless.

The maître d' approaches me with an ingratiating smile. "Your table is ready whenever you and your guest are ready, Mr. Marques," he says with a small bow.

I nod curtly and wave him away. I've no time for idle pleasantries right now.

Where could she be? Did she change her mind? I clench my jaw while unwelcome scenarios flood my thoughts. No, she agreed to come. She has to show up. Failure isn't an option tonight.

A flash of cream in my periphery pulls me from my spiraling thoughts. I see Blake gliding toward me, resplendent in the elegant maxi dress I slipped into her closet while the apartment was empty. The chatter and music fade away while I drink in the sight of her. The dress clings perfectly to every curve, the rich fabric accentuating her slim waist before flowing gracefully down her long legs. Her golden hair is swept over one shoulder, exposing the elegant line of her neck that I find myself longing to caress.

When she draws nearer I note the subtle makeup accentuating her piercing blue eyes and full lips. My pulse quickens as I imagine kissing that mouth, claiming it hungrily with my own. I have to rein in my desire when she stops before me, not wanting to frighten her away before the evening has begun.

"You look absolutely stunning tonight," I tell her sincerely.

A pretty blush stains her cheeks at the compliment. "Thank you," she says softly. "Shall we?"

I offer her my arm, which she takes. I lead her toward our table, making a mental note to call the boutique tomorrow and thank them for the dress. It was certainly money well spent.

I pull out her chair, and she sits gracefully, arranging

the skirt of her dress with care. Just after I take my seat, a waiter appears with our first course.

Blake's brow furrows.

"I selected the tasting menu for us this evening to showcase the quality of the cuisine fully," I explain.

Blake nods.

"This is a pan-seared scallop with truffle emulsion," the waiter announces as he places the dish before her with a flourish.

"It looks wonderful, thank you," she says, rewarding him with a radiant smile that irritates me. Her smiles should be for me and me alone.

The waiter retreats, and I take the opportunity to fill Blake's wine glass. "I hope you enjoy everything this evening. I want it to be a night to remember."

She meets my gaze levelly. "It certainly will be interesting," she replies cryptically before taking a bite of her scallop.

Glancing across the table at Black, I notice a soft curl has come loose from her elegant updo, and it takes all my willpower not to reach across and tuck it gently behind her ear. I want to touch her and feel her skin beneath my fingertips again. But I know one misstep could undo all my progress in getting her here with me this evening.

"Are you enjoying your meal?"

She nods, dabbing at her mouth with the linen napkin. "It's wonderful. I've never tasted scallops this fresh and perfectly cooked."

"I'm glad it meets your approval. I wanted our first

date together to be memorable." I clench my jaw, cursing myself for the slip of my tongue.

Her blue eyes flash with irritation. "This isn't a date, Gaston," she says firmly. "We're merely two acquaintances sharing a meal together."

I resist the urge to argue, inclining my head. "Of course. My mistake."

She looks a little surprised that I don't argue, and an awkward silence settles between us while I scramble for something to say to break the tension. Our waiter chooses that moment to arrive with the next course, providing a temporary distraction.

"The scallop was delicious, thank you," Blake says with another polite smile. I feel that irrational flare of jealousy again at her friendly tone.

The waiter removes our plates and presents the second course—a beautifully arranged medley of quail and root vegetables.

"This looks so good," Blake says appreciatively.

"Only the best for you," I reply, hoping the earlier awkwardness is forgotten. I lift my wine glass. "To new beginnings?"

She appraises me for a long moment before lifting her own glass with the barest hint of a smile. "To new beginnings," she agrees before taking a sip.

The sound of crystal chiming musically together settles my nerves. The evening is still young and ripe with potential. I simply need to mind my words and continue showing Blake I'm worthy of her trust. I'll make her see that I'm serious about us. That I can give her the life she deserves.

"How are you enjoying being back at Brown?" I ask, eager to learn more about this part of Blake's life. "Your studies must keep you busy."

Blake pauses a forkful of quail halfway to her mouth. She sets it down gently, dabbing at her lips with the linen napkin before responding.

"It's been an adjustment, getting back into the swing of classes and assignments after..." she trails off, leaving unspoken words between us. After being held captive by a ruthless drug cartel and then sold to me as my personal plaything.

"But yes, my coursework has provided a welcome distraction," she continues briskly, eager to move past any mention of what happened. "I'd forgotten how demanding the psychology program is. Late nights spent writing research papers, brutal exams, group projects with useless partners."

"I don't miss those days," I admit. "Though I suppose the long hours spent in board meetings and poring over earnings reports are their own particular brand of torture."

It's the closest I've come to openly complaining about my role as CEO, and Blake looks at me curiously.

"I can't even imagine the stress and pressure that comes with running a multi-billion dollar company," she says. "Do you enjoy it?"

Our conversations, save a couple, have largely centered

around my single-minded pursuit of her. It's refreshing to be seen as more than just a ruthless predator fixated on making her submit.

"It's challenging work, but yes, I enjoyed building the company from the ground up," I tell her honestly. "But there are certainly downsides, long hours, public scrutiny, Machiavellian corporate politics." I take a sip of wine. "Tell me more about your studies. What first sparked your interest in psychology?"

Blake is now disarmed by our conversation, and she describes her passion for understanding the workings of the human mind. I lean forward, genuinely caught up in her enthusiasm for what she's studying.

The restaurant fades away while we fall into an easy conversation. Our rivalry and Blake's desire to fight me is eradicated. No covert agendas, just a vibrant young woman sharing her dreams and ambitions with a man increasingly captivated by her mind and spirit, not just her physical beauty.

Blake might think I'm a monster, but I've been viewing her as more than a possession for a while now. She's a true and equal partner for me. Something I never thought I'd want, but now I've glimpsed a view of what life with her could be like, it's all I can think about.

29

BLAKE

*S*itting across from Gaston tonight, that desire for him all over again has reignited. I knew this was a bad idea.

Thanks a lot, Luna.

If it hadn't been for her encouragement, I never would've agreed to dinner tonight.

The waiter walks away after Gaston pays the bill, and I don't even want to think about how much it cost. "Did you enjoy the food?" Gaston asks.

"It was delicious. Thank you." I smile at him genuinely and see that desire flash in his eyes.

"You're welcome, mi reina."

Why do I get goosebumps whenever he calls me his queen? It makes me feel special. Something being around Gaston shouldn't make me feel.

"Are you ready to leave?"

I'm conflicted. A part of me wants this night to

continue as long as possible, but it can't. I can't let myself get swept up in the fantasy of us.

"Yes, let's leave." I grab my clutch from the table and stand.

Gaston stands too and walks to my side, placing a hand softly on the small of my back. Wordlessly, he guides me out of the restaurant and onto the sidewalk. The cool night air prickles against my heated skin, forcing me to wrap my arms around myself.

Gaston's sleek black town car is already parked out front, the chauffeur waiting by the door.

"Thank you for dinner. It was lovely. But I should really get home."

Gaston frowns, looking almost hurt. "Please, allow me to drive you home. You don't have a ride, and It's late."

I should refuse and keep my distance like I vowed to do. But before I can think better of it, I'm sliding onto the smooth leather seat. Gaston climbs in after me, and the driver pulls away from the curb.

Sitting inches from Gaston in the dimly lit backseat, the air feels charged. I'm hyper-aware of his thigh just barely grazing mine. The memories of him fucking me flood my mind, and I have to force myself to look away from him.

I can feel his eyes on me while I stare out the window, watching the city lights stream by in a blur. My heart is racing. I should ask the driver to stop and let me out on the street before I do something I regret. But something keeps me rooted in place.

When I look back at Gaston, his eyes make me shiver. It's a gaze of pure hunger and desire. The same look he gave me the first night he brought me back to his penthouse after purchasing me from Ileana.

I grip my clutch tightly in my lap while he leans in.

"Blake, may I kiss you?" he asks softly.

I'm so startled by the request I can't find my voice at first. Gaston has never asked permission for anything when it comes to my body. He takes what he wants when he wants.

Tonight has already felt like some sort of dream. And now, after too much wine, I find myself tempted.

I give a slight nod, and Gaston closes the distance between us. His lips meet mine, and a jolt of electricity courses through me. The kiss deepens, his tongue sliding against my own. My head spins from the wine, the intimacy, and my conflicted desires.

Gaston's hand comes up to cradle my jaw as he kisses me. It's frightening how quickly my body responds to his touch, my skin tingling, my heart racing. Before I can stop myself, I'm grasping at his hair, pulling him closer.

I've never felt more intoxicated than in this moment. I claw through Gaston's slicked-back locks, messing up his normally perfect style. He matches my passion with his own.

In one swift movement, I maneuver myself onto his lap, my dress riding up my thighs. I feel his hard cock even through the fabric separating us. Gaston grips my hips tightly as I grind down against him. His hands slide lower to grasp my backside, and I let out a soft moan against his lips.

This is madness. I should stop this before it goes any further. But coherent thoughts are drowned out by pure desire and the heat of his body against mine.

My hands move to loosen his tie, needing to feel his skin against mine. Gaston breaks the kiss, staring at me through lust-filled eyes.

"I've missed this," he growls, his fingers digging into my hips. "Having you in my arms, feeling your body against mine."

I don't trust myself to speak. Being this close to Gaston again plays tricks on my mind. Instead of answering, I crush my lips to his, kissing him hungrily.

The kiss deepens, becoming more urgent and primal. I grind my hips down against the hard cock in his pants, eliciting a low groan from his throat.

Gaston's hands slide lower to grip my ass, rocking me harder against his dick. I gasp at the sensation, heat flooding my core. What am I doing? This man bought me, controlled me, and treated me like an object. I shouldn't crave his touch no matter how desperately my body wants him.

My hands claw at his shirt, fumbling with the buttons in my need to feel his bare chest pressed against me. Gaston shifts beneath me, maneuvering me onto my back along the leather seat. He hovers over me, trailing rough kisses down my throat and across my exposed cleavage. I arch into him, clutching at his broad shoulders.

"We shouldn't..." I gasp as my fingers weave into his hair, pulling him closer. Gaston silences me with another searing kiss, and I surrender, wrapping my legs around his waist.

The town car hits a bump in the road, and I'm jolted against Gaston's muscular frame. His cock presses between my thighs, making me moan at the friction.

Gaston's hand slips beneath the hem of my dress, fingers dancing up the sensitive skin of my inner thigh. I shiver in anticipation, my body crying out for more.

The car hits another bump, jostling us against the leather seat. Gaston's hand slides higher, fingers brushing the damp lace of my panties. I gasp at the contact, hips rocking against his hand.

"Gaston, we can't—" I try to protest, even as my body betrays me, craving his touch.

He silences me with a bruising kiss again, swallowing my words. His fingers dip beneath the lace, stroking me with practiced ease. I whimper against his mouth, back arching.

"You feel so good, mi reina," Gaston murmurs, his voice thick with desire. "I've missed this."

He presses a finger inside me, and I shudder, clinging to him. My hips move of their own accord. I should stop this because I'm only setting myself up for heartbreak. But the wine has made me reckless, my inhibitions lowered.

Gaston's thumb finds my swollen clit, circling it in maddening strokes. Sparks of pleasure ignite within me, coiling tighter with each pass of his fingers.

"Gaston…" I moan, my voice barely above a whisper.

"That's it, cariña," he purrs, his breath hot against my ear. "Let go for me."

I'm teetering on the edge, my body thrumming with need. Just a little more, and I'll—

The car suddenly stops, and Gaston withdraws his hand, leaving me aching and frustrated. I blink at him, chest heaving.

"We're here," he murmurs.

We break apart, breathing heavily. Gaston's eyes are dark with lust as he stares at me.

"I should head in," I murmur, shifting past him and grabbing the handle to let myself out of the car.

Once on the sidewalk, I turn around to find Gaston has slipped out with me. He places a hand on my hip, pulling me against him. "Thank you for a wonderful evening," he murmurs, lips trailing down my neck. "Goodnight, beautiful, sweet dreams." With that, he slides back into the back of the car.

I watch the car disappear, still reeling from what transpired between us. I walk toward the building on shaky legs, my lips still swollen from his kisses. While I glance back to see the taillights disappear into the night, I know I've only sunk deeper into Gaston's intricate web. And the most terrifying part is, some secret part of me doesn't want to escape him.

30

GASTON

*I*t's been one week since I had Blake writhing beneath me in the back of that car—one torturous week since she slipped from my grasp and I allowed her.

I've been reduced to stalking her, watching my prize from afar because, after that night, she closed off and refused to let me get close. And it's driving me crazy.

Every day I send her flowers, a dozen red roses delivered to her door. And every day, without fail, I watch on the hidden cameras as she angrily grabs the bouquet and tosses it straight into the trash. She doesn't even stop to smell them.

Blake is feistier than any woman I've ever known and more stubborn. She has a fighter's spirit, one that refuses to break, refuses to submit. In many ways, she reminds me of myself. I've met my match in her, the one person unwilling to bend to my will.

Perhaps that only makes me want her more. There's an allure to the chase, to the challenge she presents. She is a prize worth fighting for, worth earning.

I watch Blake while she exits the university, golden hair spilling over her shoulders. She has a natural beauty about her, effortless and free. Her eyes, though, look tired, haunted almost. Is it possible she longs for me the way I ache for her? Could it be my absence pains her as much as it pains me?

My fingers curl around the steering wheel, knuckles white. I want nothing more than to go to her, to pull her into my arms and breathe in her sweet scent. To feel her soft skin under my fingertips, her lips crushed against mine. I could overpower her if I wished, but that would only push her further away.

Blake pauses on the sidewalk, glancing around warily. She knows I'm always watching, always nearby. I wonder if she feels my presence. Her shoulders straighten with determination, and she continues on her way.

My phone buzzes, and I glance down to see a text from Damien. The board is growing impatient, questioning my extended absence. I ignore it. Blake is my sole focus. I'll make her see that she belongs with me, that we're destined to be together. All other matters are secondary. I can only watch and wait for her resistance to crack.

Blake enters a small cafe on the corner she frequents nearly every day. She looks comfortable there, familiar with the baristas who greet her. I know I shouldn't follow her inside and keep my distance as she requested, but it's been one week since I've heard her voice and been close enough to catch her scent—one week too long.

Before I can stop myself, I'm out of the car and crossing the street, the little bell above the door announcing my arrival. Blake stands in line, back toward me, posture rigid as if she can sense my presence already.

I clear my throat and step up behind her. "Hello, Blake."

She stiffens, shoulders tensing, but doesn't turn around. I wait, resisting the urge to reach out and run my fingers through her golden waves. Finally, she faces me, blue eyes flashing.

"What are you doing here?" Her tone is sharp, but I detect a slight quiver. She's affected by my nearness.

I offer a disarming smile. "Getting a coffee, same as you. Thought we could sit and have a chat."

Her eyes narrow. "I've got nothing to say to you."

"I thought we had a good time at dinner. Why the cold shoulder?"

Her eyes flash and she opens her mouth only to shut it again. The barista calls Blake's name, sliding her usual chai latte and lemon pound cake across the counter. She grabs them hastily, brushing past me toward the door. I snag her elbow before she can flee, leaning in close.

"Please, just give me five minutes. Let me buy you lunch." My voice drops lower. "Don't run away again, baby girl."

Blake inhales sharply at the term of endearment, the one I would whisper in her ear while I fucked her. Heat flares in those aquamarine irises before she wrenches out of my grasp.

"Leave. Me. Alone." Each word is bitten off, venomous. Then she's gone, the tinkling bell signaling her exit.

I stand frozen, hands clenched. So close, and yet so far. Standing in line at the cafe, I'm still reeling from my encounter with Blake. Her rejection stings, but it also makes me want her even more. While I wait to order, my phone rings in my pocket. I glance down to see it's Damien. With a sigh, I answer.

"What is it, Damien?"

"Gaston, we need to talk. The board threatens to replace you as CEO if you don't return to Mexico today. I've done what I can, but they're serious this time."

I rub my temple, irritation flaring. The board has been hounding me nonstop since I came to the States.

"I'll return when I'm ready," I state firmly. "Blake and I still have unfinished business."

Damien sighs heavily. "Gaston, be reasonable. You know how volatile the board can be. If you lose your position as CEO, you'll have far less sway over company matters. Is one woman really worth all this?"

I open my mouth to argue but then pause. Damien has a point. Some distance from Blake would be beneficial for us both. If I return to Mexico for a week or two and occupy myself with work, it'll make her see what she's missing. My absence could very well make her heart grow fonder.

"Fine," I concede. "Make arrangements for the jet to

bring me back this evening. But I won't stay away from the States long."

"Of course. At least temporarily, I'm sure the board will be placated with your presence."

I end the call while the barista takes my order. I collect my coffee, considering the possibilities. This involuntary separation could work in my favor. By the time I return, Blake may be craving my touch the way I ache for hers.

A little space is all we need to stoke the fires of passion. Blake can deny it all she wants, but I know she misses me as much as I miss her. The way she kissed me in the back of that car was proof enough.

31

BLAKE

I sit in the crowded university cafeteria, half listening to my friends' chatter about classes and campus gossip. My mind keeps drifting back to Gaston and our last interaction at the coffee shop. I haven't seen or heard from him in over a week, which is strange, considering he used to be practically omnipresent.

Is it possible he's finally listened and decided to leave me alone?

I stare down at my uneaten salad, pushing around the lettuce leaves absentmindedly.

Why do I even care where he is or what he's up to?

I should be relieved that he has gotten the message to leave me alone.

"Earth to Blake!" Kali laughs, waving her hand in front of my face. "You in there?"

I blink, looking up at my friends surrounding me at the

table. "Sorry, just spaced out for a second," I say with an apologetic smile.

"Thinking about Mr. Tall, Dark, and Dangerous again?" Alice asks knowingly, raising an eyebrow.

I roll my eyes but can't stop the heat rising in my cheeks. "No, of course not. Gaston's an asshole."

"Uh-huh, sure," Kali says. "That's why you've been staring into space this lunch period."

I sigh, knowing there's no point hiding anything from them. They know me too well. "I find it weird that he's suddenly nowhere to be found after being practically obsessed with me."

Luna shakes her head. "Who cares? You should be happy you finally ditched that creep."

"I know, I know," I say. "It's just strange, that's all."

In truth, I'm worried something might have happened to him. As twisted as it was, he claimed he cared about me in his own way. And despite everything, there was a connection between us.

"Maybe he finally got the message and decided to leave you alone," Alice suggests.

Gaston doesn't strike me as the type to give up so easily. I take a bite of my salad, trying to ignore the unease. I shift uncomfortably in my seat while Kali fixes me with a knowing look.

"What?" I ask defensively.

"Do you have feelings for him?" she questions, eyes searching mine.

"What? No!" I scoff, shaking my head. "Of course not. He's a monster who bought me. I hate him."

Kali continues to stare at me, clearly unconvinced. "I wouldn't blame you." She runs a hand across the back of her neck. "My relationship with Matias is complicated, too."

Alice and Luna glance between us curiously. Matias is a true psychopath, and Kali still seeing him is fucking wrong on so many levels. But I don't think any of us can really understand what our experience did to us mentally.

And Luna seems to be completely wrapped up in Thiago, the other brother, who, while not as bad, is still an immoral piece of shit who 'trained' many women before us in horrific ways.

"I'm serious," I insist, avoiding their gazes. "Gaston is cruel and controlling. I want nothing to do with him."

But even as the words leave my mouth, I know they're a lie deep down. There's always been an undeniable connection between us, some dark magnetism. But I pushed him away not only because of the face he bought me like a slave but because he scares me. His power over me has nothing to do with his purchase of me.

I shake my head. "I don't have feelings for him," I repeat firmly. "He's in my past now. I never want to see him again."

My friends look unconvinced but don't push me further. The conversation moves on to talk about an upcoming party. I try to listen, but despite my best efforts, my mind keeps drifting back to Gaston.

"I've got to get going to my psychology class," I announce, standing and shouldering my bag. "I'll see you guys later back at the apartment."

"See you later," Luna says, waving.

Kali nods while Alice gives me a small smile. Walking out of the cafeteria, I'm grateful for the reprieve. The conversation about Gaston has left me feeling unsettled.

I breathe in the fresh air while I walk across the sunny quad toward the social sciences building, enjoying the moment of solitude. My mind feels cluttered lately in a way it hasn't felt since I was off my meds.

Entering the lecture hall, I sit near the middle, setting my backpack on the floor. Students continue to file in as I take out my notebook, ready to focus on the lecture and give my brain a break from its relentless analysis of Gaston.

Just then, an attractive guy with tousled brown hair and warm brown eyes slides into the seat next to mine, flashing me a grin. Before my ordeal, he was the kind of guy who would have caught my eye.

"Hey there, I don't think we've met before. I'm Liam," he says, extending his hand.

I return his smile, shaking his hand. "Blake. Nice to meet you." I tuck a strand of hair behind my ear as Liam smiles at me, his brown eyes twinkling.

"So, Blake, what's your major?" he asks.

"Psychology," I reply. "What about you?"

"Business," he says. "Not nearly as interesting as the human mind, if you ask me."

I let out a small laugh. "Psychology has always fascinated me. Trying to understand people's motivations and behaviors."

Liam nods. "I can see the appeal in that. You must be really intuitive."

"I like to think so," I say with a grin.

"I'll have to be on my best behavior then, or else you'll be analyzing my every move," he jokes.

I chuckle. "Don't worry, I only psychoanalyze with consent."

Liam leans in. "Well, feel free to analyze me anytime."

I feel my cheeks heat at his flirtatious tone. Liam seems nice, and I'd probably be into him under different circumstances. But I can't help comparing his boyish flirtation to Gaston's smoldering confidence. When I meet Liam's friendly gaze, I feel nothing. It contrasts with the fire Gaston ignites in me whenever he looks at me.

"What made you decide to take this class?" I ask, steering the conversation to safer waters.

"I needed another elective credit," Liam explains. "And psychology seemed way more interesting than statistics or geology."

I nod in agreement. "Good call. I think you'll find it fascinating, even as a non-major."

"With you as my classmate, I'm sure I will," he says with a wink.

Before I can respond, the professor calls the class's attention and begins his lecture. I focus on my notebook, jotting down notes and pushing thoughts of Liam's flirtation from my mind.

After class ends, Liam turns toward me. "Are you going to the frat party tonight at Alpha Phi Alpha?" he asks."You should stop by with your friends. I'd love to see you there."

"Maybe I'll have to see what they're up to," I reply noncommittally.

Liam smiles again. "Well, I hope to see you later, Blake."

I nod, gathering my things and heading out of the lecture hall. While Liam seems nice, I know I'm not interested in him. I am too preoccupied with a dark, dangerous man to consider him. But, a party might be the thing to keep my mind off Gaston Marques.

When I get to the apartment, Luna and Kali are already there. Alice has a late class, so she won't return for another hour. "Hey, have you heard about this party at Alpha Phi Alpha?"

They turn to me, brows furrowed. "No, did someone invite you?" Luna asks.

"Yeah, this guy Liam from my psych class asked if I was going," I explain, setting my backpack on the kitchen counter. "He seemed really into me and said I should stop by with my friends."

Luna's eyes light up. "Ooh a frat party, that could be fun! We haven't gone out since we got back."

Kali nods eagerly. "I'm so down! We need a girls' night out. Are you into this Liam guy, though? Don't want him getting the wrong idea."

I roll my eyes as I grab a soda from the fridge. "Don't

worry, he's harmless. Just a normal college guy looking to party. Not really my type anyway."

"Uh-huh, so you're not into the whole clean-cut, boy-next-door thing anymore?" Kali teases.

"Stop," I retort, feeling my cheeks flush. "This has nothing to do with him. I'm just not interested in Liam."

"Mhm, sure," Luna says sarcastically. "So tall, dark, and psychotic is still on your mind then?"

I glare at her over my soda can. "Absolutely not. I already told you I want nothing to do with him."

Kali and Luna exchange a look that makes it clear they don't believe me.

"Anyway," I continue, "are we going to this party tonight?"

"I'm so down!" Kali says excitedly. "We need to get dressed up. I call dibs on the bathroom first!"

She darts off down the hall toward the bathroom.

Luna chuckles and shakes her head. "I'm excited too. We could all use a carefree night out. We'll have to convince Alice to untangle herself from Taren for one night. Those two are fucking inseparable."

I nod in agreement. A night out is exactly what I need to get my mind off of certain things. Things I definitely should not be thinking about anyway.

"Ooh, let's pregame a little!" Luna suggests, heading to the liquor cabinet. "Shots?"

"Yes, please!" I say enthusiastically. The slight buzz will help me relax.

Luna pours out two shots of vodka and passes one to me. "Cheers to a girls' night out," she says.

We clink our glasses together and throw back the shots. The alcohol burns going down but immediately starts to warm my veins.

Yeah, a night out dancing and letting loose with my best friends is exactly what I need. No more thinking about intense gray eyes and strong, commanding hands. I just want to have fun like a normal college girl again.

Luna pulls me in for a hug. "We're gonna have the best time tonight!"

I grin and hug her back. "Let's party!"

Kali emerges from the bathroom, already dressed. "Come on, bitches! Let's get you all dressed up too. Tonight is gonna be wild!"

We head to my bedroom giggling, ready for a carefree girls' night. I push away any lingering dark thoughts, determined to enjoy myself and stop over-analyzing everything. The party awaits. Time to forget about the sociopath who has taken up residence in my brain.

GASTON

*T*he jet's wheels finally hit the tarmac, and I let out a deep sigh of relief. This past week in Mexico has been nothing short of torture without Blake. Though I needed to get the board off my back, each day dragged on endlessly. I longed to be close to her again.

Now, while the plane taxis toward the terminal, I feel anticipation in my chest. Soon, I'll be reunited with my precious girl once again. I've missed her, and being away has only intensified my craving.

I need to feel her soft skin under my hands and hear those sharp intakes of breath whenever I caress that sensitive spot on her neck. The desire to pin her down and take her repeatedly until she's a whimpering, shaking mess beneath me is overwhelming.

The plane stops and I gather my belongings, eager to get through customs and to my car. The drive to her apartment can't go fast enough, and each red light is pure agony. All I can think about is throwing open her door, pulling her into my arms, and crushing my mouth against hers.

When I finally pull up outside her building, I have to take a moment to collect myself before going up. I need to remain in control. Smoothing my shirt, I run a hand through my hair and head inside.

My heart pounds while I ride the elevator to her floor. I knock sharply on her door, barely able to contain my smile. I am still waiting for someone to answer the door, irritating me.

Where is she? It's nine o'clock at night.

Standing in the hallway contemplating my next move, a preppy-looking guy walks by. "Hey, man. Are you looking for the girls from this apartment?"

I grind my teeth. "Yes, I'm looking for Blake."

"I saw them heading out about thirty minutes ago, all dressed up. They were heading to the frat party at Alpha Phi Alpha."

"Thanks," I reply, clenching my jaw in annoyance. A frat party? She's supposed to be torn over me, not out living it up with her friends. I've tried to be patient and give her space, but clearly, it's not working.

The thought of other men ogling her at some party without me there to protect her drives me insane. I turn on my heel and head for the elevator, my mind racing. And then I head straight toward the frat house. Once there, I storm inside, scanning the crowded rooms for any sign of my Blake. The pulse of shitty pop music pounds in my ears while I push through throngs of drunk college kids.

Where is she?

There—a flash of blonde hair. I glimpse her in the kitchen, chatting with her friends. She's wearing a tight black dress that hugs every curve, her hair cascading down her bare shoulders. I knew I should've kept her on a shorter leash.

I watch Blake from the shadows, keeping my eyes locked on her while she laughs and drinks with her friends. As frustrating as it is to see her out like this, I've got to admit she looks stunning. The way that dress clings to her body, accentuating every curve, is maddening.

I shouldn't have let things go this far. I never should have left her alone after bringing her back from Mexico. I thought giving her space would make her miss me.

My hands curl into fists when I see some frat boy sidling up next to her. He's practically undressing her with his eyes, and now he dares to put his hand on her lower back? Fuck no. That's crossing the line. She's mine, and it's about time I remind her of that fact.

Before I even realize what I'm doing, I'm striding across the room toward them. The crowd seems to part for me while I zero in on my target. Grabbing the kid by the shoulder, I spin him around to face me. He stumbles a bit, eyes widening.

"Get your hands off her," I snarl through gritted teeth.

The kid looks utterly terrified. He glances at Blake with confusion.

"S-sorry man, I didn't know she was with someone," he stammers.

I pin him with the coldest, most threatening glare I can muster. "Now you do. So I suggest you turn around and walk away before this gets ugly."

The kid practically trips over himself, scrambling away from us. Good. Now, to deal with Blake.

She whirls around, eyes wide. "Gaston? What the hell are you doing here?"

I give her my most charming smile. "I wanted to see you, of course." I pull Blake close and grab her hips. "I thought you'd be happy to see me, baby girl."

She meets my gaze, her cheeks flushed from alcohol. "I thought you were done with me. That you were finally going to leave me alone."

I tighten my grip on her waist, savoring the feel of her body against mine. "Done with you? Impossible. I've missed you every single day since I left." My hand drifts down to the curve of her backside, and I can't resist giving it a gentle squeeze. "You've been all I can think about."

Blake's breath catches, and I see a flash of longing in her eyes for a moment. "You need to go, Gaston."

I tsk softly, drawing her back in. "You don't mean that, mi reina. I think you missed me too." My fingers trace the delicate line of her jaw, making her shiver. "You missed the fire and the passion."

She bites her lip, her resolve wavering. I can see the conflict warring within her, the desire battling against the resentment. Slowly, she relaxes into my embrace, her arms sliding around my neck.

"I did," she whispers, her voice barely audible over the music.

A thrill runs through me at her admission. Leaning in, I nuzzle the soft skin of her neck, reveling in her familiar scent. "Then stop fighting this. Stop denying what's between us."

I pull Blake closer and sway her to the music. Her nearness intoxicates me, and that familiar floral scent floods my senses. I run my hands up and down the smooth curves of her body, reacquainting myself with her shape. She doesn't resist, instead melting into my embrace. Her fingers curl into my shirt while our hips move in sync, our gazes locked.

"I've missed this," I murmur, my voice low and husky. "Having your body close to mine."

Blake parts her lips to respond, but I capture them in a searing kiss before she can speak. Her hands fist my shirt while our mouths fuse together. I kiss her hungrily, passionately, all the longing from our time apart pouring out.

My fingers tangle in her golden locks, angling her head to deepen the kiss. A soft moan escapes her, muffled against my lips. When we finally break for air, her eyes are glazed, cheeks flushed.

"Now, do you understand, mi amor?" I ask huskily. "You belong with me."

She trembles against me, breath coming fast. I know

I'm getting through to her, piercing that wall she's tried to build between us. Leaning in, I nuzzle her neck and whisper in her ear.

"Let's get out of here, baby girl. I want to be alone with you."

Blake hesitates, conflicting emotions warring in her gaze. But finally, she gives a subtle nod. Triumph surges through me. I take her hand and lead her through the crowded party, impatience rising with every step.

Soon, we'll be behind closed doors, just the two of us. And I fully intend to remind Blake of where she truly belongs tonight, beneath me with my cock inside her tight little cunt and my name tumbling from her lips.

33

BLAKE

he tension radiates between us while Gaston leads me to his car. It's a strange sensation. A mix of excitement, apprehension, and something else I can't quite put my finger on.

Climbing into the sleek, black vehicle, the air is thick with desire. I glance at Gaston, taking in his strong jawline and piercing eyes. There's a hunger there that both thrills and terrifies me.

He starts the engine and pulls out of the parking lot, his hand resting possessively on my thigh. I shiver at his touch. The ache to be close to him has finally won out tonight.

The drive to his hotel is silent, save for the engine's hum. I can feel Gaston's gaze on me periodically.

When we finally arrive, he leads me straight to the elevator, his hand never leaving my lower back. We ascend to his floor while the tension between us builds, electric and undeniable. I'm acutely aware of his proximity, the warmth of his body, the scent of his musky cologne.

The elevator doors open, and Gaston guides me down the plush hallway to his room. He unlocks the door, and I take a deep, steadying breath. This is it—I'm choosing this, choosing him, for reasons I can't quite fathom.

He ushers me inside, his gaze burning into me. I turn to face him, my heart pounding in my chest. There's a raw vulnerability in his expression that catches me off guard. Before I can overthink it, I reach up and pull him into a searing kiss.

Gaston responds immediately, his arms wrapping around me as he deepens the kiss. All my reservations fade away while I lose myself in him.

We stumble into his hotel room, lips locked. My mind is hazy, drunk on the taste and feel of him. He guides me to the king-sized bed, gently laying me down before climbing over me.

"You're the most exquisite creature I've ever met." He kisses my lips quickly. "Your beauty goes far beyond the physical because your spirit truly captivates me." He presses soft kisses on my throat, moving lower. "When I first saw you, I was transfixed. Your eyes drew me in with their spark and fire." He bites my collarbone, making me gasp. "You're a goddess. My goddess. And you deserve to be worshiped daily for the rest of your life. I want to be the man to worship you."

God damn it. How can I resist him when he says things like that?

I know I'm done for when he kisses me again. The man who purchased me hasn't only kept me captive but stole my heart in the process. Desperately, he works the zipper down on my dress and pulls the fabric from me. I'm not wearing a bra, and his eyes darken when they fix on my breasts. Slowly, he lavishes attention on each of my nipples, swirling his tongue around them. I arch into him, wanting him more than I've ever wanted anything.

Gaston's lips trail lower, leaving a path of fire in their wake. His fingers trace delicate patterns on my stomach while he plants soft kisses just below my navel. I shudder in anticipation, every nerve in my body attuned to his movements.

He removes my panties, his eyes never leaving mine. I feel exposed and vulnerable but more desired than ever. Gaston kisses the inside of my thighs, his stubble leaving pleasurable friction against my sensitive skin. My breath catches when he moves closer to my pussy.

"Please, Gaston," I beg, arching my back when he's mere inches away.

He smiles, clearly enjoying the effect he's having on me. "Please, what, baby girl?"

"Lick my pussy. I need to feel your tongue on me."

"Good girl," he purrs before stroking his tongue through my aching center. He alternates between broad strokes and flicks against my clit. Pleasure rockets through me because this man knows how to play my body like an instrument, finding every sensitive spot and exploiting it masterfully.

My fingers tangle in his hair, soft moans escaping my lips. Gaston brings me to the precipice repeatedly, only to back off and draw out the exquisite torture.

Before long, I can't take it anymore.

"Please," I gasp, my fingers digging into his shoulders.

He meets my gaze, eyes dancing with wicked delight.

"Please, what, baby girl?" His voice is like velvet as his hands continue their maddeningly slow exploration.

"I...I need..." I trail off.

Gaston chuckles. "Use your words. Tell me exactly what you need from me."

"I need to come. Please make me come."

"Mmm, that wasn't so hard now, was it?" Gaston purrs, trailing kisses down my torso. "Since you asked so nicely..."

His tongue circles my clit, making me cry out. I'm beyond words now, reduced to primal sounds of pleasure. Gaston works me steadily toward release, fingers joining in to stroke and tease.

"Come for me," he growls against my flesh. "Give yourself to me completely."

His words send me over the edge, and I come undone, shuddering violently. Gaston continues lapping me up while I ride out my climax, wringing every last tremor from my spent body.

"Such a good girl," he murmurs. "I've missed you so much."

Gaston shifts off the bed, leaving me sitting on it. I watch him remove his jacket, tossing it carelessly to the floor. His movements are slow, building anticipation with each discarded item. When his shirt comes off, my mouth waters at the sight of his perfectly chiseled chest and the dark ink covering his tanned skin. I've missed seeing him like this.

Gaston pauses a hint of a smirk playing on his lips. He kicks off his shoes and removes his belt next. I catch myself holding my breath when he pops the button on his pants, slowly lowering the zipper before discarding them on the floor along with his boxer briefs.

"Did you enjoy the strip tease?" he asks, standing there in his naked glory, his big thick cock standing upright and ready. The ache deep within becomes impossible to ignore.

"Yes, sir," I breathe.

I can't tear my eyes away from Gaston. He really is a god of a man. I find myself utterly captivated by him.

Gaston's eyes burn into me, full of hunger and possession. Slowly, he joins me on the bed, settling between my thighs.

"You're exquisite," Gaston murmurs, his breath hot against my throat. His teeth graze my skin, nipping sharply. I gasp, arching into him instinctively.

"Please," I whisper.

"Please, what?"

I meet his smoldering gaze steadily. "I need you inside me. Now."

Gaston's eyes blaze. Unable to resist any longer, he positions himself at my entrance. With one powerful stroke, he fills me completely.

I let out a low moan, my body yielding to him. This feels right. All the fighting and what for when every time he's inside me, I feel whole?

Gaston begins to move, his powerful body working above mine. His thrusts start slowly but quickly gain momentum, each hitting that sweet spot inside. I wrap my legs around him, drawing him in deeper, craving more.

"Goddamn, your cunt feels better than I remember," Gaston growls, his fingers digging into my hips painfully. I relish the sting, knowing he'll leave bruises.

He dips his head to capture one of my nipples in his mouth, and I cry out, sparks of pleasure shooting through me.

I meet his thrusts eagerly, our bodies slapping together in a primal clash. He's rough and unapologetic, slamming into me with such force it steals my breath.

Gaston hits a particularly sensitive spot, and I clench around him, nails raking down his back. He hisses, quickening his pace.

I can feel my climax building, a steady pressure that grows with each of Gaston's powerful thrusts.

"I want to feel your tight little cunt come around my cock," he rasps in my ear. "Be a good girl and come for me."

Squeezing my eyes shut, I tumble over the edge. "Oh God! Gaston!" I scream his name, white-hot and searing pleasure arcing through my veins. A flood of liquid squirts around his cock.

He grabs my throat and squeezes. "Look at me when you come," he demands.

My eyes snap open, and he continues to fuck me through it, keeping his hand around my neck like a collar. And it makes my pleasure heighten, building me toward another explosive orgasm.

"Mmm, that's it, baby girl. Let me feel every inch of your sweet pussy clenching around my cock again," Gaston growls, his grip on my throat tightening ever so slightly as he thrusts deeper. "You're such a good fucking girl."

He groans when I start to tremble beneath him again, my body on the verge of another release. "I want to see those pretty eyes roll back in your head when you come for the second time. Look at me. Look at me while I make you mine."

The Gaston I hated to love returns. All dominance and dirty talk. And fuck if I don't love every second of it. Every dirty word from his mouth.

I can barely catch my breath when Gaston's relentless pace continues. My body feels like it's on fire, every nerve ending singing with pleasure. I'm completely at his mercy, yet I've never felt more alive.

His grip on my throat tightens, just shy of cutting off my air supply, and I let out a strangled moan. The threat of danger heightens the sensations rocketing through me. I'm drowning in his scent, his touch, the sound of his ragged breathing.

"That's it, baby girl," he growls, his hips thrusting into me hard. "You're so close, aren't you? Your pussy is so wet and tight." He leans in closer, his breath hot against my ear. "I want you to come for me. Show me how much you love being my little slut."

My nails rake down his back as another earth-shattering climax rips through me. Gaston swallows my cries with a bruising kiss, his tongue plundering my mouth as ruthlessly as his cock is claiming my body. The pleasure makes me almost black out from the pleasure. "Fuck, fuck!" I cry, unable to believe how intense it is.

"Fuck, you're so goddamn tight," Gaston grunts, one hand on my hip while the other remains around my throat. "I'm going to fill you up with my cum and breed you like the little slut you are." He leans in, his teeth grazing my earlobe. "You're going to take every drop and beg for more." His words send a shiver down my spine, and I feel my pussy responding, knowing he could shatter me again, and I'm hopeless to resist.

"Fuck, yes, take it all," Gaston grunts, pumping his cum deep inside me. "Every. Last. Drop." He groans, his cock twitching as he empties himself completely.

He kisses me then, passionately and tenderly, the act so at odds with the rough fucking. And yet, it feels right. Everything about Gaston has felt right from the moment we met.

When I finally come down from the high, I'm left

feeling shattered and exposed. Gaston gazes down at me, his gray eyes burning with triumph.

"You're so beautiful like this," he murmurs, brushing a stray lock of hair from my face. "Flushed and wanton and completely at my mercy."

I want to lash out and tell him I'll never be at his mercy. But the words die on my lips as he rolls his hips, sending another jolt of pleasure through me.

"Accept it, Blake," Gaston whispers, his breath hot against my ear. "You're mine. You'll always be mine."

Gaston shifts, pulling out of me. I can't help the whimper that escapes my lips at losing that delicious fullness.

"Don't worry, my love," he murmurs. "I'm not done with you yet. Not even close."

He rolls onto his back, tugging me on top of him in one swift motion. I gasp as he fills me once more, stretching me to the brink.

"Ride me," Gaston commands, his hands gripping my hips. "Show me what a good girl you are."

And in that moment all my doubt melts away. This is where I'm supposed to be. My body joined with this man's, who has utterly claimed me, heart, body, and soul.

I move, riding his cock. Gaston releases a guttural groan, digging his fingers into my flesh.

"That's it," he praises, his voice strained. "Just like that."

I lose myself in the rhythm, in the sensation. In this moment, there's only Gaston and the delicious torture he inflicts. And the nagging voice in my mind tells me I'm falling in love with a man who doesn't deserve it.

Gaston presses kisses across my breasts while I rise and fall on his thick cock. Despite everything, we're not a captor and a captive in this moment, but simply two people falling for one another.

34

GASTON

*W*hen I wake, Blake is nestled in my arms, her golden hair cascading over the pillow. I gaze upon her peaceful, slumbering form, feeling a deep sense of triumph. Finally, she's mine, body and soul.

Yet, I know all too well that her willingness to fuck me doesn't equate to her love. That's the one thing I crave above all else. Her love. I need it like a man dying of thirst needs water. She's become my entire world, the center of my universe. The thought of existing without her is unbearable.

Carefully, I extract myself from the bed, mindful not to disturb her rest. I stand and look down at her, committing every detail to memory. The soft curve of her lips, the gentle rise and fall of her chest, the way her lashes flutter against her cheek.

Moving silently, I retrieve my robe and wrap it around myself. I need to think and plan. I cannot simply bask in this victory. No, I must find a way to truly capture her heart and make her love me as desperately as I love her.

I step out onto the balcony, taking a deep breath of the cool morning air. The city below is beginning to stir, mirroring the turmoil within me. I pace back and forth, weighing my options. Threats and domination have brought me this far, but I know that's not enough, not for her.

Returning to the bedroom, I watch her sleep for a moment longer. Then, with a deep sigh, I lean down and press a feather-light kiss to her forehead. "I'll make you love me, mi reina," I murmur. "No matter what it takes."

I watch Blake stir from her slumber, her eyelids fluttering open as consciousness returns. She looks at me, her blue eyes still clouded with sleep.

"Did you say something?" she murmurs, her voice husky.

I shake my head, stroking her hair gently. "No, mi amor. Just watching my beautiful girl sleep."

She seems to accept this, nuzzling into my hand. But then her eyes fly open wide, panic flashing across her face.

"Oh my god, what time is it?" she gasps, bolting upright. "I'm going to be late for class!"

I can't help but chuckle, watching her scramble from the bed, hurrying to gather her clothes.

"Relax," I say. "It's not as late as you think. I'll drive you to campus. We'll get you there in plenty of time."

She pauses, looking back at me uncertainly. I give her a

reassuring smile. "Trust me. I won't let you be late. Now come, I've got some clothes for you."

"Clothes?" she questions.

"Well, I'm not going to let you go to class in that sexy as fuck dress you wore last night, am I?" I tilt my head. "I brought some clothes from the penthouse back here in case you stayed the night."

She nods, following me to the closet. I pass her a pair of jeans and a pretty yet conservative blouse. I pull on my own clothes, then guide her out the door of the hotel, my hand pressed against the small of her back.

While we drive to campus, she fidgets nervously, checking the time every few minutes. I take her hand, stroking my thumb over her knuckles.

"See? No need to worry," I say when we pull up in front of campus. "Now go learn something brilliant, mi amor. I want to see you later. Can I pick you up?"

She smiles. "Yes, I'd like that." She leans over and kisses my cheek. "See you later, sir," she murmurs a seductive tone to her voice, and then she's gone, hurrying up the steps of the building.

I watch her until she disappears inside, marveling at how perfectly she fits into my life. Pulling away from the curb, a part of me already yearns to have her by my side again. This woman has become my whole world in such a short time.

My musings are interrupted by the shrill ringing of my cell phone. I glance down to see it's Damien calling. I growl under my breath before answering.

"This better be important," I snap. "I just left Mexico yesterday, Damien."

"Lo siento, jefe, but we've got a situation," Damien says, his voice tense. "There's been an accident at the construction site for the new office complex. A fire started last night, and the whole thing is condemned."

I grip the steering wheel tightly, rage boiling up inside me. This was no accident. I know exactly who's behind it— Pablo Estrada. He's trying to send me a message, attempting to interfere in my business.

"Pinche cabrón," I curse. "This wasn't a fucking accident, and we both know it. Estrada is behind this, trying to get back at me for rejecting his offer on my land."

Damien sighs. "I assumed as much. What should we do?"

I consider for a moment before responding. As much as I want to stay here with Blake, duty calls.

"I'll come back for the weekend to deal with this personally," I decide. "Have the jet ready tonight, I'll leave as soon as possible. We must send our message to Estrada —one he won't soon forget."

"Understood. I'll make the arrangements," Damien says.

I end the call, pounding my fist against the steering wheel. My anger at Estrada is at war with my longing to remain here with Blake.

Taking a deep breath, I dial Blake's number while I head back toward the hotel.

"Hello, is everything okay? My class is about to start?"

"Mi amor, change of plans," I say breezily. "I must fly back to Mexico for the weekend to deal with some business. Come with me tonight, I'll have you back in plenty of time for Monday's classes."

I hold my breath, awaiting Blake's response, hoping she agrees to accompany me back to Mexico for the weekend. I know she may be reluctant, given our complicated history, particularly since I held her captive in my penthouse. No doubt the memories give her pause.

"I don't know..." she says slowly, and I can hear the hesitation in her voice. "Mexico just brings up a lot of difficult shit for me, you know?"

I nod even though she can't see me through the phone. "I understand. But I promise it'll be different this time. I want you by my side. We can spend the weekend exploring if you want, order in your favorite foods, lounge by the pool..."

I trail off, hoping to entice her. When she doesn't respond immediately, I pull out all the stops.

"Please, Blake," I say softly. "I need you with me. I sleep better with you in my arms. And next weekend, I'll take you anywhere you want to go—Paris, Tokyo, Antigua..."

I hear her sharp intake of breath at the mention of Antigua and know I have her.

"Well, Antigua does sound nice..." she says slowly.

"It's settled then!" I declare. "I'll pick you up after your classes today and fly out tonight. Don't worry about packing. I'll have everything you need waiting in the penthouse."

"Okay," she agrees after a moment's pause. "I'll see you later."

I can't help but grind, ending the call. She's coming with me willingly. I've got her exactly where I want her. Mine, in every way that matters. This weekend in Mexico will only draw her closer to me. Another step to making her love me.

35

BLAKE

I'm rushing across campus to my next class when I practically slam into Luna. She grabs my arm to steady us both.

"Well, well, look who it is," she says with a wink.

I feel my cheeks flush with embarrassment. Of course, she noticed I never returned to the apartment after running into Gaston at the party.

"It was a late night," I mutter, avoiding eye contact.

"I bet it was!" Luna laughs. "I saw you leave the party with him, Blake. What was that all about?"

I sigh, unsure of how to even begin explaining the complicated situation with Gaston. "It's complicated," I say finally. "I don't even know where to start."

Luna loops her arm through mine as we walk across the quad together. "Just tell me the truth. Do you like him?"

I hesitate before answering quietly, "Yes. As much as I hate to admit it, I really do."

Luna nods thoughtfully. "But you feel guilty about it because of everything that happened between you two before?"

"Exactly," I reply. "He's dangerous, controlling, and morally corrupt. I should want nothing to do with him. But I can't stop thinking about him. It's like I'm addicted or something."

"Love and attraction don't always make sense," Luna says gently. "The heart wants what it wants, even when the head knows better."

I shake my head in frustration. "I hate myself for feeling this way. He's bad news, but I still have all these feelings for him."

Luna gives my arm a supportive squeeze. "Don't be so hard on yourself. You've been through a traumatic experience with him. It's normal to feel drawn back to that intensity. Just be smart and keep yourself safe." Her jaw clenches. "Believe me, I know how you feel from firsthand experience."

"Right. Thiago. How's that going?" I ask.

She sighs. "I'm hooked on him despite knowing he's dangerous and bad for me. A bit like you and Gaston, I guess?"

After everything we went through, having feelings for one of our captors seems crazy.

"I thought it was Stockholm Syndrome at first," Luna says quietly. "Being attracted to Thiago after he held us captive. But even now that we're free, I still have feelings for him."

She pauses, looking down at the ground. "We've been dating since we got back to Providence. And as much as I try to deny it, I really like him."

I nod in understanding. "I know how confusing it is. With Gaston, I feel so drawn to him, but I also know he's dangerous. It goes against all logic."

"Exactly," Luna agrees. "With Thiago, he acts all tough and menacing. But when we're alone, he's different. I see this whole other side to him."

"Gaston can be like that too," I reply. "He has this magnetic pull that I can't resist. And when we're together intimately, he makes me feel..."

I trail off, a blush rising in my cheeks. Luna smiles knowingly.

"Yeah, the sex is pretty mind-blowing, right?" she says with a laugh.

I grin sheepishly. "I mean, that's definitely part of it. But it's more than just physical attraction. I feel like he really sees me, you know? Like he understands me."

Luna nods, her expression growing serious again. "With Thiago, I feel like I can tell him anything. He listens and doesn't judge me." She bites her lip. "I don't know if it will last. But for now, it feels right being with him."

"I get it," I tell her supportively. "Just be careful. We've seen his dangerous side firsthand."

"You too," Luna says, linking her arm through mine

while walking. "I know you'll make the right choices for yourself."

I smile at her gratefully, glad I've got such an understanding friend to confide in. Our relationships may be unconventional, but the heart wants what it wants. For now, we'll just take it one day at a time and see where it leads. "I'm going with him to Mexico tonight for the weekend. He must return for a work matter, so I agreed to go with him." I glance over at Luna, noticing the concerned look on her face.

"Mexico?" she asks incredulously. "Are you sure that's a good idea? Going back where..."

Her voice trails off, but I know what she's implying. Mexico is where we got captured and where Gaston bought me from the cartel and kept me captive in his penthouse. Just thinking about it makes my stomach twist into knots.

"I know," I say with a heavy sigh. "Believe me, going back there with Gaston gives me major anxiety."

Luna reaches out and gives my hand a supportive squeeze. "Then why go back there with him?" she asks gently. "That just seems like you're asking for trouble."

"I thought the same thing at first," I admit. "But Gaston swears it'll be different. He wants me to come so we can spend time together."

Luna raises a skeptical eyebrow. "And you believe him?"

I chew my lower lip uncertainly. "I mean not completely. But I guess I want to believe him."

"Blake…" Luna says warningly.

"I know, I know," I admit. "It goes against all logic to trust Gaston. But honestly? For some crazy reason, I do."

Luna looks at me like I'm absolutely insane. Which, to be fair, is understandable.

"He bought me and held me captive," I continue. "By all accounts, I should hate his guts. But…"

"But you care for him," Luna finishes.

I nod, feeling that now familiar mix of guilt and desire. "I can't explain it. When we're together, it's like nothing else matters. The rest of the world just fades away."

Luna nods. "Just promise you'll call me if you need anything?"

"Of course," I assure her. "Don't worry, I'm going into this cautiously. Mexico brings back many bad memories, but maybe making some good new ones will help me move on."

Luna pulls me into a tight hug. As nervous as I am about returning there with Gaston, I know I'm doing what feels right in my heart. I just pray I won't end up regretting it.

36

GASTON

Tension radiates off Blake in waves while the jet soars through the skies, descending into Mexico City. Her fingers fidget with the hem of her skirt, and her eyes dart nervously out the window. I reach across the plush leather seat and gently place my hand over hers, stilling her movements.

"What's wrong, mi reina?" I ask, my voice low and soothing. "You seem uneasy. Talk to me."

Blake worries her bottom lip between her teeth, a habit I've noticed she does when she's deep in thought. "I...I don't know," she admits finally. "I guess I'm more freaked out than expected about returning to the penthouse. So much happened there, you know?"

I nod slowly, understanding. Of course, she would feel apprehensive about returning to the place where I kept her captive.

"Blake," I murmur, threading my fingers through hers

and gently squeezing her hand. "I know you were scared when I brought you there. But things are different now. You're not my captive. You're here with me of your own free will."

Her eyes meet mine, filled with a mixture of emotions. "I know. It's just confusing. All of it."

I lift her hand to my lips, kissing her knuckles softly. "I understand. But I promise you, you've got nothing to fear. The penthouse is your home now, as much as it is mine. And I'll do everything possible to ensure you feel safe and comfortable there."

Blake nods. "Okay," she murmurs. "I trust you."

The words thrill me, and I can't resist pulling her from her seat and into my arms, cradling her against my chest.

The jet begins its descent, and I tighten my hold on Blake, drawing her closer. She melts into my embrace, her head resting on my chest above my heart. I can't resist brushing a kiss across her golden hair, breathing in the sweet floral scent of her shampoo.

The plane lands, and we get up, exiting the plane hand in hand. I squeeze her hand, a subtle reassurance. The midday sun beats overhead, and Blake lifts a hand to shield her eyes.

"Welcome home, Mr. Marques," Langston greets me. I give him a brisk nod before opening the door to the waiting town car when the first shot rings out, echoing across the tarmac.

I react on instinct, grabbing Blake and shoving her down behind me and the car, using my body to shield hers.

More shots, closer now. I risk a glance around the car and see at least half a dozen armed men advancing on us. Estrada's doing, no doubt.

Smoke grenades explode nearby, enveloping us in a haze. I pull Blake tighter against me, ready to fight our way out if needed. But then I feel her being wrenched from my grasp.

"No!" I roar, lunging for her, but hands seize me, holding me back. I struggle violently, desperate to get to her. Through the smoke, I see them dragging Blake away. She's fighting, too, eyes wide with panic as she meets my gaze.

"Blake!" I bellow, throwing my elbow back and catching my captor in the nose. He curses and loosens his hold, allowing me to break free. But it's too late. Blake is gone, disappearing into the smoke and chaos.

Rage wells inside me, white-hot and visceral. Estrada will pay for this. I'll rain down hell on him for daring to lay a hand on her. And I will find Blake, no matter what it takes. I'll get her back and destroy anyone who tries to keep her from me.

I feel the adrenaline coursing through my veins when Langston shouts at me to get in the car. My every instinct screams at me to stay, fight, and get Blake back. But I know I'm outnumbered. Estrada planned this ambush perfectly. If I stay, I'll be captured or killed. And then I'd be no use to Blake at all.

Cursing under my breath, I dive into the backseat of the town car and slam the door behind me. Langston peels away from the runway with a squeal of tires. I crane my neck, trying to catch a glimpse of Blake through the rear windshield while we speed away, but the smoke has enveloped everything.

"Drive faster, damn it!" I bark at Langston, slamming my fist against the leather seat in frustration. We need to get back to the penthouse where I can regroup and figure out a plan to handle this situation.

Langston weaves expertly through traffic, pushing the powerful car to its limits. Within minutes, we're away from the airstrip and merging onto the highway headed downtown. Only once Mexico City's towering skyscrapers come into view do I allow myself to lean back against the headrest, chest heaving as I try to calm my racing heart.

I take a deep breath, trying to steady my nerves as the town car speeds through the crowded streets of Mexico City. My heart is pounding, adrenaline still coursing through my veins from the ambush. I failed to protect Blake. Estrada's men took her right out of my grasp.

With a growl of frustration, I grab my cell phone and call Damien. He answers on the first ring.

"Damien," I bark without preamble. "I need every loyal man we have, everyone who can handle themselves in a fight. Get them to my penthouse NOW. Estrada has taken Blake. I need to get her back."

"Understood. I'll take care of it."

The line goes dead and I shove the phone back in my pocket, leg bouncing nervously while I watch the city racing past. I should never have brought Blake back to

Mexico City, where my enemies could get to her. Estrada must have had people watching, waiting for the perfect opportunity to strike, and I played right into it.

Clenching my jaw, I make a silent vow to myself. I'll make Estrada suffer for daring to take her. He has no idea who he's provoked. When I'm through with him, death would seem enticing.

The car pulls up to the towering glass facade of my building. I'm striding through the lobby before Langston has even put the car into park, barely glancing at the doorman as he scrambles to open the door. The elevator can't move fast enough, whisking me to the penthouse floor. I pace the small space like a caged panther, desperate for the hunt.

When the doors slide open I'm moving again, crossing the marble foyer of my home in quick, purposeful strides.

I storm into the kitchen, rage, and adrenaline still coursing through my veins. Damien and my men gather around the table, pouring over blueprints. They look up, faces grim, as I enter.

"What do we know?" I bark.

Damien taps the blueprints. "These are all of Estrada's properties around the city. Warehouses, apartment buildings, and office spaces. If he's keeping her somewhere, it will be at one of these locations."

I nod, studying the documents. I hacked Estrada's servers weeks ago, so I'm familiar with most of his assets.

"She'll be at one of the warehouses," I say decisively.

"Somewhere secure, where he can control access. He'll want to keep her isolated."

Damien circles a cluster of warehouses down by the docks with a pen. "This would be my guess. They're isolated, lots of space, easy to defend."

One of my men, Alvaro, speaks up. "We scouted the area earlier today anyway, as we've been keeping tabs on Pablo as instructed. There's definitely unusual activity around here." He indicates a warehouse right on the waterfront. "Guards patrolling with assault rifles, lots of vehicles coming and going. It's got to be where he's keeping her."

I feel a spark of hope cut through the rage. We've already zeroed in on where Blake likely is. Now, we need to figure out how to get her out.

"Alright," I say. "Let's talk strategy. We'll need a distraction. Draw some of the guards away from the building. Then, a small team can infiltrate while they're occupied. Get in, get Blake, get out."

The men nod. I can see the anticipation on their faces. They've been waiting for an opportunity to hit back at Estrada. And none of them want to face my wrath if we fail to retrieve Blake.

For the next hour, we meticulously plan the operation. I know these men would die for me; their loyalty has been proven repeatedly for me and my company. And I know they'll stop at nothing to get Blake back safely.

By the time we finish ironing out all the details, night has fallen over the city. The perfect cover for our mission. I feel adrenaline beginning to flow again in anticipation of the action ahead.

It's time. I nod to my men. "Let's go get her."

We move out into the night, a well-oiled machine focused on a single purpose. In a few hours, Blake will be back where she belongs. And my enemy will understand why he should never provoke a beast.

37

BLAKE

This can't be happening again. Clearly, Mexico and I aren't meant to be. The second time in the country and the second time kidnapped.

One minute, I was with Gaston, feeling somewhat safe, and the next, I was being yanked away and shoved into the back of this van. The panic in Gaston's voice as they pulled me from him was absolutely terrifying. I've never heard him sound so desperate.

The van bounces so much that I can barely keep my balance. I try to peer out the windows, but it's too dark to make out anything. All I can hear is the rumble of the engine and the muffled voices of my captors up front. My heart is pounding in my chest, and I'm struggling to keep my breathing steady.

Who are these people, and what do they want?

Gaston's enemies, maybe? But how many enemies can a billionaire have? Whoever they are, I'm fucked. I don't know how I'll survive if this is anything like the first time I was captured.

Despite my hands being tied, I push myself toward the back of the van and spin around, trying the doors.

Locked.

It was worth a try. Suddenly, the van takes a sharp turn, throwing me against the wall and onto the floor. I let out a small cry of pain.

"Shut it, puta!" one of the guards calls back from the front.

Biting my lip, I lean against the side of the van, feeling totally useless. Tears prickle my eyes, but I don't let them fall. The last thing I want is to show these bastards how scared I am.

While the van careens down the dark roads, I lean into the wall to avoid being thrown about. It feels like they're driving forever until the van abruptly stops, the tires squeaking before the engine turns off.

The slam of the van's doors opening and shutting prepares me, and I coat my nerves in steel, staring at the door. This is it. Suddenly, the doors swing open, and men in balaclavas grab me and yank me out of the van before I can so much as utter a word.

"What the fuck?" I cry in protest, trying to fight.

"Stay still, bitch," one man says, forcing a thick cloth hood over my head. "And keep up."

They drag me along an uneven surface, my feet stumbling with each step. It's obvious once we've entered a building as the air changes and our footsteps echo off the walls.

Roughly, I'm yanked to a stop, and then heavy hands fall on my shoulders, pushing me down onto the cold metal of a chair. Someone wrenches my arms behind me and binds them tight with what feels like a rope. I fight against it, trying to pull my arms free.

A heavy hand comes down across my cheek, shocking me. "Keep still, puta!" a man growls.

Bastard.

My cheek throbs, telling me it'll bruise before long. Blindfolded and bound, I'm now completely at their mercy. I squeeze my eyes shut beneath the blindfold and focus on breathing. I strain to pick up any sounds or voices that might give me a clue about where I am or who's taken me. But all I can hear is the shuffling of feet and some muted voices speaking rapid Spanish.

Suddenly, heavy hands land on my shoulders, and I flinch. Only for the hood to be yanked off my head and fluorescent lights overhead to blind me. When my eyes adjust, I see we're in an empty warehouse with tall metal columns lining the perimeter.

A quick scan of the space shows no obvious exit routes or items I could use as a weapon in an escape attempt. Great. Three armed men stand around me with their faces obscured by black ski masks.

One of them steps closer, looming over me. I meet his gaze through the eye holes of his mask, acting confident.

"Who are you?" I demand, my voice echoing through the empty space. "And what do you want?"

He doesn't speak, grabs my chin, and jerks my head from side to side as though he's examining me. He releases me, turning away. And then he and the other men move to the other side of the warehouse, conversing in hushed voices.

I test the restraints binding my wrists, but they don't give at all. The men disappear out of the door, leaving me alone.

At least, that's what I believed until I heard the echo of footsteps behind me. The sound reverberates off the cold concrete walls of this cavernous warehouse. I crane my neck, trying to see who's approaching, but my view is obstructed.

The footsteps grow louder, and I feel a presence right behind me. My heart pounds against my ribs. A large hand grips my shoulder, making me flinch.

"Well, well. We meet again, mi bonita."

I freeze at the sound of that familiar voice. Pablo steps around and stands before me, an amused smile on his lips. The cartel leader who eyed me like a predator at the charity gala with Gaston. Just the sight of him sends a chill down my spine.

"What do you want?" I ask, keeping my voice steady.

"You shouldn't ask questions you don't want to know the answer to." His eyes are dark and cold as he stares at me.

I glare at him. "Why wouldn't I want the answer?"

His eyes peruse my body slowly, making me feel sick. "I can think of many things I'd want from a beautiful gringa like you."

"Dream all you want. That won't be happening."

Pablo raises an eyebrow, looking mildly impressed by my nerve. He leans in close, his breath hot against my cheek. "We'll see about that, bonita," he whispers. I recoil from him as much as my bindings will allow.

Pablo straightens up, regarding me with that predatory stare.

"Why did you take me?" I demand. "Is it some sort of revenge plot against Gaston?"

Pablo shrugs. "Something like that. See, your lover has something I want. I tried to negotiate, but he refused my offer. So you're the perfect leverage against our friend Gaston."

Shit. Agreeing to come to Mexico this weekend with Gaston has landed me in the middle of a war he's waging with the cartel.

"For the first time in his pathetic life, Marques has someone to lose," Pablo continues. "And I fully intend to exploit that weakness."

"I think you overestimate how much he values me," I lie, despite knowing Gaston will come for me. I'm sure of it. And that terrifies me more than anything else because he could die.

"I don't think so, bonita." He shakes his head.

Drawing a deep breath, I glare at him. "He'll never submit to you."

Pablo's eyes flash. In an instant, he's around the desk, grabbing me by the hair and wrenching my head back, making me yelp in pain because it feels like he's trying to pull the follicles from my scalp.

"You'd better hope he does," he hisses in my ear. "Because your life depends on it." Pablo leans close, his fingers trailing along my jaw. "But that doesn't mean we can't get to know each other better in the meantime."

I jerk my head away, shuddering with disgust because this guy is older than my father.

Pablo chuckles. "I'll be back for you soon, Blake." He says my name slowly as if savoring it. "We're going to have a lot of fun together."

Leaving that sickening promise, he turns and walks away, his footsteps echoing through the warehouse. Am I asleep and having a ridiculously realistic nightmare?

It's hard to believe that this happened to me twice. Something tells me this time will be far worse unless Gaston finds a way to save me.

38

GASTON

*a*drenaline courses through my veins as I strap on the Kevlar vest and check the ammunition in my pistol before sliding it into the holster on my thigh.

Alejandro approaches, his face etched with concern.

"Jefe, I really think you should sit this one out," he says. "Leave the rescue operation to us. We've got the tactical training for this."

I shake my head firmly. "I'm going, Alejandro. That's final."

He sighs. "It's going to be extremely dangerous. Estrada's men won't hesitate to kill you. And if something happens to you..."

"I don't care about the danger," I interrupt. "Blake is in there. I need to be the one to get her out."

Alejandro presses his lips together in a thin line. He knows better than to argue with me when my mind is made up.

"I know you care about her," he says quietly. "But Estrada took her to get to you. If he captures you too, then we've lost everything."

"He won't capture me," I say coldly. "The only thing I care about right now is getting Blake back safely. Nothing else matters."

Alejandro nods slowly. "I understand. But please be smart in there. Don't take any unnecessary risks. We can't afford to lose you."

I place my hand on his shoulder. "The only risk is leaving Blake in Estrada's hands a moment longer. Now let's move out."

Alejandro sighs again but doesn't argue further.

I slide into the passenger seat of the van. An unbelievable flood of adrenaline pounds through my veins. My men file into the back, strapping on their gear and checking their weapons one last time. I nod to Alejandro and he turns the ignition, bringing the van's engine to life.

We pull out onto the street, and I take out my phone. With a few taps, I open up the hacked security feed from inside the warehouse where Blake is.

There she is. My Blake. Tied to a chair right in the middle of the open space, directly under a dangling light. Even with her head slumped down, I'd recognize her anywhere.

Seeing her like that, restrained and helpless, makes my blood boil. I clench my jaw so hard it hurts. Estrada will pay for putting his filthy hands on her.

I zoom in on the camera, examining Blake closely. She

looks unharmed, except for some bruising around her wrists from the ropes. Small blessings. As long as she hasn't been violated, Estrada still has a chance to come out of this breathing.

Blake stirs, lifting her head. The light glints off her blonde hair, and I'm struck by a surge of possessive rage.

Alejandro glances over, noticing my white-knuckled grip on the phone. "We'll get her out safely."

I nod, unable to tear my eyes from the screen.

The van rounds a corner and the warehouse comes into view up ahead. My heart pounds wildly in my chest.

Hold on, mi amor. I'm coming for you.

Once parked, we slip out into the shadows and approach. I grip the handle of my silenced pistol tightly while Alejandro and Miguel lead us toward the warehouse's side entrance. We stick to the shadows, moving closer.

Two guards stand smoking outside the warehouse. Miguel gives the hand signal to freeze, and we blend into the darkness. In perfect sync, they clamp their hands over the guards' mouths and slit their throats smoothly. The only sound is the soft thump of the bodies hitting the ground.

Two down, and there's still more inside. We advance toward the door and then stack up. Alejandro tries the handle and it's unlocked.

He holds up 3 fingers, then 2, 1...

The door swings open, and we all rush inside with weapons raised to find the corridor empty. We clear the first couple of rooms methodically, finding nothing. My heart pounds louder with every step that takes me closer to Blake.

Voices drift from a room ahead on the right. Miguel peers around the corner and holds up two fingers. Two more guards. He places a finger to his lips and then signals to move around the corner.

The guards barely have time to react before Alejandro and Miguel put bullets between their eyes. The silenced shots make a sound barely more than a cough while the bodies slump onto the table, blood gathering in a pool.

That's four down. But Estrada will have more men guarding Blake. I steel myself, my grip on my gun tightening. We continue, all our senses heightened for any sign of the remaining guards.

The hallway opens into a larger room, which is empty except for stacked crates on one wall. We scan the area, but it appears deserted.

Where is everyone?

The cocking of guns makes us all freeze. "Drop your weapons!" A voice barks.

We spin to see six of Estrada's men emerging from behind the crates, weapons trained on us.

A trap.

My heart pounds, staring down the barrels of six guns.

How could I have been so stupid? Estrada must have a rat in my organization feeding him information. He knew we were coming.

"Drop your weapons, now!" the leader repeats.

I raise my hands slowly, signaling for my men to do the same.

"Take it easy," I say evenly. "Let's talk about this."

The leader spits on the ground. "The time for talking is over, Marques. You should have stayed away. Now drop your guns before we drop you!"

I bend slowly, placing my pistol on the ground. Alejandro and the others follow suit reluctantly.

"Good, now kick them over," the leader orders.

We comply. Two of his men come forward, patting us down roughly for any other weapons before shoving us to our knees.

"Where is she?" I ask through gritted teeth.

The leader smirks. "Wouldn't you like to know? Don't worry. We're taking good care of her."

My blood boils at the thought of any men touching her. I should have killed Estrada when I had the chance at that fucking charity gala.

"What do you want?" I force out.

"It's simple. Pablo wants the land for the girl's life," he replies. "An even trade."

I shake my head firmly. "Let me see her first."

The leader shrugs. "Suit yourself. We'll just kill all of you then."

"Stand down, Jorge!" Pablo's voice slices through the air. "I think it's time that Gaston and I had a level-headed discussion in my office."

The audacity. Nothing about this fucking mobster is level-headed. He's an idiot, but I can't deny that I've been blinded on this occasion, walking straight into a trap. Normally, I'm more meticulous.

Jorge looks to Pablo hesitantly but steps aside when Pablo says firmly, "I will handle this personally."

I want nothing more than to put a bullet between Pablo's eyes, but I force myself to remain calm. Killing him now won't get me any closer to Blake. It'll get me killed.

"Fine, Let's talk."

Pablo clears his throat. "Stand!"

We all stand, and his men prod us with guns and force us down the corridor toward another room.

Pablo has the upper hand, but he wants the land from me. As long as Blake's life hangs in the balance, I need to play along.

Pablo opens the door to an office and waves me inside. I hesitate briefly, then step past him into the spacious room. The decor is lavish but tasteful, with dark wood furnishings and ornate rugs.

Pablo circles around the large desk and takes a seat in a leather chair. He gestures to the seat across from him. "Please, have a seat, Gaston."

I sit slowly, my muscles taut. Pablo laces his fingers on the desk and regards me with an infuriating smile.

"I'm so glad we can discuss this like civilized men," he says.

My hands curl into fists under the desk. I force myself to unclench them. As much as I want to leap across this desk and throttle him, I need to restrain myself for Blake's sake.

"Let's cut to the chase," I reply coldly. "What do you want?"

Pablo raises an eyebrow. "Straight to business then. Very well." He leans forward, steepling his fingers. "It's quite simple, really. I want your land."

I shake my head. "That land is worth over fifty million dollars. You really think I'm going to hand it over to you?"

"For the girl's life? Yes, I do," Pablo says matter-of-factly.

My blood turns to ice in my veins. The implied threat hangs heavy in the air between us.

"So, we have a deal?"

I clench my jaw, barely containing the rage boiling within. "That land is worth far more than the girl," I reply coldly, buying time while my mind races. There has to be another way.

Pablo shrugs. "Perhaps to most. But I'm not the one hopelessly obsessed with some little blonde puta." He smirks. "We both know you'd pay any price to get her back safely."

I dig my fingernails into my palms under the desk. How dare he talk about her that way.

Pablo leans back in his chair. He knows he has me cornered. "Well, Gaston? I'm waiting."

I force myself to take a slow breath. "I want proof of life first," I say evenly. "I'm not handing over anything until I know Blake is unharmed."

Pablo considers this for a moment, then nods. He picks up the phone on his desk and punches in a number.

"Bring the girl to my office. Now."

He sets down the phone. "Proof of life, as requested."

The rage within feels like a living entity I struggle to control. When I get Blake back, Estrada will pay for this in blood. I'll—

The door opens. Two armed guards enter with Blake between them. My heart leaps into my throat at the sight of her. She looks disheveled with bruises on her wrists but otherwise unharmed.

Our eyes meet across the room. Relief floods through me, mixed with a fresh wave of possessive anger. Estrada will regret the day he took what's mine.

"Satisfied?" Pablo asks wryly.

I nod, not taking my eyes off Blake. "For now. But if you hurt her..."

He holds up a hand. "Please, there's no need for threats. I'm a businessman like yourself. Cooperate, and she'll remain unharmed."

"I want time to have my lawyers draw up the land transfer paperwork," I say evenly. "Forty-eight hours."

Pablo considers this and nods. "Very well. Forty-eight hours, and then I expect everything to be in order." He stands. "A pleasure doing business with you."

Two guards grab my arms and haul me out. While they escort me down the hall, I drink in the sight of Blake until she disappears from view.

Don't worry, mi reina, I'll rescue you if it's the last thing I ever do.

39

GASTON

I pace the floor of my office, seething with rage. That smug bastard Estrada thinks he's won, that I'll roll over and hand him fifty million dollars' worth of prime real estate. He has no idea who he's dealing with.

My lawyers are drafting the transfer paperwork to buy some time, but I can't sign anything. Estrada wants to play hardball, which is fine. I can play, too.

I pick up my phone and dial Damien's number. "Damien? It's time. Shut down all of Estrada's servers, everything. I want that whole operation dark."

Damien may be my second in command of operations here, but he's also the best hacker I know. If anyone can cripple Estrada's network, it's him.

"Consider it done," Damien replies. "Is there anything else, sir?"

I run a hand across the back of my neck, looking at Estrada's personal offshore account. "There's an account.

Can you funnel two hundred and seventy million from it and place it into an encrypted wallet?"

"Piece of cake," he affirms.

"Good. I'll send you the details. I want you to do it now. I want this wrapped up with Estrada tonight."

"On it." He ends the call.

I allow myself a grim smile, envisioning Estrada's panic when he realizes what I've done. Without his precious servers, his whole criminal operation will halt. Communications, security systems, transactions—all frozen with a few keystrokes. And when he realizes the amount of money I stole from him, he'll lose his shit.

Estrada won't know what hit him when his liquid assets are drained. I almost wish I could see the look on his face. Almost.

And once I have Blake safely back, Estrada will regret the day he tried to challenge me. I'll raze his operations and drive him from this city for good. When I'm through with him, he'll scramble back to whatever hole he crawled out of, penniless and broken.

No one takes what's mine. And Blake is mine. I claimed her body and soul long ago. If Estrada wants to challenge that, he'll learn the hard way with a bullet in his skull.

When this is over, Estrada will have nothing left but ashes. He will rue the day he decided to cross Gaston Marques.

And Blake will be back where she belongs—on her throne beside me.

* * *

I'M SITTING at my desk when my phone rings, the caller ID flashing Pablo's name. I feel a surge of satisfaction knowing he's likely calling to scream at me for crippling his servers and draining his accounts.

"Pablo," I answer smoothly, "To what do I owe the pleasure?"

He's practically sputtering with rage. "You son of a bitch! Do you have any idea what you've done?"

I make a tsking sound. "Such language. I thought we could be civilized about this."

"Civilized?!" he roars. "You attacked my network, my finances..."

"Collateral damage," I say dismissively. "You took something of mine, so I took something of yours. Though I'd say what I took was a bit more substantial."

Pablo is breathing hard. I can envision the veins bulging in his forehead. "I will kill that blonde bitch for this," he hisses.

At that, my amusement vanishes. My voice drops to a deadly soft tone. "Careful, Pablo. Threaten her again, and you'll never see your two hundred and seventy million dollars again."

He pauses. "What are you talking about?"

"The money I drained from your account? It's not gone. Merely relocated. To a place only I can access."

Pablo is silent, the gravity of the situation sinking in. He thought he had all the leverage, only to discover he's the one who's been outmaneuvered. He didn't know yet about the money.

"Here's what will happen," I continue calmly. "We will meet at midnight at the abandoned airfield outside the city. You'll hand Blake over to me unharmed. Once she's safely away, I'll give you access to your funds."

"You manipulative bastard," he whispers.

"Sticks and stones. Do we have an understanding?"

I can hear Pablo grinding his teeth. "Fine. The exchange will happen at midnight."

"Excellent. I look forward to our meeting." I end the call, allowing myself a satisfied smile. Estrada tried to play me and failed spectacularly. Now, he'll have no choice but to return my property and slink away in disgrace.

I pick up my phone and dial Damien's number. As usual, he answers after the first ring.

"Gaston," he says briskly. "How can I help?"

"Assemble the team for tonight," I tell him. "Same men as the warehouse raid. I don't anticipate any trouble from Estrada at the exchange, but I want to be prepared."

Damien makes a noise of affirmation. "Smart thinking. That snake might try to pull something."

"Exactly my thoughts," I agree. "Have the men outfitted with vests and armed to the teeth. I want us to out-gun Estrada's crew three to one if it comes to that."

"Consider it done," Damien says smoothly. "What time is the meet?"

"Midnight. The abandoned airfield outside the city."

"We'll be ready and waiting," he assures me.

"Good. And make sure you secure a vehicle for extracting Blake once I have her. Something fast, with bulletproof windows. I don't want to take any chances."

"Will do. I'll make the necessary arrangements."

"Excellent," I say. "I knew I could count on you, Damien. Let's end this thing tonight and show Estrada what happens when he crosses us."

"With pleasure," Damien practically purrs. I can tell he's looking forward to it.

I end the call and lean back in my chair, steepling my fingers together. Blake will be back where she belongs in a few hours, by my side. And Estrada will learn once and for all that I'm not a man to be trifled with.

40

BLAKE

*D*eja vu has never felt so terrifying. Only this time, I'm alone. My wrists are bound in front of me, and they've kept the hood on my head. The silence is deafening, save for the occasional creak of the building.

Gaston came for me, but it backfired. Pablo is in a strong position and is blackmailing him for my life. All I can do now is wait two days here and hope all goes to plan.

The slam of a door startles me. It's followed by heavy footsteps approaching. A rough hand grabs my arm and I'm yanked to my feet. Whoever has me doesn't say a word while he leads me God knows where. These guards are assholes.

It's only been a few hours since I was last dragged into Pablo's office in front of Gaston. The guard stops suddenly, and the hood is ripped from my head. My eyes strain as it's bright. Then I see those gray eyes, and the terror eases.

Why is he back so quickly?

A few of his men flank him, facing off against a group of Pablo's armed men.

Gaston's eyes flash when they meet mine, but he remains passive in his expression. Something tells me he's got a plan to get me out of here.

The asshole of a guard shoves me forward, making me stumble. Pablo appears from the left, sneering at Gaston.

"Stealing my cash was creative, Gaston." Pablo runs a hand through his hair. "I'll give you that."

"I told you not to mess with me," Gaston replies.

Pablo approaches me, making me tense. I notice how Gaston clenches his fists by his sides when Pablo grabs my chin, forcing me to meet his gaze. "Your boyfriend's a clever one, puta," he spits. "Somehow, he drained my bank account and demanded your release in return for my money."

"Pablo," Gaston's sharp voice cuts through the silence. "Call her puta again and see what happens," he growls.

My heart pounds while the tension in the air thickens to the point I can't breathe. Deep down, I fear this standoff can only end badly. Tensions are high, and all the men in this room are armed. Pablo's men are restless as they grip their weapons tighter.

"You think you can threaten me, Marques?" he growls. "I own this city. I could end you with a snap of my fingers."

Gaston scoffs. "End me? I'd like to see you try, Estrada. You're nothing but a two-bit thug."

The insult lands, and Pablo's face twists in rage. In a

flash, he pulls a gun from his waistband and levels it at Gaston. My heart leaps into my throat.

"Give me one reason I shouldn't blow your brains out right here," Pablo hisses.

Gaston doesn't flinch. "Go ahead," he says evenly. "But then you'll never get access to that money."

Pablo wavers and I let out a shaky breath.

The fear I feel at seeing this man point a gun at Gaston is worse than anything I've experienced. The idea of him getting hurt threatens to tear me apart.

Gaston presses his advantage. "Here's how this is going to go," he says. "You're going to let Blake walk out that door with me. Then I'll give you the access to the account it's in."

"Bullshit," Pablo spits. "How do I know you won't just take the girl and the money?"

"You don't," Gaston says coldly. "But those are my terms. Take them or leave them."

Pablo is fuming, but he lowers the gun. I feel relieved, but I know we're not out of danger yet. "You are one lucky puta."

Gaston growls because he hates him calling me that, but I meet Gaston's gaze and try to reassure him with one look. Let him call me what he wants if we leave here alive.

"Maldito bastardo!" He spits, pacing back and forth.

His men are exchanging nervous looks. Everyone is on edge and waiting for Pablo to give the order. Is he going to let me go?

He stops pacing and looks directly at Gaston. "You may

have won this round, cabrón," he snarls. "But this isn't over. I'll find a way to make you regret this."

Gaston simply stares back coolly. "Let her go, Estrada," he says, his voice low and commanding. "We have a deal. The moment you give her back, the money will be returned."

Pablo hesitates. And I'm pretty sure everyone in the room is holding their breath. Finally, he nods to the man holding me. "Get her out of my sight," he orders through gritted teeth. The man holding me begins marching me toward Gaston and his men.

I'm scared that one wrong move and everything could go to shit. My heart pounds when my eyes meet Gaston's. He keeps cool; there's nothing readable in his expression. All I want is to run into his arms.

The guard shoves me the last few feet, and I stumble into Gaston. He steadies me, pulling me into his arms, and I've never felt such relief.

"Let's go home, mi reina," he murmurs loud enough for me to hear. Then he turns, guiding me away from my tormentors and toward the exit. I cling to him, feeling so many emotions as the floodgates break, and I sob, clawing onto him.

We step into the cool night air and I take a deep breath. Freedom. Gaston pulled out all the stops, and he got me out quickly and safely. It's hard to believe the man who held me against my will has become my savior.

* * *

GASTON HASN'T SAID a word since we got into the back of the car. The silence is suffocating.

I study him, trying to understand what's going through his mind, but his expression is inscrutable as always. The only indication of emotion is the white-knuckled grip he has on the door handle.

My mind races, wondering what he's thinking. Is he angry at me? Disappointed? Relieved?

The tension is putting me on edge. I fidget with the buttons on my blouse, resisting the urge to speak.

I know from experience it's better not to push Gaston when he's in one of these moods. Still, the not knowing is maddening.

I take a few deep breaths, trying to calm my nerves. We're safe now, I remind myself. Estrada and his thugs can't hurt me anymore. I'm free.

So why doesn't it feel that way? Why do I still feel so anxious and unsettled?

Maybe it's the lack of resolution. Estrada is still out there, and surely he'll want revenge against Gaston for stealing his money and rescuing me.

Or maybe it's Gaston himself. This man who came for me against all odds risked everything to get me back. He's still such an enigma to me. I don't know where we stand or what any of this means.

I can't take the tense silence anymore. I have to know what he's thinking.

"Gaston," I say tentatively.

He doesn't respond, doesn't even glance my way. His jaw is clenched, his eyes fixed out the window.

I try again, louder this time. "Gaston, please. Talk to me."

Finally he turns, regarding me with an inscrutable expression. "What is there to say?" His tone is clipped, detached.

I frown, confused by his aloofness. "You seem upset."

He lets out a bitter laugh. "Upset? Yes, I suppose you could call it that."

"Why?" I ask gently. "We got away, didn't we? Estrada didn't win."

Gaston closes his eyes briefly as if gathering patience. When he opens them, I'm startled to see a flash of raw emotion in their gray depths.

Fear.

"I've never been more afraid than I was today," he says quietly. "When Estrada took you, I..." He trails off, jaw working.

I've never seen Gaston like this before. He's always so controlled, so stoic.

"You were scared for me?" I whisper.

He nods. "I would've given that bastard anything to get you back safely. My company, my home, all of it. Your life is worth infinitely more to me."

I'm touched by his admission. I reach over and lay my hand on top of his. After a moment, he turns his palm up to intertwine our fingers.

"But I couldn't let him see weakness," Gaston continues gruffly. "I had to outmaneuver him, or he would've used it against us again and again. He needed to understand not to cross me."

His silence and tension are not anger at me but residual fear and stress from the ordeal.

"It's okay," I murmur. "We're together now. That's all that matters."

Gaston lifts our joined hands and brushes his lips over my knuckles. The tender gesture sends a shiver down my spine. "The thing is, Blake, I have spent my life keeping emotions at a minimum, never caring about anyone because it's the worst thing in the world when you lose them."

My brow furrows. "What do you mean?"

"My family." His jaw clenches. "My parents and sister died in a car accident when I was eight. I survived. And from that moment on, I vowed to never care about anyone else. Until you."

My heart aches for him. "That's terrible. I'm sorry."

He raises his hand. "I don't want any pity; I'm merely telling you so you understand me a bit better. Understand why I always kept relationships like business transactions."

"I understand." I press my lips to his, overcome with emotion. He kisses me back gently, almost reverently. His usual demanding, dominant demeanor is absent. Instead, his touch is soft and caring.

My heart swells, and I'm unable to hold back any longer. I pull away just enough to whisper against his mouth, "I love you."

The words hang in the air between us as we study each other's faces. His eyes search mine, seeming to look for any dishonesty. After a moment, his expression softens. He brushes a strand of hair from my cheek and tucks it behind my ear.

"I hoped with everything in me that you did," he murmurs. "But I didn't dare believe it until I heard you say it."

I've never seen Gaston so exposed, so vulnerable. "I tried to fight it," I admit. "I didn't want to care about you. But I couldn't help myself."

He nods, looking pained. "I know I've done unforgivable things to you. I won't insult you by asking for forgiveness." His jaw tightens. "But I vow to spend the rest of my life trying to be worthy of your love."

My eyes fill with tears. After everything we've been through, all the pain and darkness, could this really be happening? Could Gaston truly love me despite his flaws?

I cling to him, burying my face in his neck. His strong arms envelop me like he never intends to let me go. "I know you've done bad things, but you also risked everything to save me. That has to mean something."

"It means you make me want to be better," he says gruffly. "I've never felt that before." He tilts my chin up to look earnestly into my eyes. "I promise you, Blake, I'll do whatever it takes to make you happy." He crushes me to him in a fierce kiss that steals my breath away. I cling to him, dizzy with happiness, hardly believing this is real.

After everything, somehow, we've found love in the darkest of places. And I know then that we'll face it together no matter what comes next.

41

GASTON

I cradle Blake in my arms while my private jet cruises back to the States. Her head rests gently against my chest, and I savor the feeling of having her close. When I felt her ripped from me on that airstrip, it felt like my world was ending.

I would've given Pablo anything to ensure Blake's safe return, but I couldn't show weakness in front of my adversary.

Instead, I outmaneuvered him. Pitted his greed against him to negotiate Blake's release and came out on top. The stakes had been high, but thankfully, I read Pablo right. Money is the most precious thing to him.

Blake shifts and glances at me. "What happens now?" she asks softly. "How will this work with you in Mexico City and me at Brown?"

I run my fingers through her golden hair. "You let me worry about that, mi amor. I'll come to Providence as often as I can. I've already rented an apartment where we can spend time together when I visit."

Blake furrows her brow. "But won't you have to go back to Mexico City regularly for your business?"

"Yes," I reply. "But I'll travel back and forth. Nothing is more important than being with you."

There's uncertainty in Blake's eyes. Our relationship has been turbulent so far, to say the least. I know she has reservations, given our history. My treatment of her at the start was my usual treatment of the women I buy, but at the time, I didn't want to admit how special Blake was.

"Sit on my lap," I demand.

She arches a brow but doesn't question me, swinging a leg over mine to straddle me. I pull Blake closer, my arms encircling her slender waist, pulling her lips to meet mine in a deep, passionate kiss.

She responds eagerly, her fingers threading through my hair.

The feel of her soft curves and perfect tits pressing against me ignite a familiar fire. I savor the taste of her. The sweetness of her tongue dancing with mine. My hands slide down to caress the flare of her hips, and I squeeze, drawing out a little whimper.

She grinds herself on my dick, making me groan. I want her—all of her. To possess her completely, to claim her as mine for the rest of our lives. It will be different now. No more games.

Her face is flushed when I break the kiss. "Blake," I

murmur. "You may have only been captured less than twenty-four hours, but I've fucking missed you."

She kisses me, undulating her hips. "I need you."

"Fuck, how can I say no to that, baby girl?" Standing with her in my arms, her legs wrapped around my hips, I lower her onto the floor of the jet, tearing her clothes off like a beast.

Her shirt rips open, buttons scattering across the jet's floor like confetti.

"You're mine now, truly," I growl, my mouth watering at the sight of her perfect breasts. "Every fucking inch of you belongs to me." My hands roam greedily over her body, squeezing her tits and sliding down to her soaked pussy. "You're so goddamn perfect," I mutter, my voice thick.

I tear her panties off and dive my fingers into her cunt, making her moan louder. "Did you miss this while we weren't fucking? Did you miss having me inside you?" I ask, my thumb circling her clit as I pump my fingers in and out of her.

She arches her back, rocking her hips in time with my thrusts. "Yes, sir. I missed it so much."

I lean down to nip at her earlobe. "Good girl," I praise before claiming her mouth in another hungry kiss.

Unzipping my pants, I free my cock. It springs out, slapping against her stomach.

"Gaston," she moans my name as she gazes down at my dick which is leaking precum onto her skin.

"God, I missed this sweet little cunt when you were avoiding me." My fingers work her clit while I line up my cock with her entrance. "You're so fucking wet for me, baby. You want it, don't you?"

She bites her lip, eyes dilated as she nods.

"Use your words for me, baby girl," I demand.

"I want it so bad, Gaston; please fuck me."

"Mmm, that's it," I groan, my cock twitching with anticipation. "Tell me how much you need this cock inside you." I trace the head of my dick through her slick folds, teasing her clit before slowly pushing just the tip inside. "Is this what you dream about? Being filled up by me?"

She grunts in frustration. "Gaston, please. I need it so bad. Fuck me. Please fuck me."

Chuckling, I thrust forward with one swift movement, filling her completely.

Blake arches her back and cries out as I start moving, setting a rough pace immediately. I pull back almost all the way, then slam back in, loving the feel of her tight, wet pussy squeezing me. "You were made to be fucked by me, baby girl. Made to be mine."

"Yes!" She cries. "I'm made for you and only you."

Hearing her words sends a jolt through me. "Fuck, yes, you are," I snarl, flipping her over onto all fours and slamming into her even harder. "Say it again, Blake. Tell me you're mine forever." I grab a handful of her hair and yank her head back, exposing her neck to my lips. I suck and bite at the sensitive flesh, leaving marks.

"I belong to you for the rest of my life. You've got me forever," she moans, meeting each thrust with a roll of her hips.

I kiss her neck softly, savoring the taste of her skin before biting down hard. "You're doing so well, baby girl," I murmur, my voice filled with pride. "Taking every inch of me like you were made for it."

Her body trembles. "Gaston! Fuck, I'm so close," she whines.

I can feel myself getting closer to the edge, too. "Then come for me, Blake. Show me how much you love having me inside you." I grind my hips against her ass, hitting her G-spot with each thrust. "Let go, baby girl."

"Fuck, Gaston!" She screams as I push her right over the cliff's edge. Her body convulses, and she arches her back more, forcing me even deeper inside her cunt.

Her orgasm triggers my own, and I explode inside her with a primal roar, pulsing deep while my cum paints her insides.

I pull out, watching as my release drips down her thighs. "Look at you, covered in your owner's cum," I say, reaching between her thighs to scoop some up. "Face me."

She remains on all fours but turns around to face me, allowing me to bring the cum to her lips. "Open up, baby girl. Taste what you do to me."

She opens her mouth eagerly, allowing me to slip my fingers into her mouth so she can suck them clean.

"Mmm, so good," I groan, watching her hungrily suck on my fingers. "You know what else tastes good?" I ask, pulling her toward me with a hand around her throat, gazing into her eyes.

"No, what?"

I smirk and lift her off the floor, setting her on the lounge chair on her back and parting her thighs.

"That sweet ass," I murmur, kneeling before her and spitting on her tight hole, spreading it around with my thumb.

"Oh fuck," she breathes, eyes fluttering shut.

I press the tip of my tongue inside her, working past the initial resistance until she's relaxed. "Just remember to relax, baby girl," I coach in a low voice, plunging it in again. "I'm going to make you feel so good."

My fingers plunge into her abused and fucked pussy, getting them wet and ready for her ass.

"You're such a good girl," I praise, my voice low. Withdrawing my soaked fingers, I press one against her asshole. "I'm going to get your ass ready for my cock." Slowly, I inch two fingers into her ass. "Does that feel good, baby?"

"Yes, it feels amazing," she moans.

I add a third finger alongside my thumb. "I bet you're wishing this was already my cock, aren't you? Beg for it. Tell me how badly you want my cock in your tight little asshole."

She whimpers and arches her back. "Please, sir. Please give me your big hard cock in my ass. I need you to fuck me hard and rough."

"Fuck, that's all I needed to hear," I rumble, withdrawing my fingers from her ass and standing to grab some lube from the dresser in the jet and generously coat my cock, making sure it's slick.

Dropping to my knees, I guide myself toward her

waiting opening and press my cock against it, giving her a moment to adjust.

"Oh, fuck. I've craved this again ever since the first time," she moans.

My dirty little anal slut. I thrust forward, releasing a deep groan while I fill my baby girl completely, her muscles clenching around my cock deliciously.

I start with slow, deliberate strokes. "Do you know why I bought you?" I ask.

She shakes her head. "No, sir."

"Because no one is allowed to experience this perfection but me. The moment I saw you in that fucking cell, I knew my life had changed forever." I pick up the pace gradually, building a steady rhythm, making her moan with every stroke.

"I'm yours always," she breathes, deepening my possessive need to claim her.

"That's right, beautiful," I growl, spanking her hard. "And when I'm done with you tonight, there won't be an inch of your body that doesn't bear the proof of that." I grip her hair, pulling her toward me so her back is pressed against my chest, her ass still impaled on my cock.

Holding her close, I fuck her harder and faster, my hand around her throat like a collar. "I'll never tire of seeing you at my mercy, baby girl."

"I love being at your mercy," she admits.

I squeeze her throat tighter, restricting her airway enough to make her shake. "You're so fucking beautiful when you submit to me." I thrust deeper into her ass, feeling her body shake.

"Gaston, I'm coming!" She screams, tumbling over the edge suddenly and violently. Her tight ass clamps down around me so fucking hard she forces me over with her.

"Fuck," I growl, slamming in once more and spilling my cum deep, my hips bucking wildly. "Such a good girl taking my cum in your tight little ass."

I release her throat, and Blake gasps for air, her body shaking. Slowly, I pull my cock from her ass, loving how it gapes.

She whimpers when I lift her off the chair and sit down with her in my arms, cradling her naked body. "That was fucking perfect," I whisper into her ear.

"It was," she breathes, resting her head on my chest. After a short while, she gazes at me with those brilliant blue eyes I've fallen so deeply in love with. She kisses me, and I kiss her back. Our kisses are soft and unhurried, a direct contrast to the intense fucking we just shared.

We cuddle on the plush leather seat, knowing I've never felt happier. "I never thought I'd find this, mi amor," I breathe, brushing a lock of hair from her face. "Never believed I was capable of love."

She tilts her head. I'm painfully aware I've not yet said those three words to her. "What are you saying?"

I press my forehead to hers. "I'm saying that I love you."

The smile that lights up her face is so fucking angelic I know I don't deserve her. "I love you, too."

Her words make my heart swell. After starting out as her worst nightmare, I vow to be the opposite.

I kiss her as if my life depends on it, breaking away only to press kisses across her collarbone and neck.

I know there are still challenges ahead, and I need to gain her trust, but I have faith we'll pull through. With Blake by my side, I can weather any storm.

42

BLAKE

*G*aston lingers behind me as we agree while I unlock the door to the apartment. Luna will wonder why I'm back early.

The moment I step through the door, her head snaps up, and her brow furrows. "Hey, what are you doing here? Aren't you supposed to be in Mexico with Gaston until Monday?"

I sigh, dropping my bag on the floor. "Yeah, that was the plan. But things got complicated."

Luna looks concerned. "What happened? Is everything okay?"

"We were attacked at the airstrip when we first got there. Armed men came out of nowhere and grabbed me. Gaston tried to stop them, but they were too quick. Next thing I knew, I was blindfolded and tied up in some dingy warehouse."

Luna gasps, her eyes widening in shock. "Oh my God,

Blake! That's terrifying to have it happen for a second time." She shakes her head. "I can't imagine what went through your mind at that moment. How did you get away?"

I rub my temples, the stress of the last 48 hours hitting me. "Gaston tracked me down and negotiated my release. It's a long story, but the guy who took me wanted access to something Gaston owns. There was a standoff, but Gaston got me out safely."

"Wow," Luna says, shaking her head in disbelief. "I'm so glad you're okay. That must have been so traumatic for it to happen again."

"Yeah, it was really intense," I reply. "Honestly I'm still kind of processing everything that happened."

Luna stands and pulls me into a tight hug. "I'm so relieved you're safe and back home," she says.

I hug her back. "Me too."

She breaks away and moves toward the kitchen. "Do you want a coffee?"

"Sure, thanks." I move toward the kitchen.

"What about Gaston?" she asks before she enters the kitchen.

"What about me?" Gaston demands, his deep voice sending shivers down my spine.

Gaston's strong arms wrap around me from behind, pulling me against his solid chest in a possessive embrace. A shiver runs down my spine at his touch, and I lean into him.

Luna turns to give me a questioning gaze. "Gaston and

I are moving in together," I admit, my voice barely above a whisper.

Luna's eyes widen in surprise. "Moving in together?" she echoes, her brow furrowing in concern. "But, Blake, are you sure that's a good idea? After everything that's happened..."

I swallow hard, glancing at Gaston. His jaw is set, his expression unreadable. "It's what I want," I say, trying to sound more confident than I feel. "I'll still be covering my share of the rent for this place, and I might stay over when Gaston is in Mexico, but..."

Gaston's grip tightens around me, and I can't help but feel a sense of security in his arms. Part of me is still terrified of him, of the power he holds over me. But another part has grown to care for him deeply and yearns to be by his side.

"Are you certain?" Luna asks, looking unconvinced.

I nod, reaching out to give her hand a reassuring squeeze. "Yes, this feels right. Gaston and I, we love each other."

Gaston's lips brush the side of my neck, and I shiver. "I did tell you I'd win you over in your own country, didn't I?" There's a cocky timbre to his voice. "And look at you, wrapped around my finger."

I glare at him over my shoulder but don't feel hatred anymore. "I think it's the other way around."

Luna clears her throat. "I can't really say anything since I'm with Thiago."

A deep voice calls from the kitchen. "I heard that, angel!"

I chuckle. "Yeah, where's Kali?" I ask, my brow furrowing because I haven't seen her in ages.

Luna's expression turns serious. "She's living with Matias now. God knows where. Neither of them will tell us. They've completely disappeared."

Thiago walks into the room with an apron, and I almost want to laugh. The man who was part of our kidnapping looks so domesticated. "I'm afraid when my brother doesn't want to be found, he's practically impossible to track down." He runs a hand through his hair. "Either of you hungry? I've made enough Enchiladas to feed ten people."

I bite my inner cheek, wondering if Gaston will agree. "I wouldn't mind staying for some food." I glance over my shoulder at him.

"If you want to stay, we'll stay, baby girl."

I can't help but feel a bit uneasy following Thiago into the kitchen, Gaston's strong arm wrapped possessively around my waist. It's still so surreal to me that the four of us—me, Luna, Kali, and Alice—were all kidnapped in Mexico, only to end up entangled with our captors.

Thiago dishes heaping servings of his homemade enchiladas while Luna chats animatedly with him.

I can't help but feel for Kali.

How can she love that monster, Matias?

I can't imagine that living with a man so psychotic is a

healthy situation for her. Out of the three men, he was the worst.

Taking a deep breath, I push those dark thoughts aside while taking the plate Thiago hands me. "Thank you," I murmur, offering him a small smile.

Gaston tugs me closer, his fingers tracing patterns on my hip. "Eat up, mi reina. You must be famished after everything that happened."

I nod, taking a bite of the enchilada. The flavors burst on my tongue, and I can't help but release a soft hum of appreciation. "This is delicious," I admit, glancing at Thiago.

He grins, puffing out his chest a bit. "I'm glad you like it. Cooking is one of my few guilty pleasures."

"Aren't you and Matias supposed to be handling the Navarro Cartel's operations here?" I ask, eating more of the delicious food. "How come you can't find Matias?"

"We were handling it until he went off the rails about five days ago and sent me a text message," Thiago says.

"What did it say?" I ask.

Thiago exchanges a wary glance with Luna and stays silent.

"Come on, Thiago. Spit it out," Gaston says, a hint of amusement in his tone.

"It simply said, going primal with my mate."

My brow furrows. "What the hell does that mean?"

Gaston chuckles. "Poor Kali."

I grind my teeth. "What does it mean, Thiago?"

He looks a little flustered. "When he says he's going

primal, it literally means that. He's probably shacked up in some makeshift cabin or something in the woods fucking Kali like an animal."

My stomach drops. There was a time when I was confused by Matias's dominance while captured by them, but he's the worst kind of man.

Kali is so sweet and they just don't make sense. They're complete opposites in every way.

While eating, I feel Gaston's gaze occasionally shifting to me. Turning, I meet his gaze, and my heart skips a beat at the adoration in his expression.

"What are you thinking about, mi amor?" he murmurs, his thumb caressing my cheek.

I swallow hard, searching his face. "Just how strange it is that we all ended up here. Alice with Taren. Me and you, and Thiago and Luna, and..." I trail off, not wanting to voice my concerns about Kali and Matias.

Gaston's expression shifts. "Perhaps it's fate. I never believed in it before, but what happened happened for a reason."

I nod, leaning into his touch. As much as I want to believe him, I can't shake the feeling that the danger is far from over for my friends. They're entwined with two men heavily involved in the cartel. But for now, I'll savor this moment of peace, surrounded by the people I care about most.

43

EPILOGUE

BLAKE

Ten Months Later...

I sit beside Kali, waiting to be called up. We've finally done it. Graduated from Brown. My heart is racing because my parents and Gaston are here. They don't know about Gaston yet since I had no idea how to explain him.

Hey, Mom and Dad, I'm dating a billionaire from Mexico City after he bought me from the cartel.

Today is the day I will reveal him to them and tell them I'm moving to Mexico City to be with him. Kali, Luna, and Alice tried to convince me to stay, but my home is where he is—my dark captor, the man who somehow captured my heart with sheer persistence.

"Blake Carter," the steward calls.

I swallow hard and walk onto the stage to accept my diploma.

My heart pounds in my chest with each step I take, knowing this should be one of the happiest moments of my life, but all I can think about is what comes next.

How will my parents react to Gaston?

That a man who bought me, who held me captive for so long, is now the man I've fallen in love with? Not that they'll ever know that part of our story.

My parents smile and cheer while I accept my diploma, blissfully unaware of the coming storm. I search the crowd and find Gaston's piercing gray eyes. He nods and smiles, making my heart swell.

After the ceremony ends, my parents pull me into a massive hug. "We're so proud of you!" my mom gushes.

"Thanks, Mom." I hug her back.

"It will be so good having you back home and working with Dad."

Guilt coils through me, but I shake my head. "I'm not coming back home. I'm moving to Mexico City." I announce.

Mom's brow furrows. "What?"

I sigh heavily, already dreading this conversation. Gaston approaches, placing an arm around my waist. He's older than me, and Dad's jaw clenches when he sees Gaston touch me. "Who are you?"

I take a deep breath. "Mom, Dad, there's someone I want you to meet." I glance a Gaston. "This is my boyfriend, Gaston."

Shock registers on their faces. I continue quickly, "I know this seems sudden, but we've been together a while.

He's very important to me. I know this is a lot to take in," I say gently.

Dad's face is growing redder by the second. "You mean to tell me this man is your boyfriend? How? When?" He turns on Gaston. "Just how old are you anyway?"

I squeeze Gaston's hand tightly, willing him to stay calm. The age gap I knew would be an issue. Gaston is thirty-four. "He's twelve years older than me. And we've been dating for ten months." I look at Gaston pleadingly.

"Sir, I care deeply for your daughter," Gaston says. "Our relationship may seem unconventional, but my intentions are honorable. I'd never do anything to hurt your daughter." If only they knew how we met, they'd have me admitted to a mental health facility.

My mom shakes her head in disbelief. "This is so unlike you. Is everything okay? Has he pressured you into moving in any way?"

"No, of course not!" I insist. "I know to you it seems sudden, but this is why I didn't tell you. I knew this is how you'd react to our age difference." I take a deep breath, willing myself to stay calm. "Believe me, I never expected this to happen either. But Gaston and I click in a way I've never experienced before." I glance at him, taking strength from his steady presence. "He challenges, supports, and understands me like no one else. It's like the rest of the world fades away when we're together."

Mom shakes her head, brow furrowed in concern. "Blake, you're only twenty-two. How can you know this man is right for you after a few months?"

"It's complicated," I hedge. How can I explain our tangled history to my parents? "But the connection we have, the bond we've formed is deep."

Dad's face is still flushed with anger. "This is unacceptable," he snaps. "You won't be moving to another country to live with some older man we don't even know!"

I feel my temper rising. "You can't tell me what to do anymore. I'm an adult." I take Gaston's hand firmly. "I've made my choice. I will move to Mexico City with Gaston, with or without your approval."

Mom's eyes fill with tears. "Please, Blake, be reasonable..."

Gaston squeezes my hand. I know he can tell how difficult this is for me.

"I'm sorry you feel this way. I wish you could understand. But I have to follow my heart." I look between them pleadingly. "I love you both so much. I hope you'll come to accept Gaston too. But right now, this is what I need to do."

Dad shakes his head angrily and storms off. Mom lingers a moment longer, eyes searching mine for answers.

"I hope you know what you're doing," she says softly before following my dad.

I let out a shaky breath, watching them go, heart aching. But I meant what I said. I need to follow my heart. I need to do this for me.

"Come on, baby girl. Let's go to the restaurant and meet your friends and celebrate. Your parents will come around."

I take Gaston's hand, and he leads me on foot to the restaurant where we've booked a table to celebrate. After the confrontation with my parents, my heart is in my throat.

We walk in, and the moment I see my closest friends gathered around a large table, smiles lighting up their faces, some of the hurt eases.

Kali jumps up to hug me. "There she is! I'm so proud of you."

I grin, squeezing her tightly. "Proud of you too!"

Alice and Luna get up, too, and we share a group hug. This might be the last time we're all together for a while.

"We're starving. Let's order!" Luna says.

I nod in response, taking my seat beside Gaston. Kali sits beside Matias who still creeps me out. However, they seem happy together as Matias drapes an arm over Kali's shoulder.

Luna smiles at Thiago and I notice her slide her hand into his on the table.

Alice sits beside Taren, looking more vibrant and confident than ever. At the same time, Taren leans toward her and kisses her cheek.

Gaston's hand slides onto my thigh, squeezing possessively.

"Let's order a few bottles of champagne," Gaston says.

Luna raises a brow. "If you're paying, I can't afford champagne."

Gaston chuckles. "Of course. Taren and I agreed to split the bill."

Kali nods. "Then, let's get the most expensive champagne on the menu," she jokes.

"Go ahead," Gaston says smoothly. After all, he's not exactly short on cash.

The waiter comes, and Gaston orders three bottles of their most expensive champagne. When it comes, we all toast to our futures and fall into a comfortable conversation.

It's hard to believe how far we've come. A year ago, we were prisoners of a cartel, thinking we may never be free again. Now, we sit with the men who took part in our capture. It's a little ironic. But now we're here, free and in love, celebrating our graduation together.

"A toast!" Thiago declares, raising his glass. "To new beginnings."

"To new beginnings," we echo, clinking our glasses.

Matias, as always, doesn't join in, but he does clink his glass with ours. Gaston's arm encircles my waist, and I lean into him contentedly. There's still much uncertainty ahead. Painful goodbyes will come while we all prepare to start our new lives after Brown.

But for tonight, none of that matters. Tonight is about celebrating our successes and our friendship. We've got unbreakable bonds, and that won't change no matter where our paths lead next.

Kali nudges my shoulder. "No parents?" She asks.

I swallow hard, shaking my head. "No, I told them about Gaston, and let's say they weren't exactly thrilled." I glance at the two empty chairs at the table because we'd invited them to dinner.

She winces in sympathy. "Yikes. I can't say I blame them, though. If I told my parents I was moving to another country to live with an older boyfriend, I'd only known for ten months..."

"They'd completely lose it," Matias finishes. "But hey, you're an adult. You don't need their permission."

"That's what I told them," I say. "I just hope they'll come to accept it."

Luna reaches over the table and gives my hand a comforting squeeze. "They will. Just give them time to process." Her eyes twinkle mischievously. "Besides, how could they not love Gaston once they get to know him better?"

Gaston chuckles. "I don't know about that, but I appreciate the sentiment."

His arm tightens around my waist. "Your parents care about you. They want you to be safe and happy. We'll win them over eventually."

I smile at him, leaning into his solid warmth. Conversation flows easily around the table while we continue to celebrate. Kali tells the guys funny stories from our college years. In contrast, Luna tells us about the coding job she recently landed in California.

"I'm so proud of you!" I tell her, beaming. "That startup is lucky to have you."

She grins. "Thanks! I'm crazy excited. But I'm really going to miss you all." Her eyes turn sad for a moment before she shakes it off. "We'll just have to meet up for reunions all the time!"

"Absolutely," I say firmly. As hard as the goodbye will be, I know our bond is unbreakable. We've been to hell and back together; nothing can truly separate us now.

After a great meal, everyone says their goodbyes, and Gaston and I stroll through the streets of Providence.

Gaston's fingers squeeze mine. "What now, baby girl?" he asks, his voice husky.

Instantly, my mind goes to the gutter when I look at him, biting my bottom lip.

He chuckles. "So dirty, aren't you?" He pushes me against the wall of the restaurant, a hand circling my throat. "Where do you want me to fuck you?"

My thighs dampen, and the idea of being fucked somewhere public makes my stomach tighten. "Somewhere we might get caught."

He smirks. "I know the perfect place."

My breath catches while Gaston's fingers tighten around my throat.

"Come," he growls, grabbing my hand and leading me down the dark street. I hurry to match his urgent pace, my heart racing.

We round a corner into an alleyway, the distant sounds of the city fading away. Gaston presses me against the cold brick wall, his body firm against mine. His hand trails up my thigh while he peppers my neck with kisses. "I'm going to fuck you right here," he rasps into my ear. "Right out in the open where anyone could see."

My pussy throbs at the thought. "Gaston," I gasp, arching against him.

Gaston's fingers slide under my dress, stroking me through my soaked panties. I whimper, grinding shamelessly against his hand. With a sharp rip, the lace tears away.

"So ready for me," he growls. His belt buckle clinks as he frees himself. Gripping my hips, he lifts me effortlessly, poised at my entrance.

Gaston's passionate kiss leaves me breathless while he presses me against the brick wall. Despite our public location, I melt into his touch, my body craving more. His hands trail fire across my skin, and I gasp against his mouth.

"Tell me what you want," he commands.

We shouldn't be doing this out here, where anyone could happen upon us, but the illicit thrill sets my pulse racing.

"I want your thick cock stretching me," I confess in a whisper. "Every inch deep inside me where anyone could see."

A smile flickers across his face before his expression grows serious. Still pinned against the wall, I watch him reach between us and rub the head of his cock through my soaking pussy. It bumps my clit, making me cry out.

"Please, Gaston. I need you to fuck me."

He chuckles. "So ready for me, aren't you?" The grin he gives me is utterly devilish. "I love how your body responds to me, how your pussy weeps for my cock." He pushes the head in only an inch, making me whimper. "So fucking needy. Beg me for it. Make me believe you want it."

I look up at Gaston, my eyes pleading. "Please, I need you so badly. I'm aching for you."

He smirks, clearly enjoying having me beg for him. "Tell me how much you want it, Blake."

"More than anything," I whimper. "I need that big cock of yours stretching me out. I want you to fuck me so deep and hard against this wall that I can't help but scream your name for the whole of Providence to hear."

Gaston chuckles darkly. "Mmm, I do love hearing you scream for me."

I gasp, trying to push my hips closer, but he holds me firmly in place. "Please, Gaston, give it to me. I'm begging you, fuck me right here and now."

"Keep begging," he growls. "Maybe if you're convincing enough, I'll give you what you want."

"Please, please, I'm desperate for your cock," I beg. "I want you to pound my tight little pussy until I can't walk straight. Until I'm a whimpering mess. Please, Gaston, I need you so fucking bad."

He seems satisfied with my begging, gripping my hips tightly. I brace myself against the brick wall behind me, ready for him to finally claim me. "Such a good girl. My good girl." And then he slams every inch deep, making me scream.

His hand clamps around my mouth, stifling the noise since we're in public. Gaston's hand muffles my cries as he pounds into me relentlessly. The faint chance we could be discovered only heightens my arousal. I wrap my legs around his waist, taking every deep thrust.

"That's right, take my cock," he growls. "I know how much you love being fucked in public like a dirty little slut."

I can't deny it. The illicit thrill sends heat flooding my core. My back scrapes against the rough brick with each powerful snap of his hips. The pain mingles exquisitely with the pleasure.

Gaston moves his hand from my mouth to grip my throat. "You're mine," he rasps. "This pussy belongs to me."

I gasp out a yes, barely able to breathe with his large hand around my throat. The possessive, feral look in his eyes makes my insides clench around him.

He pounds into me relentlessly, my body slamming into the unforgiving wall. I'm sure my skin will be marked and bruised tomorrow.

"Harder," I manage to beg. "Fuck me harder."

Gaston complies, his fingers tightening further on my throat as he rails me. My vision starts to blur from the lack of oxygen. The danger only amplifies my pleasure.

I feel the pressure building, each powerful thrust edging me closer. Just as I'm about to climax, Gaston releases my throat and pulls out.

I whimper at the loss, my legs unsteady as he lowers me down. Gaston turns me around to face the wall, pressing my cheek against the rough brick, and then he forces me to my knees, which scrape on the rough concrete.

"Hands behind your back," he commands.

I obey instantly. Gaston gathers my wrists with one hand and slides another arm around my waist, bracing me as he kneels, too, rubbing his thick cock against my pussy.

I brace myself against the rough brick wall, my heart pounding. Despite our risky location, my body craves more. His strong arm wraps around my waist, holding me steady while his hard length presses between my thighs.

"Please," I whisper, anticipation coiling inside me.

Gaston's lips graze my ear, his warm breath sending shivers down my spine. "Tell me what you want, Blake. I want to hear you say it."

I swallow, knowing I should stop this before we get caught. But the words spill out before I can stop them.

"I want you inside me again. I need to feel you stretching me, filling me up."

He chuckles, low and dangerous. "What a dirty girl you are, begging to be fucked in public." Gaston's grip tightens on my hip, holding me firmly in place. The tip of his cock teases my entrance, and I push back desperately.

"Please," I gasp again.

Mercifully, he slides into me, letting me feel the delicious stretch. I cry out, quickly muffling the sound with my own hand.

Gaston pauses, his ragged breath warm against my neck. "We have to be quiet, mi amor. Unless you want the whole city to know what a naughty girl you are."

I shake my head, biting my lip to keep silent as he resumes his slow thrusts. Even just the first few inches make me feel deliriously full. He pulls back and then sinks deeper. I clench around him, shuddering with the effort to stay quiet.

"That's my good girl. Take every inch," he murmurs.

My body is pressed against the wall, utterly helpless to do anything but let him claim me in this alley. And despite the risk, I want nothing more than to feel him bury every inch of his thick cock inside my aching pussy again.

Gaston gives me a moment to adjust before drawing his hips back. His first real thrust knocks the breath from my lungs. I press my cheek into the rough wall, surrendering completely.

Each deep plunge stretches me to the limit. I clutch desperately at the brick, dizzy with pleasure and pain. I can't hold back my moans of pleasure.

"That's it, baby, let me hear how good I make you feel," Gaston growls. He releases my wrists, and a large hand clamps over my mouth, muffling my cries.

I fall forward and place my palms against the rough brick wall, rocking my hips back desperately, chasing the building orgasm.

Gaston's movements become more erratic, his ragged breath hot against my neck. "You feel so fucking good wrapped around my cock. I'm getting close."

I nod, right on the brink myself. Gaston's next angled thrust pushes me over, my orgasm crashing through me. I cry out into his hand, my inner walls spasming around him.

With a guttural groan, Gaston follows me over the edge. His final powerful thrusts prolong my pleasure as he spills deep inside me.

We stay locked together, both gasping for breath. Gaston turns my face toward his, capturing my lips in a searing kiss.

"I love you," he murmurs. "More than I ever thought possible."

My heart swells, tears pricking my eyes. "I love you too. So much."

Gaston wraps his arms around me, enveloping me in his warmth. We stay like that for long moments, simply holding each other close.

Despite our precarious start, what lies between us now feels so right. After everything, I know with utter certainty that I belong here in his arms. The arms of a beast, but he's my beast.

THANK you so much for reading Beast. I hope you enjoyed following Blake & Gaston's story.

The next book will follow Alice's friend, Kali, as she somehow falls in love with a man so savage, they call him the wolf.

<u>Wolf: A Dark Captive Cartel Romance</u>

WHEN I TOOK a vacation to Mexico, I never could have imagined the deadly game of hunter and prey waiting for me...

Kidnapped by the cartel along with my friends, I'm thrust into a brutal world where survival depends on submission. Matias, one of the cartel's most feared enforcers, also known as the wolf, is tasked with breaking me. He's wild, untamed, and fixated on me. Every instinct screams to hate him and resist, but he's relentless, stalking me like a predator.

In the midst of this nightmare, I begin to see another side of Matias beneath his savage exterior. His primal nature both terrifies and mesmerizes me, igniting a forbidden attraction that defies reason. While I struggle to maintain control, the line between captor and captive fades, and I find myself caught in a dangerous game of cat and mouse.

When the leader of the cartel is murdered by her second in command, a chance for escape emerges. With the help of the new leader, Matias, and his brother Thiago, we make a daring bid for freedom. But Matias isn't ready to let me go. He follows me into my world, determined to claim me as his own. I insist our twisted bond can't survive outside the nightmare we shared, but he's resolute. Love, especially one born from such primal instincts, doesn't follow the rules.

Wolf is the Sixth book in the Once Upon a Villain Series by Bianca Cole. This dark, cartel captive mafia romance explores themes that may be disturbing to some readers. No cliffhanger and a happily-ever-after ending means this book can be read as a standalone.

ALSO BY BIANCA COLE

Once Upon a Villian

Pride: A Dark Arranged Marriage Romance

Hook: A Dark Forced Marriage Romance

Wicked: A Dark Forbidden Mafia Romance

Unhinged: A Dark Captive Cartel Romance

Beast: A Dark Billionaire Romance

Wolf: A Dark Captive Cartel Romance

The Syndicate Academy

Corrupt Educator: A Dark Forbidden Mafia Academy Romance

Cruel Bully: A Dark Mafia Academy Romance

Sinful Lessons: A Dark Forbidden Mafia Academy Romance

Playing Dirty: A Dark Enemies to Lovers Forbidden Mafia
Academy Romance

Chicago Mafia Dons

Merciless Defender: A Dark Forbidden Mafia Romance

Violent Leader: A Dark Enemies to Lovers Captive Mafia Romance

Evil Prince: A Dark Arranged Marriage Romance

Brutal Daddy: A Dark Captive Mafia Romance

Cruel Vows: A Dark Forced Marriage Mafia Romance

Dirty Secret: A Dark Enemies to Loves Mafia Romance

Dark Crown: A Dark Arranged Marriage Romance

Boston Mafia Dons Series

Empire of Carnage: A Dark Captive Mafia Romance

Cruel Daddy: A Dark Mafia Arranged Marriage Romance

Savage Daddy: A Dark Captive Mafia Romance

Ruthless Daddy: A Dark Forbidden Mafia Romance

Vicious Daddy: A Dark Brother's Best Friend Mafia Romance

Wicked Daddy: A Dark Captive Mafia Romance

New York Mafia DonsSeries

Her Irish Daddy: A Dark Mafia Romance

Her Russian Daddy: A Dark Mafia Romance

Her Italian Daddy: A Dark Mafia Romance

Her Cartel Daddy: A Dark Mafia Romance

Romano Mafia Brother's Series

Her Mafia Daddy: A Dark Daddy Romance

Her Mafia Boss: A Dark Romance

Her Mafia King: A Dark Romance

New York Brotherhood Series

Bought: A Dark Mafia Romance

Captured: A Dark Mafia Romance

Claimed: A Dark Mafia Romance

Bound: A Dark Mafia Romance

Taken: A Dark Mafia Romance

Forbidden Desires Series

Bryson: An Enemies to Lovers Office Romance

Logan: A First Time Professor And Student Romance

Ryder: An Enemies to Lovers Office Romance

Dr. Fox: A Forbidden Romance

Royally Mated Series

Her Faerie King: A Faerie Royalty Paranormal Romance

Her Alpha King: A Royal Wolf Shifter Paranormal Romance

Her Dragon King: A Dragon Shifter Paranormal Romance

Her Vampire King: A Dark Vampire Romance

ABOUT THE AUTHOR

I love to write stories about over the top alpha bad boys who have heart beneath it all, fiery heroines, and happily-ever-after endings with heart and heat. My stories have twists and turns that will keep you flipping the pages and heat to set your kindle on fire.

For as long as I can remember, I've been a sucker for a good romance story. I've always loved to read. Suddenly, I realized why not combine my love of two things, books and romance?

My love of writing has grown over the past four years and I now publish on Amazon exclusively, weaving stories about dirty mafia bad boys and the women they fall head over heels in love with.

If you enjoyed this book please follow me on Amazon, Bookbub or any of the below social media platforms for alerts when more books are released.